The Curse of the Moonless Knight

an Alyson Bell novel

It is the season of Samhain, also celebrated as Hallowe'en. The crisp of Fall is in the air. Spirits are amiss in the town of Hollow Creek when a portal that should've stayed closed, is accidentally opened. A medieval knight, misplaced in time, links sixteen year-old Alyson to an extraordinary discovery about herself, and her family.

Embarking on a quest for knowledge, Alyson learns that sometimes in this magical world, you have to close your eyes... to see. And in order to forgive, you must first open your heart.

Thus befalls this bewitched tale...

The Curse of the Moonless Knight

an Alyson Bell novel

Kristin Groulx

The Tenth Muse Books

This book is a work of fiction. Names, characters, businesses, organizations, places, events, and incidents either are the product of the author's imagination or are used fictitiously. Any resemblance to actual persons, living or dead, events, or locales is entirely coincidental.

The Curse of the Moonless Knight

Copyright © 2008 by Kristin Groulx

ISBN 978-0-9811315-1-1

Published by The Tenth Muse Books

www.thetenthmusebooks.com

All rights reserved. No part of this publication may be reproduced, stored in a retrieval system, or transmitted in any form by any process – electronic, mechanical, photocopying, recording, or otherwise – without the prior written permission of the copyright owners, and from the publisher.

Copy Editor: Eric D. Goodman
Guest Editors: Monique Goguen, Chantelle Russell, Marie Bergsma

Cover and Interior Design: Moonspinner Designs
Back cover art: "Mystic Caravan" by Janet Liston Watkins ~ Ontario

This book is set in the font Garamond
Titles and embellishes: Initials with Curls, Dollhouse, Maiandra GD, Minya Nouvelle and 1942 Report (typewriter), Blackadder ITC, First Order (text on scroll)

Thank you to the Karen E. Troeh and the Kansas City Renaissance Festival for use of elements from their famous poster (original by Renae Taylor). Poster adaptation by Moonspinner Designs. Font is Vegacute.

DEDICATION

I've decided to dedicate this book to a classmate of mine from MIZZOU,

Glenn Stephen Kuhlman (1970-2002)

Look to the stars; history is written in them

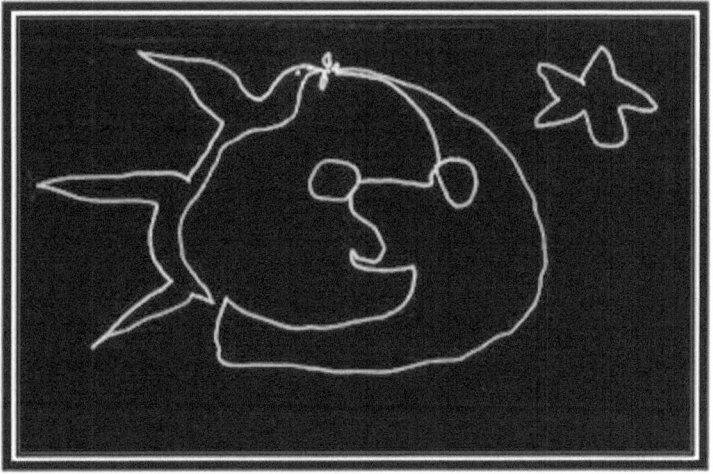

Peace, inspired by John Lennon.

I was 9 years old in December 1980, when the world lost John Lennon, a great musician, visionary and father.
Thank you for letting your spirit live on and reminding us to use our ...

ATIONS.

Also, John O'Donahue, author of *Anam Cara* who passed during the time this book was written. His work is inspiring and taught me about wisdom, and to listen to the wind, and trust my heart when my eyes failed me. An Anam Cara is a 'soul friend' ... the friends we feel the strongest bonds to. It's a mystical connection. A true friendship is something felt. Even the blind can see it.

Acknowledgements

To my friends,

Thank you for taking the time to review and peruse my work, which is essentially a collective diary of meditative thoughts and memories, put to a modern story of a teenage girl on her own path towards wisdom and truth, and finding the magic within. I've also included some poetry of mine in this book, as well as creative "spells" to add to the magic. Be wary of reading this book out loud, haha. Don't say I didn't warn you ;) I can't be held responsible if you accidentally end up in the wrong time or conjure up an imp underneath your own bed. But, if you enjoy the book, please let me know. This book is best read under the covers and by flashlight, on a dark and stormy night.

The artwork was done by me, with the exception of the lovely illustrations included throughout the pages by such talented artists as:

"Owl" by Christine "Chrys" Rodrigue, Phd. ~ California (chapter header)

Featuring an exclusive print made just for this book:
"Mystic Caravan" by Janet Liston Watkins ~ Ontario (back cover)

"Kansas City Renaissance Festival poster" ~ original design by Renae Taylor (page 90-91) adapted with permission

Congratulations to the VIP's from the contest held last Fall, from my website. All of whom are in the book, as students, teachers ... or ghosts :)

* * *

This book is playful, but dark. 13+
It's not meant for those less than thirteen years of age, truly. Use your best judgment. Enjoy.

Table of Contents

Prologue – THE PORTAL ~ PAGE 1

1 – PANDORA'S LOCKER ~ PAGE 13

2 – THE CAPRICIOUS ELEVATOR ~ PAGE 43

3 – DO YOU WANT TO KNOW A SECRET? ~ PAGE 65

4 – THE DUMB-FOUNDED DRESS ~ PAGE 79

5 – FEST SHINANIGANS ~ PAGE 87

6 – INTO THE PAST ~ PAGE 115

7 – A FAMILIAR PLACE ~ PAGE 125

8 – EVERYTHING IS NEVAR WHAT IT SEEMS ~ PAGE 133

9 – BRUSH STROKES OF MIDNIGHT ~ PAGE 143

10 – A ROGUE ATTACK ~ PAGE 161

11 – THE ILLUSION OF NIGHTMARES ~ PAGE 177

12 – ONE LAST GOODBYE ~ PAGE 191

13 – DISTURBED GRAVES ~ PAGE 209

14 – MEMORY LANE ~ PAGE 223

15 – THE SECRET ROOM ~ PAGE 237

16 – A TRICK OR TWO ~ PAGE 243

17 – THE DAY THAT JUMPED ~ PAGE 249

18 – ELDERQUAKE ~ PAGE 263

19 – THE GRAVEDIGGER'S SECRET ~ PAGE 281

20 – ANCESTRAL VOICES ~ PAGE 297

21 – FROM INSIDE THE BLACK HOLLOW ~ PAGE 309

I called out to the Uni-verse,
the one language,
The mother tongue that speaks to us all

O Great Elder of Wisdom

I wish to speak the language that is not yet spoken
And to tell it
As it should be told
So that we as a humankind
Can move forward
And not backwards
It is time to bring the past into the future
Before it is forgotten and lost
In the sands of time

So mote it be

It is an ancient language.
Our mortal ears cannot hear it.
Poetry and prophecy

The three words whispered… "I am here"
I am the voice of the wind that whispers through the tree
And awakens the spirit within
I am the voice that seeks the seeker
Giving light to the blind
Singing music heard by deaf ears

I am the unseen one
But I am felt

"I am here," says wisdom

Use the key

"Now the door is opened ... a portal has been unlocked"

You cannot un-turn a key, that's kept a door shut for so long

But now you know what lurks behind the locked door
And have opened it and seen with your own eyes

And heard words unspoken where magic hides, in the corner waiting for the cue

To leap forth and protect all that is righteous and true
A great battle looms in the distance

Prepare yourselves

Prologue
THE PORTAL

wilight. The blue hour. A magical transition betwixt the intense light of day swallowed into the darkness of night. A chill passed through the autumn air of mid-October. Crisp, fallen leaves rustled all around us and blew gently in the wind. All of my attention went to Ethan. I loved him.

My hand rested gently upon his heart. His chest rose and fell with each breath. I studied every muscular curve outlined on his grey t-shirt that my hand discovered hiding underneath his woolen sweater. He practically lived in his Irish Aran sweater, which represented the Reilly clan of his family lineage. I'd spent many afternoons tracing the various basketweave, cables and honeycomb stitches that ran vertically up the sweater.

His presence made my heart skip and occasionally I had to pinch myself. *Remember to breathe.* Breath is everything. It's sacred. To share it with someone, you share a little piece of your soul with them, and they with you. I could kiss Ethan – *forever.*

Ethan lay back with his eyes closed. Caught up in the afterglow of an afternoon full of lingering kisses, I studied him with close observation the way any girlfriend would of her boyfriend. Everything about him fascinated me. He had stubble. Most of the senior guys had stubble. I found myself counting them and looking at the myriad of colours, even gold and copper. My eyes centered upon his lips. I know why they call it a 'cupid's bow'. I never wanted to stop kissing them. As if the Goddess Aphrodite had cast a spell on us herself. I thought about our first kiss, and slow dancing with Ethan. The corner of his lip turned up and he let out a soft laugh simultaneously with my eyes staring at them. The clouds passed *so slowly* ... as if time didn't really exist.

"What are you dreaming about?" I whispered softly, rolling onto my stomach on the blanket beside him. Ethan had his eyes closed and he smiled complacently. I tickled the tip of his nose with the fuzzy tip of a shaft of wheat grass, which there was an abundance of during harvest season.

"Hey. Stop." He giggled swatting at his own face, before opening one eye and giving me a flirty glare, a smirk of his lip and a raised eyebrow to behave myself. He settled back down and closed his eyes, but the smirk remained, like he held onto a secret.

"Tell me. Or I'm going to have to tickle it out of you." The sun disappeared beyond the horizon.

He sat up, his silhouette slowly fading into the indigo blue of the oncoming night sky. He looked first to the newly arriving stars, and then to me. The intensity of his eyes captured me. "Slow dancing with you under the stars, kissing you for the first time."

I dusted away the hair from his eyes and my gaze lingered longingly upon them, lost in them.

"You know, I like you a little bit."

"Well I like you a little bit … *a lot*," he said.

I could only smile. My eyes caught his and my heart stopped beating for a few moments. He still took my breath away. Everything around us and within us was changing. Metamorphosis. No one ever said being a teenager was easy.

Darkness began to settle upon us. The grass was still warm, where we spent the past few hours in each other's company playfully bantering in our courting of one another. I'm sure to an outsider, we would have appeared as two playful kittens, romping about in our teenage whims and desires. Holding each other, watching the clouds disappear; replaced by a starry blanket, as day turned to night. No more ghosts peered out from the forest trees, or worries that Hremm Nevar would swoop down over us. Ethan, still very much unaware of any events that had transgressed within this forest, or in the mirror and land of dreams, lay peaceful in his contemplative thoughts. He had no recollection of Sadie kissing him as a ghost, weakening him to near death, or the dark discovery and transformation of Hremm Nevar.

A month had passed since that fateful day, and another full moon came and went uneventfully, although it became a secret date night for Ethan and me. I clasped my hand around my lapis lazuli pendant, and there within my palm, I held the universe. All of the gold-flecked stars on the blue stone reminded me that my dreams really were within my grasp.

Of course, even the most stellar-connected teenager still has obvious questions. How did Ethan and I find each other? Were we like the earth and moon, clandestined to orbit around each other for all eternity? Was it just dumb luck that I should stumble upon the most perfect boyfriend? I glanced from the sky over to Ethan, lying next to me, who watched the evening clouds pass over, blanketing the stars. We didn't need words. It went beyond words. He smiled at me. Both of us, listening to our own music as nature played out its symphony. I decided living away from the city really wasn't so awful. I'd found harmony with Hollow Creek. It was rural suburban living in a century old haunted house. It was home.

Ethan, while he was my faithful companion, could never fight my battles for me. Those damsel-in-distress days were over. Nowadays, it seems it's the girls who have to rescue the boys. As a dark cloud passed over and blocked out the moon, I knew my moments in bliss would not last forever. There were still things to do; still battles to be won. However, with the awareness given to me by the Elders and my guardian Emily, I knew I would not face them alone.

My world existed because I wanted it to. If I hadn't wished to know the magical world, would it still have revealed itself to me? Would I still be the same boring Alyson that hung out at the beach and stared out across the ocean, across the universe in its nighttime reflection? Wondering how far it stretched in all directions, including below and above, because in the water there appeared to have no end or beginning?

"I should get going," I said, standing and letting out a subtle stretch.

Ethan stood and smiled. "I know. Where'd the day go? I bet Grams is wondering where I'm hiding."

"No doubt, unsuspecting of her grandson rolling around in the bushes with the neighborhood witch –." I laughed and gasped when I saw Ethan's expression. I then realized what I'd just said, which made me laugh even more. A witch, *in love*.

"What did you say?"

He hadn't heard me, or perhaps he did. My head was in the clouds and I didn't care what Ethan thought. Still, I thought now was not the time to make such splendid revelations. *Cough.* "Race you." I tagged him and ran towards the path. Ethan snagged the blanket and ran after me. He easily caught up to me in the chase and he pounced on me. His tackle ended up in more of a full body combat move, resulting in both of us on falling clumsily to the ground. Ethan stared down at me awkwardly. I felt very uncomfortable. I'd landed on a rock.

"Ouch," I moaned. "Guess you win."

"Sorry. I kind of thought it would've been a soft landing, you know, with the blanket and all." He gave puppy dog eyes. I couldn't resist those. "I'll walk you home," he said, taking my hand as we walked.

"I forgive you," I said and kissing him sideways as we continued walking. We kept walking until we arrived at my parent's doorstep. I turned around and faced Ethan, keeping his hands in mine. Looking at him made me blush a little.

"I can still hear the music," he whispered as he leaned in and looked me deep in the eyes.

"Music?" I said as a flutter of nervous butterflies tickled my stomach. Him looking so deeply at me made my soul stir. Serious moments like this with boys made me nervous, so I let out a small giggle and hoped he wouldn't notice my nerves. I knew the ground beneath my feet existed, but I didn't feel it. It felt like I floated several inches above it.

"From slow dancing with you. I could stay here, in this moment with you forever, Alyson." His voice was solid and sincere.

Our eyes stayed locked in each other's gaze, as though holding hands and slow dancing again with dazzling meteors shooting above us. I still remember those moments etched in my memory. I will never forget. My heart strings tugged tightly. A love this deep would surely kill me if it ever broke.

This romantic tension made me really nervous, but still I stared at his lips in anticipation. I closed my eyes and leaned in. But instead of a kiss, he smiled and put his finger up to my lips. I opened my eyes in surprise. His eyes went soft and dreamy. "I know this sounds really old-fashioned," Ethan said, "but I want us to go steady."

"Go steady?"

"Yeah, you know. I want to be your only guy and you my only girl. You know, I want you to be the only candy in my trick or treat bag," he said, which resulted in both of us giggling.

"Okay. I mean. We kind of were already, weren't we?"

"Well yeah. But I want to make it official." A moment of seriousness passed between us. The words felt like vows.

I smiled and brushed a stray hair off his face. His hair was very soft. I didn't want to go inside, but I knew I had to, and Ethan saw it in my eyes.

"See you tomorrow," he said and gave me a soft kiss on the forehead. Ethan walked away. I stared at the way he walked. He was not hard to look at by any means. He shoved his hands in his front pockets and as he walked, he paused to look back at me and caught me watching him. He blew a kiss, followed by a wave. I was lost to him.

"See you in my dreams," I said to myself. I pushed open the magnificent door of the Finch Estate, now my home, and went inside. As I closed the door, I let out a teenage sigh of bliss, caught myself in a twirl, and leaned back against the door to keep myself from falling.

* * *

Sunday morning came abruptly, shining powerful sunlight through my bedroom window. I shielded my eyes from under a blanket. I opened them long enough to see a blur of black feathers zoom by my window too close for comfort.

"Emily, did you see that?" I exclaimed. "I – I thought for a moment... it might've been... it could've been..."

A bundle of grey fur leapt down from the windowsill and out of view from the window. "Yes, I saw it. I know how you feel. It gave me quite a fright. He's still very much a part of my nightmares."

I inhaled a deep breath and let out a nervous giggle of relief. I didn't need Hremm Nevar interrupting my peaceful weekend. "At least we know it's not you-know-who," I said smiling in the confidence that he stayed locked safely behind the walls of a mirror and forever existing in a land of infinity.

"Yes. I suppose there is comfort in knowing we've put him exactly where he belongs: in prison." Emily's grey fur along her back still stood softly on end, and slowly lowered itself to its normal height as she let her guard down. "Still, I have so many questions and so little answers. There must be more to him than we have knowledge about. Where did he come from? Certainly there were others before Sadie that he seduced." Emily hopped up to the edge of my bed and tilted her head sideways at me, twitching her whiskers.

"He's seduced his last victim. He can't harm anyone else." I slipped a sweater over my head.

"For now. I believe the Elders are still evaluating his powers. He is quite powerful, but how powerful? Are there others like him?"

A twinkling mist-like shimmer of stardust appeared in my bedroom and formed what resembled a cat's eye. At the center, the eye's iris opened, making a portal. Its twinkles beckoned Emily. She looked back at me. "The Elders have summoned me. I must go speak with them. I will let you know when I have returned. Watch over the painting." Watching Emily transform from cat to human form never ceased to amaze me. It only took seconds for her to morph. And into the portal, the girl with the beautiful auburn hair stepped inside, and disappeared, taking the portal with her.

"Bye Emelia. I'll miss you," I said, hoping she'd somehow hear me.

My feet descended the stairs with an effortless trample and stepped outside for some fresh air. It was a beautiful last day of the weekend, all was quiet and I couldn't be happier. Crunchy leaves crackled beneath my feet as I walked down the country dirt road of Colby Drive. The colours of the changing fall leaves were everywhere among the tall oaks and maples. The apple trees were ripe with their harvest. I pocketed a few acorns and pinecones, snagged a juicy apple and took a bite.

The tiny stone bridge was a halfway mark between Ethan's and my houses. The creek became nearer. I was close to it. The Kissing Bridge. I'd hoped to find Ethan sitting there. I peered over into the water. There was only one person there; one person staring back at me. My heart sank a little as I looked at my own reflection. Standing alone. My every waking moment, from breath to breath, had thoughts of Ethan somehow drifting in them. Being with him made everything feel so magical. He made everything feel complete and without him, I just wasn't myself. I wasn't complete. *How do you describe a feeling like this?*

A fallen leaf traveled swiftly down the current of the creek towards me but as it neared me, it seemed to perpetually suspend in slow motion until it passed under the bridge below. I spun around to check the other side of the bridge to see if it would appear and instead came face to face with Ethan. My apple fell into the creek with a *plunk* sound.

"BOO," he said smiling with his nose quickly pressing back at mine. *How could he possibly have snuck up on me like that?*

My heart jumped. "Ethan!" I giggled out of fright and pounded on his chest. "Ugh! Don't do that! How come I didn't hear you?"

Ethan laughed. "It's a secret. Actually, I was just down below and heard you coming, so I hid." He pointed to a tree nearby. I smirked. "So, how's your day going?" he asked, leaning his back against the bridge railing behind us.

"My day's going good, Sneaky. You know I like to be scared from time to time. BOO backatcha!"

He laughed. "I sensed you were outside. It's too nice to be stuck inside. I took a chance and walked here. And here you are! Either way, I was headed to your place to show you this. It's from my mom in Paris," Ethan pulled out a postcard with a picture of the Eiffel Tower in the background and a gargoyle atop a building in the forefront. "She took the photo herself and made it into a postcard. It's really cool."

"Your mom's really talented. I bet you miss her."

He nodded.

"I love gargoyle statues. They're so mysterious. She's really good. I love photography, especially black and whites, and silhouettes." A chill rushed us in the air and ran up my arms. Ethan took off his jacket and wrapped it around me. "Thanks," I said, feeling the warmth of Ethan's body heat still lingering inside the jacket as it hugged all around me.

"You're welcome." Ethan leaned across to kiss me.

It wasn't just a crush. My lab partner in biology class is just a crush. Ethan was extraordinary and unexpected. I never meant to fall in love. It just happened. Supposedly if we had known each other before, maybe there was a reason we felt connected. Maybe the stars really did look down upon us.

"Catch you later?" he said, slowly walking away backwards with his hands shoved in his pockets. He left his jacket around me.

"But wait. You just got here," I pleaded.

"I know. I wanted to see you. And now I have. My day is complete." He stopped for a moment to face me. "Plus, I promised Grams I'd keep my grades up if I stayed with them under their roof. And you! You're just a very deliciously kissable distraction Miss Alyson Bell. You have no idea what you do to me," he said with a grin and continued to step backwards, still facing me. I kept waiting for him to trip, but he eventually turned around and walked front ways. He giggled and mouthed the word 'bye' as he walked away back to his side of Colby Drive.

I bit my lower lip and smirked. *I made his day complete.* I beamed from the inside out and all the world could see it. My heart felt like it had a song all its own. I'd never been this way before. Was this love?

Most definitely. All I wanted to do was dance, and keep dancing to this song stuck in my heart.

I made it home and opened the door, dashing up to my room to greet Emily. Mom and Dad were busy with their usual Sunday activities. Emily hadn't returned yet.

I sat on my bed and felt very alone in my room. It was still only late morning. The silence deafened me, broken only by the sound of the clock ticking in the hallway. Hypnotically, it lulled me like a metronome. I fell asleep listening to it sway back and forth and back and forth, like the sound of a tide glazing the sands of the shoreline. The beach. The smell of salt in the air, the seagulls, collecting rocks and shells. The sounds of the tide. *One day I'll go back*.

As the clock ticked away, time felt incredibly distorted. Even my dreams seemed to move at different speeds. I tossed and turned aggressively in my sleep and woke up startled and looking around the room for intruders. *Nothing. Just my imagination.* An hour had passed. Time for my nap to be over.

As I rolled over on my side, my hair ruffled. A breeze had suddenly entered the room. I glanced over my shoulder to see my window wide open.

"How did that happen?"

I crawled out of bed and slammed it shut tight, and slid the latch into the keeper of the brass lock between the two panes. I caught a glimpse of my own reflection in the window. I looked different. I looked older, and more old-fashioned looking. I stared at my reflection. That is, until my eyes looked back into mine, and changed. It was no longer just a reflection. I took my hand off the lock and sat back on the bed, pulling the covers back over me and still focused on the window.

That wasn't just my reflection. It had spirit. It was older. It was a woman. But *it* was me.

Had I just had a vision? Tempted, I contemplated leaping from bed and looking into the glass of my window again, but nervous who I'd find staring back at me.

"This is silly. Of course it was just my reflection." I let out a nervous giggle as I pulled back the sheets and placed a foot to the floor. "Who else would it be?" I recalled seeing Sadie as a ghost several times outside my window. I sensed my comfort in things just passed would soon run out. She was still there, waiting for me.

Curious, but not afraid, I stood facing my reflection once again. She smiled. I didn't. Her eyes were my eyes, but who was she? She raised her hand and pointed in the direction of the lake. I looked beyond her image into the darkness of night and down at the yard.

There was something out there. Something or someone watched me.

Chapter 1
PANDORA'S LOCKER

The darkness intensified the difficulty to see properly out the window. The woman was no longer there. In her place, sitting perched on one of the trees was the silhouette of a small animal. A small, rotund bird. It let out a whistle and then a *hoot, hoot, hoot.* Then it went silent and flew off. My eyes had difficulty following its shadowy figure in flight against backdrop of the night sky.

A noise came from above, like a rustling of leaves in the attic. The whoosh was followed by a creak and then a poof, and then *silence.* The owl returned into the view of my window. Its feathers looked severely ruffled, as though it had been through a fight.

All of my attention focused on the owl. My room , positioned on the second story of the house, was high up compared to the downward slope that led to the lake. The owl appeared to be solid black, as though it had rolled in the soot of a fireplace. It was barely visible. I had to squint. "Do black owls exist?" I whispered to myself. I'd never seen one before, though I'd not seen very many owls to begin with. Its presence in my tree was peculiar and probably linked with magic I suspected.

A loud booming crash of an unknown object came from above, and hit the floor above me, and rolled until it crashed into a wall. I ducked down instinctively. A quick scurry of footprints echoed across the ceiling.

"Okay. Now I *know* I heard that! Who's in the attic? Where's the door?"

I ran into the hallway, checked Sadie's room, the bathroom, my room… nothing. Passing between the hallway midpoint between the sister's rooms, I stopped. I turned towards a small, antique table of mahogany wood, adjacent to a Grandfather clock. From the wall behind it radiated an energy I'd not felt before. I placed my hand to the wall – and it tingled. Something waited beyond that wall. A void and something more. I saw boxes. *No, – It's a stairwell.* Where was the entrance?

Pressing my ear up against the wall provided little details. The footsteps I'd heard before were there, but very muffled. They stopped abruptly and then came closer. The sounds of them descending the stairwell echoed through the other side of the wall. I moved away from the wall, half expecting the footsteps to come crashing through, but they stopped just before it.

Ghosts don't make footsteps, and Sadie was still in the painting. Who was it? Was this the woman I had seen the reflection of? *Was it a ghost?* A shiver ran up my spine, but I did not waiver in fear. I stared at the wall – and waited.

My eyes scanned the wall for a door knob or a lever, even a secret one, possibly revealing an entrance to the attic. Nothing. I let out a heavy sigh of frustration and stared blankly at the wall. The wall stared back at me. There were eyes just on the other side of it. I felt them pierce through. But I didn't feel threatened by them. I was just aware of them. Once the acknowledgement was made, the clock started to chime. I felt the strange visitor on the other side of the wall walk back up the stairs, and then it was gone. Silence.

Feeling anxious, I went in my room and sat atop my bed. "Probably just squirrels," I contented myself. "Or mice. Could just be mice in the walls. Oh, hurry back Emily." I got up and closed my door to block out the hallway. "There."

A breeze ran across my feet; a very cold breeze. I spun around baffled. My window had been pulled wide open. "Impossible! I latched it myself!"

On the window sill perched the owl. It hooted at me again and then flew off. It startled me. I ran over to the window to slam it shut. As I did, I noticed a light shining from above and reflecting onto the trees. Looking out my window, I carefully slid it open again and leaned my body out. The distance of falling from such a height would certainly be unforgiving. I rotated my head to an angle so I could see the area of the house just above me. There, above my room, was a window. It had a light on. The owl hooted from the trees, distracting me and almost made me lose my balance. I re-gripped the windowsill and leaned out again to look at the window. Not only was the light not on anymore, but the window too, was gone. It had disappeared.

Rain began falling, thwarting any further attempts at looking above me. I crept back in to my room and closed the window.

"What's going on here? I must be having a dream or a hallucination or something." I sat on my bed and a crumpled piece of paper below me made a noise. I looked underneath me and found a note. I looked up to see the clock of the hallway. My door had been opened. I quickly unfolded the note.

"You're not dreaming. We'll talk soon. I am here." – Abigail

Abigail?

My questions had only just begun to be asked.

The owl hooted again, coinciding synonymously with the large Grandfather clock in the hallway. The clock chimed 10 p.m. "That's crazy. I went to bed at 10 p.m. and that was hours ago. It has to be at least 2 a.m. That old clock needs to be wound or something." I pulled the covers over my head and drowned out the sounds.

I woke to the sounds of Mom shuffling around downstairs and then fleeing upstairs and barreling into my room. "Alyson! Get up! You're late for school! Come on and hustle up." She left the doorway and I caught glimpse of the hallway clock.

"8:30 a.m.?!" I exclaimed. "How did it get to be so late so quickly? I've hardly slept." Hurriedly I got dressed facing the window, when my eyes caught something surprising. The black owl perched in the trees, in the daylight, staring back at me. It did not fly off. It waited, ensuring that I noticed it.

Two beeps on the car horn sent me scurrying down the stairs, barely assembled. Typical Monday.

At school, the curious placement of the black owl perched in my mind distracted me more so than my usual daydreams about Ethan. Why was it there? Was it guarding something? Tick tock, the classes flew by. The last bell of the day rang. I was jabbed in the shoulder by Cam.

"Hey, quit daydreaming. School's over. Did you miss it?" Cam teased.

"Yeah, what's up? You seemed really lost today. There wasn't a moment that I didn't look over at you to see your head in the clouds," Sara chimed in. Sara and Cam packed up their backpacks quickly. I followed suit as I stumbled for an answer.

"Boyfriend, probably," Cam jested. Sara giggled.

"I just – I," I stammered. I didn't know what to tell them. For once, I actually hadn't thought of Ethan. I was too distracted by the owl, and the noises from the attic, and the presence of the footprints behind the wall.

We walked into the almost deserted hallway. We were the last ones to leave. Cam seemed overly anxious to talk to us about something and I was right.

"No worries. Hey, did you hear?" he started.

"What?"

"Rumour has it Jeremy's ghost is haunting the school," Cameron said in his most mysterious storytelling voice. "Friday night, after hours, the school's janitor was here late, cleaning, and witnessed an entire row of lockers open themselves simultaneously and then slam shut repeatedly until he dropped his mop and fled the hallway. His bucket and mop were still there this morning, and they found only one locker open, Jeremy's. His letter jacket still hung inside, just as it was the day he disappeared," Cameron said excitedly and seemingly all in one breath. Sara's mouth was agape. "Want to go check it out since we're here? The school play auditions don't begin until 4:30 – that's a whole hour away. I know Jeremy's old locker combo. I doubt they've changed it."

I paused and glanced at Sara, who gave me a confused look. "Oh yeah, sure… haha… let's… NOT!"

"Yeah, let's go, why not?" I said.

We wandered down the hallway on the second floor outside the math rooms. As soon as we turned the corner, there was a noticeable shift in energy. I cupped my hands to my throat and struggled to breathe.

Cameron looked down at his feet. A notebook paper with a muddy footprint lay just at the tips of his toes. He recognized the paper and the footprint. He bent over and snatched it up, balling into and throwing it in the trashcan as he stormed off in one swift move towards the locker. "*You're not going to stop me, Jeremy*," he muttered as he approached the locker. "I'm not afraid of a little ghost action. Bring it on Jeremy Fox. I can take you." Sara looked confused at Cameron's rage. Odd how in that moment, Cameron acted like Jeremy, aggressive and intimidating.

A presence in the hallway overwhelmed me. There was a ghost near, attempting to drain my energy. Vamps. My stomach felt knotted and filled with an ill feeling.

"Alyson? What's wrong?" Sara said, grabbing my arm nervously.

"I'm feeling short of breath. The air in this hallway feels so dense." Jeremy's presence was felt but not seen.

Catching my breath and sensing Sara's apprehension, I made light of the situation. "You're not afraid of a little ghost, are you?" I said, prodding her.

She looked nervous. "No, no, of course not. I don't even believe in ghosts, or UFO's or green-faced witches riding brooms. That's silly stuff for bored people who have nothing better to do than make up fantasies."

Well I didn't believe in that last one either. Witches didn't ride brooms. They teleport into the astral plane. I'd seen both Emelia and Abigail do it before. For a moment, I wished Sara was more like Emelia, someone I could talk magic with. Someone who understood what I was going through and could teach me. "Oh well that's good. At least if you don't believe in them, they can't scare you, right?" I teased. Sara glared at me. Regardless of her beliefs or not, she was not happy to be there at that moment.

"Over here," Cam called to us. "Jeremy's locker is the one with the giant anarchy symbol etched into it. They've tried to paint over it, but you can still see through this pocket-knife carving. I can't believe he never got caught. Serves him right now that he's dead. It's karma. He got his."

"Don't be mean, Cam," I scolded him.

"Why not? Was Jeremy ever nice to you?" he rebutted. *No, not really.* I couldn't recall a single episode where Jeremy was – *nice*.

We approached the locker. Cameron brought his hand to the black dial of the locker's combination lock and turned it.

"Sara, we don't have to do this if you don't want to," I said, glaring at Cameron.

"No, it's okay. I'm a little curious what's inside too. To see if he wrote anything bad about me in there on any of his notebooks. I swear, I'm happy he's gone. He was such an a -," she mummed the word as one of the math professors walked by whistling, but did not notice us, at the far end of the hallway.

"Hurry up," I jabbed Cam in the ribs.

"Let's hope all they did was close it, and not clean it out yet," Cameron mumbled. "Eight," he called out quietly, as he spun the dial clockwise. "Twelve," he spun the dial counter-clockwise. "And thirty-two." He gave the dial a final spin clockwise as the three of us waited in anticipation. "Would either of you lovely ladies like to do the honours?"

"Oh, just open it already, Cam," I said in nervous anticipation of both what was inside and also getting caught.

Cameron pulled up on the metal lever, releasing the mechanism securing the locker and it swung open. The three of us peeked inside. A miniature noose suspended across the bar. Sara looked horrified as she looked at the letter jacket hanging on the back right hook. "Too many memories. I used to wear that jacket when I was cold. How could someone so nice be so mean? So two faced?"

I think there were many things about Jeremy that no one understood but him. He only showed the world who he wanted them to see – the tough guy, the bully, the jerk. Hard to believe he ever had a nice side to him, an amiable and romantic side that charmed Sara. Visibly, she still was hung up on him.

"What is that?" Cameron noticed the corner of something poking from one of the breast pockets lining the jacket. He pulled out a tightly folded piece of notebook paper, shaped rather creatively like origami, but instead a rectangle with a corner protruding as a pull tab. It was addressed to Sara. Cameron passed her the note. She just stared at it and closed her eyes as she deliberated whether to read it or tear it up. She passed the note to me.

"Here. You read it. That part of my life is over. There's nothing he could've said that would change anything. I'll never forgive him."

Down the hallway, the door to the janitor's closet opened. We waited to see if someone would come out of it, but no one did. Slowly, a fog crept out and poured along the floor heading towards us.

"What is that?" Sara asked as she jumped backwards frightened.

"There might be a fire. It might be smoke. We should pull the alarm," Cameron said as he scanned his eyes quickly down the hall to pull the bell. The red box was just on the other side of janitor's door.

"I don't think it's a fire, guys. Look." I pointed at the closet. A shadowy figure stood in the doorway and as we stared at it, it became more and more human like. It motioned to us to come towards the door and enter the closet.

"Are you crazy? I'm not going near it!" Sara spat out emphatically, backing up until she bumped into a trash can, knocking it over. "That was *not* a ghost. It can't be. Ghosts don't exist," Sara said to herself.

"I'll go," I said in a moment that teetered finely between bravery and stupidity. I looked at the apparition. Its shape seemed familiar to me, but I couldn't pinpoint who it was. *Is it Jeremy? Can it be him?*

"Me too," Cameron said, "But someone should stay back with Sara. You stay Alyson. I'll go."

"Oh get real, Cam. This isn't the 16th century. Girls can take care of themselves," Sara said, jumpy with excitement. She took a step forward and then stopped when she felt my arm hold her back. "What?"

"Let him go. It's okay," I said to her and she backed off.

Sara looked on nervously as Cameron proceeded. He looked up at the bell on the wall and hesitated. The fog continued to roll out of the closet. As Cameron got closer, the fog rose up around him and formed smoky tentacle 'feelers' that twisted vividly into ghostly arms. Cameron stood in front of the door as the misty arms wrapped around him. I counted eight of them feeling him, rubbing across his chest and through his hair. Sara's mouth was wide open as she stood in shock and confusion over what to do next. Cameron looked at us and broke free from the foggy grip long enough to pull the switch activating the bell on the wall. Red paint splattered over his shirt. The sound of it gave short bursts of ear-shattering warnings echoing through the empty hallways.

"What the?" one of the professors ducked his head out of the math lab, followed by consecutive doors opening and mass exodus in the hallways. Things never went as they did in the fire drills.

"Run!" I yelled. Cameron ran towards us, grabbing us both by the crook in our elbows and pulling us in the opposite direction. The three of us scrambled outside.

"We are so dead!" Sara barked.

We watched and waited, to see if a flame or any evidence of a fire would expose itself. Nothing. Sirens approached the school rapidly, as red trucks and ambulances, sent as a precaution, turned hastily around the corner. One of the fire chiefs approached Cameron, who noticeably was ornamented in the tell-tale splatter of paint released from pulling the bell, similar to wearing a Scarlet Letter. He'd been labeled unquestionably as the perpetrator.

"Excuse me young man. You pulled the alarm?" the chief asked.

"Yes Sir." Cameron's voice waivered. He was nervous. We all were. "There was smoke on the second floor coming from the janitor's room."

"Okay, thanks. We'll check it out. You kids stay right here and don't go anywhere," the chief commanded us as he shouted orders to his crew. Firefighters in full uniform ran into the school, lengthy coils of water hoses trailing behind them.

Cameron looked awestruck at the spectacle of vehicles and people flooding into the school we just ran out of. He also looked very worried.

"Are you okay, Cam?" Sara asked. "What happened up there?"

"I'm not sure. I can't explain it. I felt frozen in place, like I couldn't move and there were all these hands caressing me, but they didn't feel right. I was being lured by them, seduced. They sang to me with this haunting sound. It was like being pulled underwater, caught in an undertow and drowning. For a moment, I couldn't breathe."

"Okay, that's just too creepy!" Sara exclaimed. "You can't drown if you're not actually in water, can you?" Sara looked at Cam with worry. "It's impossible, Cam."

"Anything is possible, Sara! Especially the impossible. Just because it didn't happen to you, doesn't mean that it didn't happen!" Cam bit into her. His nerves were still rattled.

"Looks like you've had your very own experience with a ghost, or several," I said, happy that I wasn't the only one with such experiences.

"So if it was a ghost, why'd you pull the alarm?" Sara toyed.

Cameron studied the red splatter on his shirt. "I saw something. I saw something inside the janitor's closet."

"What did you see? Another ghost? Jeremy's ghost?"

"Let him finish already," I barked to Sara, just as eager to know his answer to her questions.

"There was smoke. It rolled across my feet, coming from the closet."

"And?"

"And it was coming from what appeared to be an old service elevator. It had an old, black metal grating across the front."

"An elevator? In the janitor's closet?"

"Yeah. It is kinda weird, but it is an office too, and who knows what it was used for before that. This is a really old school. Maybe there was a fire in the basement or something, so I pulled the alarm," Cam explained. "It was definitely smoke. I saw it with my own eyes."

"The fire chief approached us and walked towards Cam. "Young man, there was no smoke, and we've searched the building. There's no fire. I'm having you booked for a prank call. You've wasted everyone's time with this nonsense."

Cam looked scared. He'd never done anything to break the law before. He told them the story he had told us, save for a ghostly detail or two.

"Honestly Sir, I wouldn't pull a prank. I saw smoke. I'm not sure where it was coming from. Maybe the basement?"

"This building doesn't have a basement," the Chief said.

One of his crew said, "Well, it does have a small area that was used as an infirmary and make shift morgue during the war when the local hospitals got too full. We'd send someone down to check it, but it's been closed up for years. There's no access to it."

"The building's secure, Sir," one of the firefighter's main security team tapped the chief on the shoulder, cutting him off.

"Thank you. That will be all," the Chief said and the security officer nodded and walked away.

"You kids stay out of trouble. I'm letting you go with a warning. My wife's about to have our baby and her call the *only* one I hope to receive today. Am I clear?"

We all nodded and watched as the crews packed up and left.

"Oh my goodness, Cam. You could've gotten us into so much trouble!" Sara hissed and pounded his chest.

"Why can't grown-ups take us seriously, huh? I'm not a criminal. Really. Well, hardly at all." Cameron seemed to be negotiating with himself.

"Seriously. What do you think about the firefighter's story about the school being used as a morgue?" I questioned. "Think he was telling the truth?"

"Yeah. I do. Creepy."

Cameron looked ill and hunched over holding his stomach like he might be sick. "Sorry… nerves. I don't think I want to go back into school today, but we have to."

"Maybe you could see the school nurse?"

"Yeah, just remind me not to go to the infirmary," he said sarcastically. He released some of his nerves in the form of dry heaves and hunched over. Cameron recomposed himself. "I'm okay."

"Seriously," I said. "It's almost 4:30 now. We should head to the gym. Auditions hopefully are still going on, although no doubt the entire school evacuated thanks to us."

"Yeah," Cam said shamefully.

"Don't worry, Cam. I would've done the same thing if I were in your shoes. Hey, at least your shirt is perfect for the play. You look already like Dracula got to you, with all that blood-red paint splattered over you," I said. We giggled and the heavy air lifted between us. "What role are you trying out for, Sara?"

"I am more Mina than Lucie," she said as we re-entered the school and pulled open the heavy double doors leading to the school gym. "Lucie's kind of a slut, don't you think?"

I hadn't really thought about it. I didn't give her an answer, but instead looked around the gym at its newly redecorated architecture. It had recently been renovated, and graciously funded by the parents of such honoree students as Jeremy and Jenny Fox. That explains why the gym always felt so cold.

Rows of chairs lined the floor atop the markings of the basketball court, and faced the stage. Bleachers aligned the back wall.

Our school gym was used for everything from sports to school plays to school dances. Along the ceiling still hung several trapped balloons and leftover decorations from dances past. A suspended, caged light in the far corner flickered on and off.

"Cam, are you going to audition too?"

"Umm, I'm not sure. I'm not really the actor type."

"Hey, sorry I'm late," Ethan entered the gym and walked up beside me. "I got held up in class and then the fire alarm went off we all had to go stand in the parking lot. I didn't see you, but I looked."

"Yeah. About that…" Cameron started to explain and I motioned to him to just let it go.

"It's great to see you," Ethan pulled me aside and put his arm around my waist. "Ready for a little vampire action?" He pretended to bite my neck. It gave me tingles. "I vant to suck your blood," Ethan joked in his vampire voice.

We all giggled.

A handful of other thespian hopefuls entered the gym and mulled about and Ms. Hildegarde-Snodgrass walked out onto the stage.

"Okay students. Let's get started. I will be calling you forth to read lines from the script. You will each be reading for several different roles and I will choose which one suits you best."

"Your hair looks nice that way Ms. Hildegarde-Snodgrass," Sara complimented, trying to be smart.

"Thank you. Although I do appreciate your flattery, Miss London, I recognize an attempt to bribe the judges. Show me what you can do in your audition."

Sara sulked down in her seat a little and thumbed through the script, which had all of Mina's lines perfectly highlighted in bright pink marker.

Principal Jeffries walked out onto stage. "Everyone give a round of applause to our dear principal," Ms. Hildegarde-Snodgrass led a series of loud clapping that faded quickly.

"Now the Woodhaven High School Theatre department is one of the most well-known in this country. We have some amazing talent hiding at this school, with new faces appearing every day." She looked at me. "Let me see your best work. Audition with feeling and emotion. Let's put on more than just a school play – let's make a memory that this school won't soon forget! Give it your all!" She continued on with her pep talk for a few minutes. I lost interest in what she was saying altogether and spent those moments lost in Ethan's eyes. My eyes dropped to his lips and zoomed in on the kisses that waited to be stolen.

"First up. Let's have Holden Jeffries reading for the role of Jonathan Harker and our Irish transfer student, Samantha Barry for the role of Mina Van Helsing."

"Figures he'd have his son in the lead. I may as well not even audition," Ethan said rather miffed at the possible favoritism.

Holden Jeffries was also on the football team with Jeremy, but had a darker side he seemed to keep hidden, something less public. He always appeared to me to be kind of shy and introverted, unless he was around friends. I didn't know him that well. Usually when I tried to talk to him, he'd walk by me with his headphones in his ears.

"You should audition. You'll get a good part. I feel it."

Ethan smiled and our eyes got all lovey again. "Cool. I'll do it for you then."

Jenny Fox strolled in with every ounce of her over-inflated ego leaking out of her perfectly sized pores. My jaw dropped as she approached me. Why she targeted me, I didn't know.

"So, Amanda," she began.

"It's Alyson."

"Yeah. Whatever. Like it matters anyways. Don't bother auditioning for any of the lead roles. They always go to me."

Her smugness silenced me. I'd only run into one other person who was this rude to me and I thought I'd left her back in ninth grade. I guess it didn't matter which school I went to. Girls like Jenny Fox are always around.

"I know you're like – new, so I'll cut you a break. I'm sure there are lots of supportive roles you could get. And you know, there's always scenery crew." She flashed her manicured nails at me. "Yes, my daddy makes sure I don't have to do any heavy lifting. Can't risk pulling any muscles and miss cheerleading practice, can I?"

I was speechless. "I – umm – hope you get the role you deserve."

"What's that supposed to mean? Holden and I always get leads, get it? Want to get in my way? I'll step all over you."

"Oh, back off, Jenny," Ethan said, stepping in front of me in his usual over-protective chivalrous manner.

"Fine. Why waste my beautiful voice on you losers. Except for you cutie. Can't wait to audition with you," she said as she blew a kiss to Ethan. Ethan narrowed his eyes and looked away.

"Ciao." As she started to walk off, she looked back. "Oh, and Amanda, I meant what I said," she said with a glare in her eyes that hinted her competitive nature might extend beyond cheerleading. She took a seat close to Holden and started chatting him up.

"Wow," Ethan exclaimed silently with over-exaggerated lip gestures mouthing out the word.

"Yeah, no kidding. She's a boa constrictor, that one," Cameron agreed. "Chokes the life out of you just to be around her."

"Well she doesn't scare me. I'm still auditioning, and I hope I get the lead!" I said.

"Me too," Ethan added. We both smiled and sat down again.

There was a bustle of students getting up out of their seats and collectively gathering around the lip of the stage. Ms. Hildegarde-Snodgrass got down on one knee and looked at the remainder of the students before her. She waited until she had everyone's full attention before speaking. It took a few moments for the chit chat to stop and she cleared her throat repeatedly until the chatter ceased.

"After Holden and Samantha, can we have Jess O'Meara and Jonathan Holeton, followed by Kay Smith-Gosling and Brendan Myers. Additional pairs of you will follow. Would Suzanne Archer, Sheila Gonzalez, Jennifer Flegg, Cassandra Vezina, Emily Francoeur, Ami Fournier-Smith, Annie Langlois, Asmaa Sharkawy and Morgan Blackbyrne also come to the front, please and thank you? Yes, our infamous Morgan, who played our Pirate King in last year's *Pirates of Penzance* opposite our lovely Daniela Vitagliano who played Mabel. Let's see you give us your best auditions for *Dracula* this year." She directed her attention around the room. "And our high school disc jockeys, Rahim Jetha and Mark Young, I will need your assistance with the props later on, especially the gravestones. Hopefully I haven't missed anyone. Do we have anyone else auditioning?"

Ethan raised his hand.

She acknowledged his request. "Very well then. Everyone settle down please. Now I won't be able to pick everyone for a lead, but you will all have a part in the development of the play. Everyone who has an acting scene is also part of the scenery crew, so no one is left behind. And remember, there are no small parts. Good luck. Oops, *break a leg*, students. Remind me not to undertake *MacBeth*!"

As they each reenacted their scene, I reached into my pocket to find the folded note from Jeremy. I looked to Sara as I pulled gently on the tab. I didn't feel right reading it. I retucked the tab and passed the folded note back to Sara. "I really think you should have this. Maybe it says something important?" I eluded to the notes contents. Sara took the note with a heavy sigh and unfolded it, laying it flat against her script.

She passed the note to Cameron and I read it over his shoulder. She looked humiliated. Cameron's jaw dropped.

"You mean?" he said.

"He was?" I asked. "Really?"

Sara shook her head and pouted. Her forehead crinkled with deep hurt, but also showed signs of relief. She leaned in to whisper to us, in our private group resembling a football huddle.

"There's no use in lying anymore. Jeremy and I didn't go as far as I said we did." She let out a discontented sigh. "We never had sex. I only said I did to spare my reputation. I didn't want everyone to know. It's humiliating."

Cameron gasped. Apparently it was just as much a surprise to him. "What? Why didn't you tell me? You lied to me? Of all your friends, and you can't trust your best friend? *Me*, Sara – you lied to *me*!"

Cameron looked upset and folded his arms across his chest. Sara continued to look humiliated and unsure whether or not continuing to divulge such information would prove helpful or hinder any possible future relationships, including the one she's sort of having with Cam.

We all looked at her with surprise.

"I lied to everyone. I had to! Jeremy could be really manipulative. I can't believe him! I can't believe I lied to cover up such a stupid secret! And what was he so afraid of anyways? Losing his father's money or losing his position as team captain? Why didn't he just come out himself? Oh, he angers me so much! Remember that day we put the poster in his locker? It really shook him up."

Ethan rubbed his jaw. "Yeah, I remember."

"I suppose none of it matters now anyways. Jeremy's dead," Sara spat.

Cameron was bitter. "Wow. That's newsworthy. Did everyone catch that? Not sure they heard you in the back," Cameron's snarky tone caught Sara off guard. There was anger in his voice.

Sara looked at him apologetically and shocked, but then quickly lowered her head and let out an ashamed sigh.

"So, does that mean you're still a vir-," I asked the obvious question and Sara cut me off.

"Yes," she said sharply. "Shut up already. I wasn't really ready anyways. I found that out the hard way," Sara's eyes lowered to her script again. "But nothing happened and I'm glad. I couldn't imagine – still, I had to see him every day in class."

"There's nothing wrong with being a virgin," I added.

"For you maybe. Everyone expects someone like you to hold onto it until forever, but me," Sara began.

"Oh, you can't be serious, Sara," Cameron quipped. "Someone like you? You think having sex makes you popular or something? How stupid are you?"

"But I didn't have sex!" Sara retorted.

"No, but you have a problem with the rest of us who want to wait?" Cameron barked back.

"I don't have a problem," Sara said.

"Yes, Sara. I think you have a really *big* problem!" Cameron said, holding back a shout. He turned his back to her. Sara was scorned and had hurt in her eyes.

"I can't stand this. Why is it such a big deal?" Sara asked me.

"Don't look at me. I'm still a virgin. What do I know?" I answered her sharply. Anger filled me. "Why does it matter to you so much anyhow what people think? Especially about something like that? Why would you purposely want people to think you're a slut when you're not? Sorry, Sara. I just don't get it."

Tears swelled in Sara's eyes. "But I'm *not* a slut. I *am* still a virgin – like you."

"Sara, the more I get to know you, the more I think you are *nothing* like me," I answered. The words hurt me just saying them out loud. I felt her pain. She had regret for the secret she hid from everyone to protect Jeremy and now it came back to haunt her.

"Shhh… we need quiet please while the auditions are going on," Ms. Hildegarde-Snodgrass called into the audience, "And will students Sara London and Ethan Reilly come forth please?"

"Guess we're up," she looked to Ethan, as she grabbed her copy of the script, forced a smile and headed on stage. "Time for real acting," she said. Sara's emotions weren't too hard to hide, yet she managed to read from the script flawlessly and got into her character without a hitch.

DRACULA:

SEVERAL EVENINGS LATER

T R A N S Y L V A N I A

NIGHT

Mina and Van Helsing camp outside the castle walls
HELSING: Here...you must eat.
MINA: I am not hungry.
HELSING: Mina!
Mina begins to writhe and scream
Three vampiresses call to Mina
Mina suddenly looks hungrily at Van Helsing
MINA: You've been so good to me, Professor. I know that Lucy
harbored secret desires for you. She told me. I too know what
men desire.
Mina and Van Helsing kiss
MINA: Will you cut off my head and drive a stake through my
heart as you did poor Lucy, you murdering bastard?
Mina attempts to bite Van Helsing
HELSING: No! Not while I live! I've sworn to protect you!

Ethan and Sara had to kiss in the scene. It caught me off guard. The only rescue was that Sara didn't appear to enjoy it. She still had Jeremy on the brain.

Everyone clapped. "Good good. That's great students. Well done. Very convincing work," Professor Jeffries called to Ethan and Sara. "Can we say *bastard* in a school play?"

"If it's in the script," Ms. Hildegarde-Snodgrass interjected. "After all, this is turn-of-the-century classic literature. We can't just go switching words around. It just isn't done."

We all took turns reenacting various scenes from *Dracula* until it was almost dark outside. We still had the drive back home.

"Yes, that was convincing Sara. You're a good actress," Cameron spat at her, as if to really be saying, "*You're a good liar.*"

Sara ignored the tone of his comment. "That's it for me guys. I'm outta here," She grabbed her jacket and black leather satchel and left abruptly.

Cameron ran after her. "Sara, wait up!"

I picked the letter to Sara off the floor and refolded it.

"Ready to go home?" Ethan asked.

"Yeah. I think so. Let's go."

"Want to drive?" he joked and jingled keys in front of me.

"Are you for real? You know I can't drive yet." I was surprised by him. Still, he showed some trust in me by offering.

"Yeah. I know. Maybe I can teach you someday then." He smiled and wrapped his arm around my shoulder and led me out to Grams' car.

"Cool," I said softly.

The moments before with Sara and Cam and Jeremy's revelation had all passed. Once again, being in the presence of Ethan's company made everything else disappear.

"Come on. I'll walk you home from here. It's a nice night out and a full moon." Ethan parked the car at Grams. The darkness had already found its way to Colby Drive. My parents expected me to arrive home promptly after the play auditions. We got distracted.

"You know, I enjoy acting. It's a lot of fun. But that audition kiss I had with Sara today, well, it felt really weird with you watching. I'm just glad I didn't have to kiss Jenny. Yuck!"

I nodded with similar disgust for my least favourite student. "It's okay. I know you were only doing what the scene required you to do. I'm sure if I had auditioned with you, you would've had to kiss me too."

"Oh yes, and that would've been just torture," Ethan said, grinning. We both laughed.

"Yes, completely."

"Look at that moon," Ethan said as we stood on the kissing bridge. The only traffic that ever crossed it was anyone visiting the Finch Estate, now my home.

"It's mesmerizing."

Ethan cupped his hand lightly to the side of my cheek. "Yes, *you are*." He leaned in to kiss me. My knees buckled beneath me. His kiss vibrated through me straight to my toes and made them curl. I cinched my grip on his shirt and pulled him closer to me. His heartbeat matched mine. It was no longer just a kiss in the moonlight. Passion and temptations overwhelmed us both. We were moments away from slipping into something deeper. Our breath quickened rapidly and I pulled away from his kiss to catch my breath and clear my head. I took two steps back from him.

"Ethan," I said, blushing and overheated. I looked down at my feet and then back up at him, wiping the corner of my mouth and running my finger along my lip. His kisses lingered.

"Alyson."

We stared into each other's eyes, our skin glowing a soft blue under the moonlight. I ran my fingers through his hair. He captured me. I leaned back against the railing. The body of water for which Hollow Creek was named trickled beneath us. Ethan took two steps forward and pressed me against the railing. His hand went around my waist. He kissed me again. I felt swept away in the current of the creek. He pulled my hair away from my neck and kissed me there. His breath was incredibly hot. I pressed harder into the railing for support. My thoughts didn't even seem like my own anymore – they'd lost all sense of rationale. I was lost to him. It was already past my curfew, but I'd accept any punishment to remain in this moment with Ethan. Lock me in a tower and toss out the key. Still, with every ounce of willpower I could summon, I stopped Ethan from going any further. My entire body shook. Panting heavily under headed breath, I put my hand to Ethan's chest and he pulled away from kissing my neck to look up at me. Our eyes locked. We didn't have to say anything. Body language and breath said everything.

"We – we," I said, panting too heavily to speak.

"I know," Ethan said. "I know." He paused for a moment. "But I just keep thinking about what it would be like to just –."

I laid my head on his chest as he let out a deep sigh. He closed his arms around me and hugged me. His heartbeat told me all I needed to know. It galloped. I thought of Thunder, and Harding. Every time Ethan exhaled, I felt the warmth graze the tip of my nose. I'd never really noticed how hot breath is until I felt it from someone else. As cold as it was outside, Ethan's hug and breath passed over my face and kept me warm. With every breath he took, his exhale kissed me. The scent of his breath made me want to kiss him again. But I didn't. I held it in, like a sneeze. I knew if I kissed him once again, I'd be lost.

With a deep sigh, Ethan said, "You're freezing. Come on. Let's take you home." I nodded reluctantly. It was the right choice, even if our hormones demanded more.

Ethan held my hand as we walked. I could only think about what possible punishment might await me for returning so late after curfew. Perhaps my parents worried about me too much, but I was their only daughter, so of course they only wanted to make sure I was safe. They also trusted Ethan and I didn't want that trust to be broken.

As we got closer to home, a set of headlights came into view crossing over the bridge. It was my parents' car.

"That's it. I'm doomed," I whispered to Ethan.

"It'll be okay," he said.

The car parked in the driveway and my parents emerged from the open doors giggling and laughing.

"Hi Honey. Hi Ethan. Did you get our note? Your father and I went to a movie tonight. How went the auditions?" Mom said cheerfully. I knew in that moment that I didn't get caught and Ethan was right – it was okay. Still, I gave a look to Ethan and he nodded. We'd be more conscientious of our time next time.

"Ethan, want a ride back to your house? Temps' dropping," Dad said with one hand still on the door.

"Sure Mr. Bell. Thanks," Ethan gave me an acceptable kiss on the cheek in front of my parents. In many ways, Ethan was old-fashioned, and I was very happy about that. It's like finding an old copper penny. You can feel its worth even if it looks like all the others. Its value is in what makes it different. Ethan was different. "See you in school tomorrow. Hope you got the part."

"You too! Guess we'll know soon enough. Good night." I felt my neck in the area he kissed me. Only Dracula could've kissed harder.

My parents laughed and bid goodnight to Ethan. He gave me a sincere look about what had transpired in our evening together. It went beyond any of the candid talk we presented to my parents to appear to still be on the teenage surface. But we'd gone deeper. Ethan had struck something inside of me that went to my core. Our eyes locked one last time as he held the door handle of the car. Dad looked at Ethan and back at me. He knew. I sensed one day, Dad and Ethan would have one of those man-to-man talks.

He let out a little wave as he pulled the door of the car closed and drove off with Dad.

"So, all the lights are off in the house. Have you been outside this whole time or inside, in the dark, with a boy?"

I hesitated answering, but finally just accepted that I had been caught.

"Yes, outside. Ethan's been with me until you came home. I umm – forgot my house keys and couldn't get in."

Mom pressed the lever on the door and it swung open easily. "We left it unlocked. Perhaps try pressing a little harder next time."

I'm sure my look of surprise was all Mom needed.

"Inside before you freeze to death," she ordered with a motherly smile. As she closed the door behind us she said, "You know, I didn't tell my parents the whole truth all the time either, especially about boys. Your father and I broke many curfews. Now I'm not saying that I approve of you staying out late, but I do trust you to be responsible for your actions."

I nodded.

"I am happy you made it home safely. Ethan's a nice boy and we like him. We trust you with him, Alyson. Just remember that. Trust is a very valuable thing."

Emily had returned from visiting the Elders. She sat perched on my window seat, staring down the path and towards the lake.

"What are you thinking about?" I asked.

"I was just remembering something. I guess there's a part of me that will always wonder what it would've been like to marry Harding. I miss him."

I pet the top of her head to comfort her. "He's just a boy. Don't worry. There will be others."

"Harding was not just a boy. Harding was special. He still is. My heart doesn't belong with anyone else. If I can't love him, there will be no others."

Emelia had met the one boy that had made her eternally happy. I knew Ethan was my Harding. Ethan made me happiest. I leaned back on my bed and cuddled a pillow.

Emily crawled to the foot of the bed and purred at my feet. My thoughts journeyed to what happened in school and with Ethan and my dreams wandered to somewhere beyond into what could've happened. I'd never felt Ethan kiss me so hard before. I touched my neck to where he'd kissed me. I felt my blood pulse through my veins. Just thinking of Ethan made my heartbeat quicken. My own desires scared me with how strong they were.

"Emily?"

She looked up.

"How do you know which guy is 'the one'?"

"You will know it in your heart. Just don't rush into a burning building if you can't put out the fire."

Even in riddles, Emily's wisdom spoke volumes. I wasn't about to let my own desires get the better of me. I closed my eyes and dreamt of tomorrow.

Chapter 2
THE CAPRICIOUS ELEVATOR

Anxiously I entered the school and approached the oversized corkboard bulletin boards that would announce the results of the cast for the school play. I could only read the words *Dracula Cast List* at the top of a giant fluorescent yellow paper. I didn't even know why I was nervous. I didn't particularly care whether or not I was cast.

"Congratulations," Sara said as she ran up behind me. "You got one of the leads. You're Lucie. And I got picked too, see," she said pointing to the list.

"Oh, congrats. Mina. That's a good role too – the lead! Very hot. We've both got big parts."

"Wonder if Jenny's seen the list yet?"

I scanned the list of names quickly looking for Ethan's name. 'Ethan Reilly as *Dracula*'.

"Wow, Ethan. That's awesome."

Immediately, he acted on cue, pulling up an invisible cape over his crooked arm, shielding his fangs from view.

"Oh my gosh. Jenny's got a part – she's your understudy!" Sara exclaimed.

"Understudy? I wonder why she didn't just get the lead."

"Maybe you're better than you thought," Ethan said, smiling.

Cam poked at us from behind. "Did I get a part?"

"Narrator," Sara said.

"Cool. No lines to memorize."

"How long have you been standing there?" I said.

"Long enough. Hey. Meet me on second floor after school today," Cam said jingling a set of keys in front of our faces.

"Where do those open up to?" I asked.

"I swiped them yesterday. Don't worry. They're copies. They go to the janitor's office. I thought they might come in handy on our umm… investigations. I've decided to do an undercover report on the basement. If this school has potential residual diseases or bad psycho kinetic energy lurking about, I feel the students have a right to know about it. Besides, I want to see where that elevator goes, just as much as you do. Admit it Alyson, you're more curious than a cat."

"Cam, you're insane. Your curiosity always gets the better of you. But sure, I'll go check it out with you," I said.

"I really don't want to be crawling around in the basement. What if there are mice or something really disgusting? What if we get caught? Yesterday scared me, Cam. That fire chief meant business. You could go to jail. Do you know what they do to pretty girls in jail? Huh? Do you?" Sara complained.

"Fine. You don't have to go. You can stand at the door and keep guard. Let's hope Jeremy's ghost doesn't come out and spook ya," Cam prodded.

Sara's eyes got really wide and her emotions ran somewhere between scared and pissed off. She glared at Cam. It was the first time I'd seen her really mad at him. *Could it be they're having a fight?*

"Teachers are leery of going on second floor anyways today. Did you guys hear what happened last night after the auditions?"

Sara and I both shook our heads.

"The lockers have been physically moved around, rearranged, and the numbers are all out of sequence. It's really confusing the students – they have to search for the right locker number to get into their lockers."

"Weird."

"Yeah. Some of the teachers are blaming the yearbook committee who held their meeting up there yesterday, but if you ask me what I think, I think it might've been whatever ghostly hands were all over me yesterday," Cam mimicked them rubbing his chest and Sara rolled her eyes at him.

"Oh, grow up already. Ghosts on the second floor?" Sara mocked.

"Well can you deny it? I can see the headlines now: Ghosts Run Rampant at Woodhaven High." Cameron made invisible headlines with his hands in mid-air.

"Amusing, ... *not*," Sara whined.

"I bumped into Jess. You know her – Jess O'Meara from the all state choir finals, and crew and yearbook committee? She said when she locked up the room she saw strange lights that looked like orbs float past her and down the hallway. She got scared, locked up and left. She was the last one on the floor and said no one touched the lockers."

"What about Jeremy's locker?" I asked.

"Well, that's the odd thing. It was the only locker that didn't move, however once again, it was wide open. Principal Jeffries closed it and sealed it with a big strip of yellow 'CAUTION' tape."

"Didn't the janitor hear anything? Moving lockers around would be noisy I think," Sara said.

"Nope, he didn't hear anything. It happened after he'd gone home. It must've happened sometime in the middle of the night."

"It could be vandals," Sara said, dubbing herself something between a devil's advocate and a CSI investigator.

"Vandals don't typically break into a school just to rearrange lockers. These are more pranksters. Possibly poltergeist activity," Cam said.

"And since when did you become the expert on ghosts?" I said giggling.

Sara gave him an anti-nerd glare she usually shot at him when he did something *not cool*. "How'd you find all of this out?" Sara interrupted.

"I spend a lot of time on second floor in the math labs. My Dad dropped me off early this morning and I came up to see Principal Jeffries taping Jeremy's locker shut and he told me. He was also really nervous for some reason. Principal Jeffries had a photo in his hand he got from Jeremy's locker. I couldn't see what it was, but he didn't look happy."

"Interesting," I said. Sara kept quiet, as though she knew but couldn't say anything.

The three of us looked at each other mystified. I'd had my share of ghostly activity. This seemed like it might be a playful mischievous ghost, maybe even Jeremy himself, just being bored.

"Well, it is only a few weeks before Halloween," I noted. "Don't spirits get more active around this time of year?"

"Yes. In fact, Halloween is actually from the Celtic holiday Samhain and literally means *summer's end*. This season was the beginning of the New Year in many rural areas of Europe. The time of transition, from sundown on Samhain to sundown the following day, was a "thin place" in the Celtic world, a place between-the-worlds where deep insights could pass more easily to those who were open to them. In addition to inspiration, through the portals could also pass beings of wisdom, fun, and play," Cam said. "So the easy answer is 'yes'... beings of wisdom or spirits are more active this time of year. It pays to be a bookworm. You learn a lot of stuff you wouldn't normally catch in an ordinary textbook."

"Well, if that's true, and our school really is haunted, then the night of the school play should be interesting. It's on Halloween night!" I said. "And we've all been cast, so we'll be here."

"Should be fun," I added. "I don't mind playful ghosts."

"Even if it's Jeremy Fox?" Cam said.

"Could we just stop talking about Jeremy for two seconds please, ugh! Enough already!" she spat angrily and walked off in the direction of the girl's bathroom.

※ ※ ※

The last bell of the day rang and school was adjourned. As the flurry of students made their way to their busses and cars, Sara and I nonchalantly crept up the stairs to the second floor hallway. We bumped smack into Mr. Parker, our geometry teacher.

"Oh, hi girls, nice to see you up here. Looking for your friend? He's in room 202 down the hall a little and on the right."

"Thanks, Mr. Parker. That's a really nice shirt you have on. It's a good colour for you." Sara kissed up any opportunity she got. Being every teachers "pet" didn't hurt her grades. Mr. Parker was just out of college. Couldn't have been more than twenty-three or twenty-four years old. He was distractingly handsome. He smiled and walked away as we headed towards room 202.

"I look forward to college," Sara said, hushed and giggling.

"Why?" I asked.

"Because of all the cute guys that will be there. These high school dorks are all the same and only after one thing, just like Jeremy. College guys know how to treat a lady. College guys are smarter. College guys would go through anything for their girl. They'd even change their hair and not wear a tie if I asked them too."

Her last reference was obviously a subconscious referral to Cam.

"Mmm... yeah. I guess so." I didn't really need a college guy. I had Ethan to hold onto, and he did everything right. He knew how to treat a lady, he was smart, and he was a really good kisser. *A little too good.*

I peeked through the long slit of a window in the wooden door and waved to Cam, who sat among a few other students in the computer lab. He waved to us and walked towards the door.

"Hi Cam," I said.

"Hey," he said. "Everybody cool now?"

"I don't know if this is such a good idea. Maybe we should come back later when there are no other people around," Sara said.

We stared down the hallway at the janitor's closet door. "Just try not to draw attention to yourself," he said to Sara as he walked towards the door with every intention of going inside.

"We are so dead if we get caught," Sara said.

"Then don't get caught," I said.

Sara and I leaned our backs up against the wall adjacent to the janitor's closet door. Cameron was no stranger to the second floor labs. Everyone knew him and his presence roaming the floor was not unusual. But a nervous beauty queen and her somewhat mathematically challenged friend did stand out. Sara and I made small talk and giggled uncomfortably as Cam pressed his ear against the door listening for the janitor inside. "I think the coast is clear," he whispered. "But we'll have to be quick."

He turned the key and we all ducked inside the office and closed the door behind us. Sara hyperventilated slightly as she panicked and played scenarios in her head of us getting caught and what jail would be like.

Cameron struggled to slide open the metal grate of the service elevator. "It's jammed shut. Do they even use this thing?" Cam rattled it, and the noise echoed throughout the office.

"Shhh," Sara screamed through a whisper. "I swear, Cam, I am so mad at you for making me do this."

"Then go home, Princess. I am not *making* you do this! You don't have to be here. You could be doing something that doesn't require any thinking – or danger – like *shopping*. Isn't there a sale on shoes somewhere that you're missing?" Cam snide comment snapped right at her. Sara fumed.

"You're right. I don't have to be here, but I am. I'm here for Alyson."

It's clear that Cam and Sara were in the middle of a disagreement and I decided to stay out of it. "Are you sure this is safe, Cam?" I questioned.

Cameron grunted as the metal gate gave way, reluctantly budging only enough for us to slip through. "No, I'm not sure, but yesterday this is where the fog came from. I want to see what's down there. You'd better come along in case the janitor returns."

The three of us stood in the service elevator. Sara leaned against a side wall, emotionally on edge. Cameron closed the metal gate in front of us and looked at the buttons on the wall. We were on '2'. There was a floor beneath us and below that was a faded button marked 'B'.

Cameron pressed it. Nothing happened. Already I wanted to leave. He pressed it again. We waited.

We heard the sounds of a person whistling coming from down the hallway, headed in our direction. The whistling paused and muffled voices took its place.

"Let's get out of here," Sara said with an unexplained nervous tension.

"Wait," Cameron instructed. We felt a slight shift in the elevator and on its own, it started to go down. It stopped on '1'. The door didn't open. Cameron pressed the 'B' again and we all looked nervously at each other as the elevator didn't move. It refused to go down. Cameron pressed the '1' button and we heard a ding sound, but the door did not open. The small elevator box that held us was not very forgiving. It wasn't roomy like modern hospital elevators. If they carried bodies down to the morgue, they'd have to carry them upright. I had been leaning up against one of the sides but then quickly stood up straight and away from the walls of the elevator. I felt very uncomfortable, even more so with the elevator not cooperating.

"Dammit! Go down already you stupid –" Cameron shouted at the button as he rammed it again. Finally, the elevator crept down and the doors opened to the basement. The three of us stood there and stared into the darkness. My eyes had difficulty adjusting to the darkness. Hesitantly, we all stepped out. Sara held my hand.

The air in the basement was thick with dust and mould. Sickness and decay loomed in the air. The damp and cold clung to us.

"Here. I brought flashlights." Cam gave Sara and me each our own.

"Stick together," I said. Sara couldn't even speak she was so scared. "Just stay close to me. Nothing's going to happen."

"How can you be sure?" she whispered.

"I'm not."

Cameron walked around shining his flashlight. There were rows of ordinary looking storage boxes, extra lockers, extra sporting equipment, and extra theatre props. It seemed that for a place no one used, it was actually quite full of stuff.

Exploring was only part of the excitement. Not getting caught was the other.

"Cam is mental," Sara whispered.

He glared at her.

"I think he heard you."

She smiled satisfactorily.

"Why are you so bitter at Cam? It's Jeremy you should be mad at."

We both jumped when Cam walked into a metal bookshelf on wheels.

"A gurney. Yuck! There were probably dead bodies wheeled around on this thing," Sara cried.

"Cool," Cam said as he pulled back the white cloth that had been covering it. He hopped up and tapped it, inviting Sara to come sit next to him.

"Cam, don't do that."

"Why? Scared much? Hey, why do they need straps on it if the bodies are already dead?" He prodded Sara. He then pulled the white sheet up over himself and laid flat on the gurney and quietly laid there as if he were a corpse.

The silence of the basement unnerved us all.

"Cam. Cam, get up. Stop goofing around," I told him.

He continued to lay there like a stiff.

"Fine. You want to be dead – be dead. Don't expect me to come save you," I yelled at him. Still, Cam didn't move. From under the sheet, it didn't even appear that his chest moved.

"Cam?" I walked closer to the gurney.

"Cam? Quit kidding around. Come on, enough pranks for one day," Sara said.

Echoing through the basement, we all heard the howl of a dog.

Cam sat up with a start, fumbling to get the sheet off his head. "What was that?"

"It sounded like a dog," I said.

"I knew you weren't really dead, goofy," Sara commented.

"Shhh," Cam said in a soft voice. He clicked his flashlight back on and adjusted the beam. Cameron's flashlight scanned the room and landed on a set of big black eyes so intense he couldn't move from it.

"What is that?" I yelped.

"Be still. It's not moving. I think it's sleeping," Cam said.

"Sleeping? With its eyes open?" I said. "And didn't you hear it howl? It howled!"

"I think we should leave now," Cam said as the dog lifted its mangy head and let out a low growl. "It wants us to leave now." He slid off the gurney with snakelike stealth, letting the white cloth fall to the floor.

"Hey, where'd it go?" Sara asked flustered and fumbling with her own flashlight.

"I don't know." Cam shined his flashlight to the perimeters of the basement.

"I want to leave. I don't want to be down here anymore." Sara said rattled and upset.

"Me neither. What if it has rabies?"

We backed up to the elevator. I reached behind my back and put my hand on the bars of the metal grate. But instead of opening it, I accidentally closed it. There was a tiny 'click' behind us and the elevator started to go up… without us.

"What do we do?" Sara panicked and dropped her flashlight.

"It's back," Cam said as the beam of his flashlight hit the dog's eyes once again. He covered Sara's mouth so she wouldn't scream.

"And it has something in its mouth," I added. Cameron felt for the call button and called the elevator back down.

"It looks like a bone," Sara said, pulling Cam's hand down from her mouth.

"A bone of what? That thing is huge. It's like the size of a human leg!"

"What if it *is* a human leg?" I added.

We all panicked.

The elevator arrived and the gates opened behind us. As we stepped inside, we heard a voice.

"That's Penelope. Good dog. Go fetch."

We all screamed again at the sight of the janitor.

It was the janitor. He smelled like stale cigarettes mixed with sweat, and cleaning products, and a skunk. His heavy, beige boots were all covered in dirt. He must have trouble mopping floors and not muddying them back up again in those things.

"Don't worry. I'm not going to turn you in. I see a lot that goes on in this school, and you three are a good bunch," he said. "Why are you kids snooping down here anyways? If you need theatre props, check with the theatre department first."

"Who is Penelope? Is she your dog?" Sara asked with the naïve eyes of a child.

The janitor looked Sara up and down, making her uncomfortable. She tried to hide her legs peeking out from her miniskirt from the janitor's prying eyes. Cameron stepped in front of her and the janitor backed off.

"Oh, Penelope's not a dog... *anymore*," he spoke slowly. "She's a ghost that wanders and guards the basement, just the same as the other hundreds of ghosts wandering the Boneyard."

The Boneyard? What's the Boneyard? I wanted to ask but thought better of it. Something was very off about the janitor, but I had too many nerves to pinpoint it. "She's something crossed between a wolverine and a Rottweiler, and maybe *Quasimodo*. Hard to explain."

"Funny, I think he's doing a pretty good job of explaining," Cam whispered.

"Rumour has it she belongs to the ... umm," he let out a cough, "the gravedigger that worked here back when this part of the building was a morgue. She can't really harm you, but she sure does give a good fright to intruders. I thought I was the only one who could see her, but apparently not," he said and laughed, which made all of us uncomfortable. His laugh was followed by a very hoarse cough, the kind that only smokers get. He coughed for nearly a half of a minute before composing himself again and then continuing on as if he was fine. We all looked around at each other with looks of curiosity and concern. He punched in the buttons on the elevator and it smoothly traveled to the main floor. He slid open the grate of the elevator.

"Rumour has it, the gravedigger is still around too," he said with a cocky smile. He winked at Sara. She looked disgusted and mortified.

"Ugh! I may be flirty but I'm not *that* desperate. As if?" Sara said disgruntled. "Besides, if I were going to get with a teacher, it'd be Parker," Sara leaned in and whispered to me.

"Oh – you didn't just say that out loud. That's so icky," I whispered back.

"What? Parker's not that old. He's like a senior, that's maybe graduated a few times. It's no wonder I'm doing awful in math this year. He's easy to… umm…. Listen to."

"This year?" Cam leaned in and joined us. "If it weren't for me Sara, you're grades in math over the past, say… *decade*… might prove to be a slightly different letter of the alphabet. Like eff eff eff as in fffroggg," Cam said stretching out his words, making me giggle but teeing off Sara. She snarled at him and stuck out her tongue.

The elevator arrived at the top and gave a bounce at its arrival point. I held in a tiny scream. Departure was the only thing on my mind.

We all looked back and forth as we exited the elevator. With each footstep off the elevator, it bounced a little, leaving me to wonder how sturdy the cables were. We gathered into the office again. The metal grate of the elevator closed crankily like a rusty accordion.

"A gravedigger?" I asked.

"Yes. You kids sure ask a lot of questions." The janitor smiled at us, revealing a set of bad teeth only a pirate would be proud of.

"We're students. Of course we ask questions. It's what we do," Cameron answered. "Thanks. We'll be on our way."

"How'd you kids get in here anyways? I thought I locked the door," the janitor said. "Oh well, just stay out next time." He slammed the top drawer on his desk shut which had an obvious girly mag poking out. "Scram already," he yelled to us as we let out a soft giggle.

"Sorry to have bothered you. We didn't see anything," Cam said to the janitor and the janitor nodded that he didn't see anything either. Cam's eyes scanned the room quickly and he nodded, smiled and left.

The hallway was empty now.

"Oh my gosh! We could've been in so much trouble! Cam, I am so mad at you!" Sara fumed. Cameron laughed.

"Why are you laughing?" she said irritated.

"Because of your expression. It's priceless. You're so scared and annoyed and you remind me of when you were five and on the playground and Jeremy Fox had just put gum in your hair and Jenny pointed her fingers at you and laughed."

"Oh shut up. Well, once a jerk, always a jerk. And can we all grow up already," she said.

"I mean, did you see the size of that thing? It was ginormous!" I said.

"Ginormous is not a real word," Cam corrected. "Ignoramus is a word, but ginormous isn't."

"It is and if you don't believe me, I'll give you a ginormous wedgie over your ginormous head. Isn't that right Sara?" I paused. She stood motionless in front of the lockers. "Sara?" I called to her again.

Across from us, the caution tape on Jeremy's locker began to peel off, the way tape peels if it is really old adhesive or in humidity. It fell to the floor in front of the locker. Sara stepped forward and picked it up off the floor. She stared blankly at the metal tomb that held so many of her ex-boyfriends memories. The locker made a 'click' sound and the door swung open. Sara seemed baffled as she stared inside of her old boyfriend's locker.

"Sara? Are you okay?" I said as she stood frozen, holding the tape.

"I feel – I feel like I'm staring into his coffin. He's here. I feel him around me and it's so incredibly cold. Look, his locker has cold spots in it. Feel." She reached her hand inside the locker and yanked it back out again.

"He grabbed my hand! Oh my gosh! I felt Jeremy! He's in the locker!" Sara held in a scream and looked stark white. "I still feel his hand on my hand. It's icy cold."

"Ectoplasmic residue," Cameron said.

A wisp darted out from the locker and spiraled down the hallway and around the corner out of sight. I watched it disappear as Sara looked around at the ceiling looking for answers.

"Jeremy?" She looked around questioning the presence. She reached forward to his letter jacket and noticed the corner of another note tucked in the inside pocket. She pulled it out. Just like the first, this one was marked with Sara's name across the front. She slammed the locker door shut.

"Jeremy, why don't you just leave me alone!?" she screamed and fell to her knees, holding her head in her hands. "He's tormenting me from beyond the grave. Why?" I wanted to remind her that she didn't believe in ghosts, but I'd known all along that she did. She just didn't want to appear stupid.

"Open the note," Cam suggested.

Through tears, Sara unfolded the note. This note was different. It was barely legible and written recently, as the ink was very smudged.

> Dear Sara,
> I'm sorry.
> I never meant to hurt you.
> I need your help. I'm trapped.
> I don't know where I am.
> -- Jeremy

"I don't understand. Am I supposed to believe these notes came from beyond the grave? I can't help you Jeremy," Sara said aloud in hopes Jeremy's ghost could hear her. "I can't. I don't know the first thing about ghosts. I'm not even sure I believe in them," she said to us. "I mean, ghosts can't really write notes, can they?" She looked down at her hand and gave me a look that it still felt like ice. I took Sara's hand into my own and tried to warm it up.

Cam sat on the opposite side of her. "Well, I've had more than my fair share of ghostly encounters, and I'm pretty sure we all were sane when we saw the ghost wrap around me up on second floor. Whether we choose to believe in them or not, they exist."

"That's what I'm afraid of. And Jeremy, of all people, or ghosts, is asking for my help. How can I help him?"

"Only time will tell," I said. "Come on, let's go."

Sara continued to sit and hold the note. So much sadness was written across her face. "You know, I really did love Jeremy and he said he loved me back. Hah! I would've given him all of me, but he didn't want it. I was willing to let him have me, and he didn't want me. That really stung. He actually had the nerve to lie to me and tell me he was keeping it for someone special. Like I wasn't?" You could hear the sound of her heart breaking as she spoke through quivering words. "At least I didn't listen to him. I knew there was something else. I just never guessed it would've been because Jeremy had a boyfriend. Two-timing jerk!" She let out a huff and then went completely silent. A single tear dropped, and unlocked a tormented and broken heart, as a flood of tears streamed down her face like pouring rain.

"Sara?" I nudged.

"Shh. It's okay." Cam sat back down beside her and wrapped his arms around her and just held her while she cried.

"Let go of me," she said through tears to Cam and broke free of his embrace. "I want to be left alone."

"Fine," Cam said. He got up from the floor, grabbed his bag and left.

All went quiet. Even Sara stopped crying momentarily and looked around.

"Do you sense that?" she asked.

"Yes."

Jeremy's locker opened and burst out hundreds of folded notes, all addressed to Sara. They lay scattered around her. Sara sat unsure of what to do next. The notes all simultaneously burst into flames. Sara screamed. The notes quickly burnt out and turned to ash, and then simply disappeared as though they were never there. Sara looked around to see if the fire had spread, but there wasn't even evidence of smoke lingering in the air.

Sara took heavy breaths from surprise and swallowed deeply. "He won't let me rest, will he? Why is he still tormenting me? Why does he still break my heart?" The last comment she said softly before folding her head into her hands. "I wish I didn't have to be here anymore!"

An eerie voice echoed Sara's name from the far end of the hallway. *"Saraaaaaaaa."*

I looked to the far end of the hallway. There was a large open window. I didn't recall seeing it before. A chill of the autumn breeze passed down the hallway and caught our attention. Perched on the sill sat a black raven. Its familiarity haunted me. It looked to Sara as she wept innocently.

"It's him!" I said under my breath. I couldn't believe my eyes!

Through the wind and a breeze passing through the hallway, a shuffling of stacks of papers came trailing down the hall. With it, a voice lingered hovering in the air like a bell long after it's been chimed. *"I will come for you.*" His voice reverberated off the metal lockers and bounced endlessly into my eardrums like the squawking of a thousand ravens.

Sara looked up and down the hall to the raven in the window as it flew off noisily flapping its thunderous wings behind it.

"That voice. What was that? What was that beautiful voice?" Sara looked around the hallway.

Beautiful?

I didn't like the sound of that voice, one all too familiar to me.

It was Hremm Nevar.

Chapter 3
DO YOU WANT TO KNOW A SECRET?

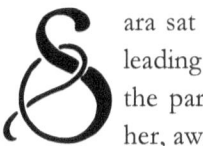ara sat quietly by herself on one of the cement steps leading down to the courtyard of the school and into the parking lot of busses. Cautiously, I approached her, aware she was quite agitated.

"Everything okay?"

It was not okay. She held her head in her hands and cried.

"Alyson. I've done an awful thing to Jeremy. He didn't deserve this kind of attention. He really shook me up. I'm not trying to be conceited or anything, but look at me -- he could've done far worse." She was right. She was a hottie.

"Forget about Jeremy. What about Cam? Cam loves you."

There was a long hesitation before she answered. "I love him too. But I loved Jeremy and look what he did. He took my heart and left his giant, muddy footprint, just like he muddied up everything else. It's not easy to lend it back out again, even to Cam, – especially to Cam. I just need to be alone, so I can think clearly."

I held out a little red square box with carnival pictures on the side of it, and offered it to Sara. "Want an animal cookie before I go?"

"No thanks. I'm vegetarian," she said through emotional tears. I felt sorry for her – I didn't know what the pain of a broken heart felt like. I never wanted to know. Clearly, Sara was distraught.

"Alright. I'll see you around." I walked to the parking lot in the rear of the school to see if Ethan was there. He was, but he was not alone. A girl stood next to him and his car. My eyes widened and I debated approaching them or just keeping my distance. I trusted Ethan. I decided to keep my distance. His eyes looked up and saw mine.

"Hey! Alyson! Over here," Ethan yelled.

She wore a very short mini skirt for October. Her legs went up to her neck. And she had a very long neck. In fact, this girl had many things I didn't have yet. I looked down at my chest and then back to hers.

"Hey," the slim brunette extended her hand and shook mine. "I'm Carly." She turned to Ethan. "Thanks so much for unloading these books. I'm sure Professor Higgins will be really happy to donate them. Give Grams my best."

"I will let her know I bumped into you." Ethan giggled. I hadn't heard him giggle around anyone else but me. I felt really awkward inside, like I'd swallowed a box of iron nails and they sat there in the pit of my stomach, jabbing me.

"Nice ride by the way. Just got my license." She leaned in and kissed Ethan's cheek. "Great to meet you. Ethan talks about you all the time in class. Well, see ya later." She waved and left.

"Yeah. You too. Bye," I said softly, watching her legs walk away and then locking eyes with Ethan. He looked at me oddly. I tried to hide my impending jealousy.

Feeling overprotective, I pulled Ethan to my lips and kissed him. "Missed you."

Ethan almost lost his balance. "Missed you too. But I have presents."

"You do?"

"Yeah, as a thank you from Professor Higgins, for all the help in physics lab, he gave me these. Tickets to Ye Olde' Woodhaven Royal Medieval Faire. It's a Renaissance Festival. You know, like Medieval Times? Want to go?" Ethan asked, presenting a pair of tickets pulled from his wallet hiding snugly in his back pocket.

"Awesome. I'd love to. When is it?"

"This weekend. There's a costume contest, so if you can find something Medieval-ish to wear, bring it. How do you feel about men in tights?"

The mental image of Ethan dressed as Robin Hood made me burst into laughter.

"Okay, so I might not go in costume, but you should. Mostly because I know I wouldn't be able to take my eyes off you."

"Oh is that so?" I didn't want to admit it, but sometimes Ethan made me nervous in a good way. I looked out to the autumn leaves to distract myself. "I can't believe it's October already."

"I know what you mean. It feels like school just started. Time's moving quickly. Hey, there's another full moon on the thirty-first. You know what that means, don't you?"

It took me a moment, "Oh cool, on Halloween. That should make things interesting and very spoooooky. That's the night of the school play. What time does it start again?"

"Five. That should leave plenty of time for the play and then trick-or-treating after. Wonder how many people will be having parties? You should throw one; you know… in that haunted house of yours," Ethan said with a grimace.

"Yeah, like that would happen. Who'd want to drive out to the country to party?"

Ethan paused to mull that idea over and nodded with a *you're right* expression.

"So, who all is going to go to the RenFest?" I asked.

"Oh, let's see, there's me, you, and another guy from my class named Matt, and his girlfriend, Carly and I've got two other tickets I can give away. You know anyone else that wants to go?"

Hearing him mention Carly had a boyfriend made me smile. "Well, I could ask Sara and Cameron tomorrow."

"Cool. Well I have to get these books over to the other side of town. Want a lift?" he asked as he held the door open.

"You bet."

As we drove home, I resisted the urge to ask him if he and Carly were ever more than friends. She was obviously his age, and also a senior. I decided to let it go. But my insides wouldn't let it go. Her image seemed to fester. Who was she? How did she know him? These were odd feelings. I hadn't felt this kind of jealousy before. Carly seemed like a threat. The way Ethan giggled with her appeared etched in my head uncomfortably. Boyfriend or not, Carly with the long legs was competition.

"You okay?" he asked.

"Yeah. Sure. I'm good." I let out a deep breath and stared out the window.

Ethan turned onto Colby Drive and parked.

"Is this about Carly?" he asked.

"Who?" As soon as I said it, I felt immature. Ethan saw right through me.

"Carly's just an old friend. That's it. There's nothing there. She's like a sister to me."

Hearing him say it made me only slightly relieved. "Oh no. I wasn't thinking about her. I'm just bothered by some ... erm... Biology notes and stuff."

"Oh. Well maybe I can help."

"That's okay. I just need to go study. Call me later?"

"You bet."

I walked home after saying bye to Ethan. *Holy awkward moment. What was I thinking? Am I really that transparent?*

My thoughts were incredibly agitated for the remainder of the day. Even my sleep was disturbed.

The next day at school I met up with Sara and Cameron, who were sitting at their usual desks, cleverly disguising the fact that they were secretly dating.

"Hey guys, guess what? I have two tickets for this weekend's Renaissance Faire, if you want to go."

"Really? Cool. Battle chess!" Cameron said excitedly and smiled at Sara.

"I've never been to one of those things. There aren't going to be a bunch of hippies bugging us, are there? Because the smell of patchouli makes me gag."

I couldn't help but laugh. "I don't think so. But even if there are, I really don't think you have much to worry about. Go with us. It'd be fun. You can go in costume if you want. Have any prom dresses and tiaras lying around?"

And with that, she was convinced. A chance to dress like royalty was enough.

"Princess, I shall escort you to your royal kingdom," Cameron jested and outstretched a crooked elbow, while he still sat in his desk. "Shh...," Sara pushed his arm away at the sight of other students entering through the door. Cameron gave her a look of confusion and hurt as he took his seat in his desk. He looked at her awkwardly, attempting to understand why she pushed him away when they weren't alone.

Ms. Hildegarde-Snodgrass entered the room. "The three musketeers are early today I see."

I smiled, Sara rolled her eyes and Cameron pulled a heavy textbook from his backpack as we continued our chatter and a few other students took their seats. Jenny Fox strolled in; her hair pulled in tight blonde, ramen pigtails. She'd been in therapy coping with the death of her brother, Jeremy. She'd been prescribed something, which worked a little too well and now made her more annoying than ever. She sat in Jeremy's old seat, which made me glance twice just as she sat. It looked like Jeremy's ghost got up from it and moved to the corner of the classroom and stood there, watching us briefly before passing through the door into the hallway. I looked back to Sara and Cam. They didn't see anything.

Jenny bounced and fussed as she sat like a nervous kindergartener. "I'm in your class now. Now you'll at least have somebody *interesting* to talk to, Sara, and won't have to hang out with these nerds," she hissed in Cam's general direction.

Cameron pretended not to hear her, when clearly he did. It hit a home run with Sara. She glanced at Cam, torn between her reputation and her relationship. One of them was going to get pulled apart and it wouldn't be pretty.

Ms. Hildegarde-Snodgrass wrote on the blackboard: SCHOOL PLAY REHEARSALS AFTER SCHOOL TOMORROW

"Cow. Why doesn't she just drop the hyphen? Just because you remarry doesn't give you poetic license to string the worst possible combo of names together. Hildagassey drives me nuts," Jenny whispered.

"Assuming those of you who are in the school play are available to meet after school for rehearsals, please take this sign-up sheet home to your parents. We still need volunteers to build props and distribute posters. If you're interested, please sign up," Ms. Hildegarde-Snodgrass addressed the students as she passed papers around.

"I heard she's still sneaking into the broom closet with Parker," Jenny snarked. "What a cougar, that one is. But I would be too. Parker's hot!"

"So what if she is, Jenny? Don't you have a life of your own? Can't you stop gossiping for one minute? Is it humanly possible for you to *just shut up*?" Cam spat at her, emphasizing the last three little words. He slammed his book shut and turned his back, staring out into the parking lot, emotions running rampant.

Jenny's mouth dropped open, but no words came out. I smiled. I guess she did have a mute button on her remote-controlled life. It used to be funny to make fun of teachers, but something about the way Jenny framed it made me look at Ms. Hildegarde-Snodgrass in a new light. She was just a human being, getting through her day, and having to put up with losers like Jenny and Jeremy Fox. And lucky us, now we had to put up with her too. I begrudgingly let out a heavy sigh and tried to ignore her for the rest of the class. Even for Jenny, she seemed overly hyperactive. I wondered if the new medicine she'd been prescribed wasn't reacting well, but I didn't want to say anything. She coped with a lot already.

She scribbled something on a piece of paper and held it up as poked Cam in the back. He turned and read it. "Don't mess with me nerd." Sara hadn't noticed, but I did. Jenny grimaced with smug satisfaction. I recalled the muddy footprint Jeremy left on Cam's paper. Jenny and Jeremy were bad apples picked from the same poisonous tree.

The bell rang and students gathered their belongings and rushed for the door, including Jenny.

Cam locked eyes with Sara and paused as he crammed his books into his backpack untidily. His eyes had serious hurt in them. He stormed out of class without saying bye to either of us. I had a hunch what was on his mind.

Sara pulled me aside and let out a sigh of frustration as she addressed what really was on her mind. "Alyson, I need your help. I've thought about this the whole class. Did you see how Cam looked at me? Cam won't kiss me. I've given him several opportunities and he's just too shy. I can't stand it. There are a million other guys at this school who would jump through hoops to just touch me, let alone kiss me, and here is my best friend and he won't. Why? Can you talk to him?"

"Umm ... maybe it's because you won't tell anyone that you're dating him?" I snapped a sharp retort in her direction. It's not like me to sugar coat the truth.

"It's *Cameron* though. Honestly, I like him a lot... he's always been there for me, *but it's Cam*! And *I'm* like the most popular girl in school. I can't be seen dating a *nerd*. Do you know how bad the other cheerleaders would tease me over this? Did you see Jenny's reaction?"

Does she actually hear herself? I began to understand more about why she made up the rumour about having sex with Jeremy. Her precious princess reputation. My head felt like the tip of a thermometer with the mercury reaching all the way to the top. I was about to burst. Words escaped my mouth like an uncontrollable explosion. "Is that all you see in Cam? He's a nerd? That's it? It never seemed to bother you before you started dating him. You know, Cam has feelings too. Did you see the look he gave you? He's hurt, Sara. It probably had nothing to do with kissing you."

She bit her lip as I continued to bite into her with words, "What if he weren't there, in your life, who would you be dating? What if Cam loses interest and decides to go out with someone else and never talk to you again… could you stand that? What if Cameron no longer wanted to be friends with you because you're treating him like dirt? It *is* a possibility and you know it. Honestly Sara, I had no idea you could be so shallow. I thought you were better than that. And who gives a rat's ass about Jenny. Her opinion is nothing to me, and you're behaving *just like her*. Seriously. I've had enough!"

I stormed off, but not before seeing Jenny overhear us. *Good. She needs to hear it.* I glared and she gave me a cold death stare. I continued walking, lost in my own thoughts and brewing with frustration. I couldn't stand to hear Sara talk about Cam like that. *He loves her. Cam practically worships her. He's devoted his every thought to her and all she cares about is her popularity and the opinion of a psycho cheerleader.*

I ran into Cameron at his locker. I caught glimpses of several titles, laying sideways on his top shelf. *Quantum Physics for Dummies… An Intro to Parapsychology … Ghostbusting 101.* Odd titles, but then Cameron still remained a bit of an oddity to me. He seemed utterly clueless about Sara, or maybe he knew and just didn't care.

"Umm, Cam, can I ask you a question?"

He pretended not to be hurt. "Sure. Need something else transcribed? I've got a new book on Norse mythology."

"No, it's not that. It's Sara."

"Oh. Yeah. Right." He lowered his head briefly and glanced up, giving me his full attention. "She's acting so weird and I'm not sure what's up. It's like, she's embarrassed to be seen with me now. Whatever. She won't even let me touch her unless we're alone, and then it's almost like she's worried someone will see us. I can't stand it. Every time I try to kiss her, she shies away. Is she playing coy or does she just not want to be with me? We've been best friends forever. I've watched her go through some pretty tough stuff with other guys, especially Jeremy. Man, he practically ruined her and she *worshipped* him because he was the most popular. But I *know* Sara. I *know* her, who she is on the inside. She's not always so pretty. Seems like those are the times she's run to me the most. When she's coping with something. I just wish… I just wish she'd figure it out." Cameron shut his locker abruptly and walked away.

I didn't know what to do with either one of them. Maybe this RenFest wasn't such a good idea for them.

Friday came and they still weren't speaking to each other. I couldn't think of anything to say to either of them, so we sat quietly. I did notice one thing however… Cameron wasn't wearing his usual neck tie. But one thing was clear; he fumed inside with anger and disappointment at the one person he loved. I felt helpless. Sara stared in the opposite direction, in her own world and not talking to anyone. Just the fact that Sara was "not talking" was probably killing her. The bell rang. Again and again, throughout the entire day of classes, I heard only the bells ring, until the last one rang and it was time to go home.

※ ※ ※

That night was agonizingly quiet. Emily had to visit the Elders one last time regarding Sadie's sentence; Dad was busy with his usual work at the newspaper and steady at his desk for the remainder of the day; Mom secluded herself to her studio to paint. Ethan and tomorrow's

RenFest were the only thing keeping me going. I cracked open a page in the journal that my dad had given me. It made a cracking sound as I opened the cover for the first time to write. It felt like the right time to begin a new journal.

"Oh hurry back Emily. I miss you. You're like a sister to me now."

I closed the journal and set my pen aside. I wandered over to the closet and opened it, browsing through the dresses that hung far to the side. They weren't mine, but I kept them there for Emily. Her life was so tragic to lose so many people; I wouldn't dare dream of throwing anything of hers away. It wasn't my house, even though we lived here, it still didn't belong to me. The dresses were all so beautiful, and I know they'd be my size. I hesitated as I tugged at one gown on a hanger and decided to not disturb it. I just couldn't. I'd just have to wear my own clothes and not go in costume. No biggie. No doubt Sara will be dressing like a royal princess anyway, and she'll probably win any contest they have.

Emily could now come and go as she pleased, as she no longer lived under the curse that Sadie put upon her. Sadie on the other hand served out her sentence living within my mother's painting, along with her guardian: her mother Abigail. Even though Sadie had been stripped of her powers, and was harmless to me, the memories of her instability and revenge over her sister still stayed with me.

I retired my thoughts for the evening and settled into my bed to dream of tomorrow; spending the day with Ethan and my friends, even if they weren't talking to one another. I closed my eyes and then opened them again when I glanced at the closet. *Emily has to have something in there. But I wouldn't feel right borrowing it. If only I had a fairy godmother and a pair of glass slippers.*

A rustling came from overhead, just the same as several nights ago when Abigail left me the note.

"Abigail? Is that you?"

I ran to the window and opened it. The cold night air splashed in and a shiver ran through me straight to my toes. Just beyond, the tiny, black owl sat perched in the trees again. The black owl. I could barely make him out if his hooting didn't reveal himself. I looked away momentarily and when I looked back, he was gone. He must've flown off. I closed the window and latched it again, and crawled back into bed.

I'd already drifted off to dreamland when a breeze trickled across the back of my neck. I rolled over to face my window. It was wide open! In its mouth sat the owl, and then he flew off. I closed my window again, just as I heard tiny footsteps run across my floor. They went unseen. I decided to leave the window ajar, so if it were something like a fairy or another one of Emelia's friends, they could come and go as they pleased.

As I slept, all was quiet. Too quiet. Sleep was disturbing. So were the dreams. I tossed and turned, keeping an ever watchful eye open for the disturbance of an owl appearing on my windowsill or a magical creature running across my floor.

The sound of shattering glass woke me with a start. It sounded as though it came from a window or a mirror. I sat up in bed and looked to the ceiling. There was an attic up there. I was determined to find it.

Chapter 4

THE DUMB-FOUNDED DRESS

I was unable to fall asleep after the sound of shattering glass had woken me. Staring at the ceiling in the dark with tired eyes, my mind drifted to various stages of lucid dreaming, and astral travel.

My hand felt the handrail of the stairwell and the wall next to it, only I was still in bed. I glided my hand down the wall as I flew over the stairs with ease. The room with the painting was in view. The painting was gone! My heart leapt and I gasped as I felt the feeling of jumping back into my body. I lay there in bed, staring at the ceiling and wondered what had just happened. A large part of me wanted to run downstairs to confirm if the painting was there or not. But I was too scared. The darkness scared me. Stairwells scared me. I decided to stay in bed and try to focus on having fun with Ethan tomorrow at the RenFest.

Morning came and I was still awake. I lingered in bed. Too many thoughts raced through my head, mostly about what to do about Sara and Cameron. I couldn't stand to see them torn apart. They'd been friends forever. If anyone was a perfect couple, it was them, even if they were both too stubborn to see it. I stood to fumble for the pair of jeans

I would wear today to the festival. My hand ran across something on the foot of my bed.

"Huh? Where'd this come from?" I touched the mysterious fabric at the foot of the bed. "What's this? A dress?! Who put this here?" It enchanted me to see such a dress. It was unlike any I had ever seen; straight out of a fairy tale. Pure white silk chiffon armlets matching a strapless gown. It had been carefully laid across my bed. "Oh wow! Thank you Emelia," I whispered aloud even though she had traveled to speak with the Elders. *How did she know? I wonder when she put it here.* It was beautiful. I couldn't wait to try it on and wear it to the Renaissance Faire. *Ethan will fall to his knees to see me in such a gown. I will be his fair Lady Juliet.*

I slipped on the white strapless gown and cinched the gold cord around my waist. It was lovely even without the detached sleevelets. Each sleevelet was encircled with a gilded threaded arm band that held it in place on either side of my newly budded breasts. The sheer sleevelets draped down each arm to the wrist, ending in the shape of a calla lily.

The full length mirror in my bedroom gave a different view as the dress wore me, and not the other way around. It was so snug in spots. I'd no idea that I'd blossomed so much over the past few months, and curves that literally happened overnight. *Wow! I'm getting hips. And, and... cleavage.* Even if it was tiny, it was there. I felt like such a woman. The beautiful white gown enamoured me. A little less so with my tennis shoes peeking out from underneath, but that didn't matter. The gown was beautiful.

I added the finishing touches to my hair and makeup and snagged a small denim purse. Okay, so I wasn't totally in costume, but at least I had a place to stash some money and lip gloss.

I could only imagine what Sara would wear. There was a knock at the door. Dad opened it and let Ethan inside.

"Ready, Peanut?" I heard coming up the stairwell.

"Yes, Dad. Be down in one minute."

It took about fifteen actually. I was seldom nervous around Ethan, but on the day of the festival I felt like I was wearing a prom gown. I didn't know how he was going to react. I took a deep sigh and headed downstairs.

I completely forgot my nerves when I saw Ethan. He didn't have a costume, but wore my favourite Irish sweater that he had on the night we first kissed. Seeing him in it again brought me back to that night, a night we almost went too far.

"Do mine eyes deceive me or have I just gazed right into the sun? For the sun would not shine so radiantly as thou art glowing today," Ethan danced in a circle and outstretched his hand, taking mine and kissing the top. "My chariot awaits for thee m'lady. And if we don't get there soon, it'll really be a pain to park and we'll have to walk quite aways to the fest gates," he added in his usual voice, which made me laugh. "Have directions to Cam's house?"

"Mm'hmm," I nodded and handed him a folded up paper from my purse. "Bye Dad. Bye Mom. Hope you have fun on your trip."

"We will. Remember tonight, you're staying at Ginny's house," Mom reminded me.

"Mm'kay. Bye," I waved hurriedly and jumped into Gram's car, which sat four perfectly.

"Hi," I smiled at him. It would be a fun day.

We drove to pick up Cameron, who lived in town, near the school. He didn't live too far from Sara. We didn't even have to knock; he watched for us in the window. He emerged from his house wearing a short sleeved tee-shirt over top of a long sleeved one, with a dragon across the front. His hair was gelled up high and glasses were off. And this was the first time I think I'd seen Cam wearing a pair of jeans… ever!

"Wow, Cam, you look *different*."

"Yeah, you said to go in costume, so I am. Guess who? I'm going as a popular. If this is what it takes to get Sara to notice me, then so be it!"

Cameron piled himself into the car, but not before I noticed he brought along an unexpected accessory… a single, long stemmed red rose. Even in his grumpiness, he loved her. I only hoped Sara could see it.

We pulled up Sara's long driveway to her huge house. It truly was a mansion. Cameron didn't want to get out of the car. He was a bundle of nerves and anger, conflicting emotions. Filled with want, the pathway leading to Sara's door must've felt like a walk to his doom. I went to Sara's door and gave it a knock. Sara would be dressed like a princess, on the off chance that any of the other cheerleaders and populars decided to go to the festival. I'm sure she had lots of gowns to wear, after being in the Woodhaven annual parade's royal court several years in a row, and hers would probably make mine look like a rag. Footsteps just beyond the other side of her door approached and she opened the door. Sara stood just inside.

I almost didn't recognize her. No makeup. Hair pulled back in a braid. Dressed down in jeans and a nerdy button-down shirt. If she wore a neck tie, I'd have mistaken her for a Cameron twin. Her mouth fell open when she saw me, and she smiled. The moment felt very humble between us. For once, I felt like the pretty and popular one.

"Alyson, you look beautiful," she said. "I thought about what you said... about Cameron, and you're right. He's the one person that's always been there for me and I can't stand to hurt him like this." Her voice shook. "I don't think I can go today. I can't face him. He's never going to forgive me." She turned to go back into her house.

"Wait," a voice said.

Cameron walked up from behind me, as I gave him a look of surprise. I didn't know he'd gotten out of the car. These two had to talk, so I stepped aside and waited by the car with Ethan.

"Sara," Cameron fumbled with words, "I really don't know what to say to you. I can't sleep, I can't eat, I can't remember when I've ever felt this, this disconnected. It's just that I've waited my whole life to be with you, and now..." He outstretched his trembling hand with the rose and presented it to her. "I love you Sara. I've loved you ever since I can remember. Every breath I take is yours, every word I speak has your name on it, I can't be without you, and I don't want this pain anymore." He paused. "I haven't been able to think straight lately. I feel like you've tied this rope tightly around my heart and you're yanking at it at your pleasure. I wanted to break up with you today. As I got dressed this morning, I couldn't stand it. Looking back in the mirror. You don't like me now because of the clothes I wear, and how I do my hair. You've always hung out with me, since ... like forever! There MUST be something that you like about me. But you're too ashamed to let your friends see us together! Because I'm a nerd! Admit it! Just admit it, Sara!"

Sara's eyes lowered to the pavement.

"Look at me!" Cam spoke firmly with her. "Is this what you want?"

Sara looked so hurt and ashamed. She couldn't look him in the eyes. She looked only moments away from collapsing into tears on her front stoop.

"If dressing like this makes you happy, then I will. I will be whoever you want me to be, as long as you will still be my best friend," Cam held back tears of his own.

I'd never seen Cameron get so angry and filled with so much emotion. Love is the strongest emotion. It feels so good to fall into and so very, very bad to fall out of.

Sara's eyes welled with tears, sending black streams of mascara down her cheeks. For once in her life, Sara couldn't think of words to say. She looked into his eyes and there was a moment between them. Something unsaid, but they both heard it. He'd rendered her speechless. Tears dropped from her eyes into tiny puddles at her feet and she lowered her head in shame.

"I am such a coward," Sara said softly through tears.

"I can't lose you Sara," Cameron rushed forward and threw his arms around her to hold her up. His lips met with hers in a long awaited kiss. Sara kissed him back and wrapped her arms around him so tightly I wanted to applaud. I felt tears of my own start to form. Cameron kissed her with every ounce of passion he'd waited to deliver for so many years, untangling her braid with his hands running through her hair.

Sara pulled away to catch her breath, but he wanted to keep kissing her. "Cameron, I – I love you. I think I always have, but I've been too stupid to notice. But you've always been there, by my side, whenever I needed you, and I've never known a time that I've needed you more than this moment. I don't want to lose you. You *are* my best friend. You're more than that. I don't know who I'd be if you weren't there, and I didn't realize that until Alyson asked me. You're the only one who knows me, my secrets, what I've been through. You're the key that holds my diary together. I can't lose that," she paused and smiled as their friendship restored. "Cameron, it's not who you are on the outside that made me love you." She let out a soft giggle through her tears. "Although I like your hair that way." He smiled and looked as though he was about to fall over.

"Will you go with me?" Cameron asked her.

"Yes. As long as you don't mind me looking like this."

"You look beautiful. Let's go."

She kissed him again and they held each other, before descending the front porch stairs. It wasn't exactly their first kiss, but still, this was a most memorable kiss that marked a new beginning of their relationship within their already strong friendship. I was eager to give them hugs.

"Oh I'm so happy you guys made up! It killed me to see you fighting."

Ethan smiled and motioned for us to pile in. "Come on, let's get there before we have to park a mile away. Nice shirt Cam. You look like a surfer." Ethan laughed.

Cam imitated some surfing moves and we all had a laugh.

The drive to the RenFest was a happy one. The energy in the car was filled with love and laughter. Ethan couldn't stop taking his eyes off me and I repeatedly had to remind him to keep them on the road instead. The back seat's lovebirds held hands and made googly eyes at each other the whole time. Cameron looked completely different out of his nerd uniform, and Sara's hair had come undone during their kiss. For the first time that I could remember, they looked comfortable to be with each other, just as they were when they were kids. Untainted by the rules of school cliques and society, they were just themselves, and that was enough for them.

Chapter 5
FEST SHINANIGANS

hoa. This place is incredible. It's bigger than I pictured it. There's so much stuff. It's going to take hours to explore everything!" I was in awe. I'd never been to a Renaissance Faire before. I'd stepped back in time several hundred years.

Rows and rows of vendors stood before us, in various stores ranging from tents, to wagons, to fixed buildings that weathered the elements and time, from year after year, until the fest would reopen its gates. I would never have expected that such work would be put into the surrounding structures. A giant maypole stood in the center of a large field, along with many children running around in costumes, dodging one another with foam swords and shields. Several actors roamed the fest camp wearing medieval costumes. A lady approached us with brochures dressed in a Queen of Hearts costume. Her healthy bosom heaved out of her corset with every breath and Cameron couldn't stop staring. Sara gave him a light smack with her purse.

"Ow," he complained.

Sara smiled satisfactorily.

"May I collect your tickets?" she asked.

We each handed her our ticket and she tore off one edge and gave them back to us. *Cool souvenir.*

"Here's a map of our fair land. Hope you enjoy your stay. If you have any questions, you can easily recognize the patrons of the merry Kingdom by the medallions they were, such as this one," she said as she slid her palm behind her pendant and showed us. It was a round bronze medallion with a dragon, very similar to the one on Cameron's shirt. Cameron was afraid to look at the medallion as it rested upon her bust and Sara smiled at her little victory.

"Thank you," we all said in unison as she smiled and walked to the next group of newcomers.

Cameron unscrolled the map and held it open so we could all view it. It was cleverly drawn. "Okay, so we're here, and there's food over here, and a chainmail shop here," he pointed to various spots on the map. "I don't know where to start, this place is so huge!" A man in a jester's costume strolled by us on a unicycle as he juggled and went out of view. In the distance there were magicians, knife-eaters, belly dancers, fire jugglers, and all sorts of entertainers. It was a little like being at a circus, only without the elephants, and with a whole lot more cleavage floating about us, stacked with stocking covered legs and pantaloons.

"Wow," I said. "This is going to be amazing."

Ethan turned to me as he held my hand and whispered softly, "What do you mean... *going to be?*" He kissed my cheek.

"I know! Check it out." Cameron pointed over to a life sized chess board, with human sized chess pieces moving about on its top. "It's so cool," Cameron squealed. "I love chess. Let's go watch."

Sara snagged his arm. "Well hold up. Check that out." She pointed to a display case of massive swords, flails, maces, daggers, and a crescent scythe that would even have the Grim Reaper eager to wield. "They almost look real."

"I'm sure they are. You want one?"

"Oh haha. Let's check out the jewelry vendors' area." Sara was always thinking about shopping.

From a nearby tower, two hefty wenches leaned out and beckoned and bantered with the fest goers. The sign dangling below their bosoms simply read *"Good for what 'Ales' ye"*. Next to that sign was a tiny sign alerting these wayward travelers that they accepted ye olde' cardes d' credit. I admired how hard the faire makers worked to make period buildings. They weren't perfect, but they added to the character of the festival.

We started to walk away when a large gentleman approached us; as he spoke to us, his whiskers and hairy beard drew my attention. It was

a coppery red and gleamed in the sunlight like the mane of a lion. "Greetings my fellow fairgoers. I am known by the name Seamus Phyfe. I am, but a wandering minstrel of these faire lands." He had a musical instrument similar to a miniature fiddle attached to him with a guitar strap and he strung a few chords as he spoke. "Allow me to entertain thee with a bardic tale and song of olden time. I shall know by your applause *or lack thereof*, if you have enjoyed the tune. And if you have, then it is not a token from you I seek, but a mending of my poor broken heart. You see, there once was this lass,

"… and she stole from me," he spoke as he strummed.

"… my heart, and although she wanted very much to freely return it, she could not. We lived our love in secret and she even bore a child. And then, before my own eyes, she vanished, but our love remains true.

"Alas, from her love,

… angelic sonnets were born.

"And when I see young love such as yours, my heart fills with both glee and sadness. Love one another, with all your hearts, for one day… that love… may be lost." He clasped a hand over his own heart and mimicked a sound of weeping for dramas sake.

" Alas my love, ye do me wrong
to cast me off discourteously;
And I have loved you so long,
Delighting in your companie. . . ."

We applauded when he concluded his song. It was well deserved. Cameron asked him, "Is that a lute?"

"Very observant. This is a type of lute called a cittern, but it comes from the same family as the lute, only easier and cheaper to construct," Seamus explained. His eyes turned to me. "Excuse me m'lady, you are one of the most lovely visions I've seen all day. Forgive me, but I've not been able to take my eyes off you since you've walked through the gates," he said as he eyed me up and down. Ethan raised an eyebrow. "I am also one of the judges for the costume contest. And that dress! It's astonishing. Marvelous handiwork. Did you make it yourself?"

"Umm... no. It was given to me, sort of. I don't know where it came from." It was the dress he eyed.

"Exquisite. I haven't seen this kind of beadwork in ages. Just look at that attention to detail. If only you had the shoes to match it. This gown is perfect. You must enter the contest. I insist! When you hear the bells chime three times, come to the arena area," he pointed to it on the map. "We will judge costumes and declare a winner. My heart will be trodden upon if you are not there m'lady. I hesitate to think of the other wenches that would stand in your place," he shuddered and placed the back of his hand across his forehead and we all laughed.

At that moment, several ladies dressed in medieval rags walked by, singing and chanting "We're walking; we're wenching," and frequently stopping to mark some unsuspecting, but very lucky gent with lipstick kisses. They were obviously actors paid to be wenches. Each was in a bosom-heaving corset, and one had a rose cleverly tucked in between her breasts. She smiled at Cameron as she walked by, and Cameron tried his best not to stare. She was missing a few teeth and had a big, brown mole on her face that was most likely fake, but added to her character.

"Hey Seamus, how's about a lil' pop tart for ye breakfast?" one of the wenches shouted with a giggle and a flash of her decorated garter, just above her knee.

"Aye m' Wendy, there must be an Alekeep missing one of its *more gifted* barmaids." A gentleman dressed as a scoundrel or rogue of some sort approached the wench and grabbed her around the waist, cinching her close to his side. "You see my friends, this here is noticeably a woman of distinction, a product of excellent procreation, a possessor of stunning, if not vaguely dubious talents and a scrumptious appetite for all things luscious and ripe, as clearly she belongs among them," he said as his fingertip trailed along the ruffles of her corset. "Normally, I would 'trade-up' to a better model of woman, but there is none finer than 'tis here Wendy. She's the prettiest rose in the whole bouquet."

Wendy smiled coyly, and pulled the rosebud from her cleavage and smelled it.

"He's a sly one, that one. A girl in every port. Duncan's got 'is own harem."

"They all pale in comparison m'lady."

Fortes Fortuna Juvat

Cameron read the words on the gentleman's medal. "What does it mean?"

"It means that I'd give my every last breath and risk life and limb for this maiden's honour. I'd cross oceans and climb mountains, why…

I'd slay dragons, pirates and even ex-boyfriends if it meant the affection of m'dearest Wendy," the rogue jested. She giggled and cooed at him. "Literally translated it reads, Fortune Favours the Brave. Ye can be possessor of one of these fine tokens should ye be successful in a jousting tournament or battle chess, or for a few coppers ye can purchase them at ye olde gift shoppe near the privvies."

"Aye Duncan, and ye are so very brave, and valiant as any knight, and mayhap ye sword needs a bit of polish?" she toyed and tapped his sword hilt lightly as it rested on his hip, and followed it with a wink as though to indicate there would be some promise of canoodling to follow. It was probably all an act, but still, they were very good at it. "Aye, I'd best be not letting them get too sober and suffer an empty cup lest they forget where to spend their monies," she jiggled her corset and it sounded like a change purse. Wendy the wench and her rogue fellow Duncan waddled off towards the tavern, arm crook in arm crook.

"You see? You must enter the costume contest. There will be prizes to be won... good prizes," Seamus winked. "What if I said prithee and promised a good word with the royal King?"

"Okay, okay, I'll be there," I said smiling shyly. It felt odd to have so much attention being paid to me instead of Sara. I looked to her to see if it was making her jealous. It wasn't. It was Ethan that seemed bothered.

The gentleman clapped. "Oh, wonderful. Remember, listen for the bells. Fare thee well." There was something oddly familiar about Seamus. I felt as though I knew him already, as though I know my own father!

Ethan's smile hid an ounce of jealousy at this man's attention being paid to me. I didn't really pay too much attention to it. The gentleman nodded and bid us farewell as he waltzed away and continued to play his wandering minstrel music to other visitors.

"Lucky you," Sara congratulated me.

"Well, I haven't won yet."

"But still," she pulled me aside and whispered, "just look how jealous it made your boyfriend." I looked at Ethan who watched the gentleman walk away and he looked back at me and smiled. It made me laugh.

"Oh come on. It was all about the dress."

"I know. It's really a great dress. I'm going to go find Cam." She giggled and walked over to Cameron and grabbed him by the hand. "Come on, let's go play chess." Sara led Cameron in the direction of the chess board.

"We'll be there in a minute or two; you guys go ahead," Ethan yelled over to them.

Carly and her boyfriend, Matt walked by us and waved at Ethan and me. They carried on very casually and Ethan didn't even bat an eyelash. Thankfully, my jealousy was quickly put to a halt.

"I saw this place when we entered. Come here for a sec." Ethan walked with me over to a jewelry vendor. I smiled. "They're very pretty," I said, mulling my hands over the rings. The vendor watched my hands and my eyes caught hers.

The woman vendor was every bit a gypsy. Her intense stare watched my hands as they grazed the jewelry. She looked away, but I still felt her eyes watching me, even though she glanced in the opposite direction. Immediately my intuition flagged and my forehead tingled gently where my "third eye" resides. There was something oddly familiar about this woman. I had no reason to fear she'd endanger us, but could sense how powerful she was. She was not a paid actress. There was something authentic about her. She was a real witch.

Ethan reached in and pulled out a sterling silver ring wrapped with copper and a tiny gem at the top. "Do you like this one?"

It was a sweet moment; Ethan wanting to give me a ring. Ever since we entered this magical place, I'd felt hopelessly in love with him. He could have been handing me a toad and I'd still have loved it. I smiled gently and nodded as he unfolded his wallet and paid the vendor, who was dressed as a gypsy with long flowing batik sarongs and scarves around her head and waist. She grabbed Ethan's hand as he held out his payment, and said in an accent, her words heavily dripping out of her mouth, "Wait. Please. You have such beautiful hands. May I?"

Ethan outstretched his hand and lent it to her palm face up. She trailed her unusually long fingernails along his lines. Her head looked up and down at Ethan as she muttered foreign words under her breath. "Mmm... yes, yes, I see. Yes, yes, it has been written."

Ethan looked surprised. "What do you see? What's been written?"

"I will not tell you what I see. It might influence your decisions. But I will tell you this," she paused and looked at me, but leaned in to Ethan and whispered to him quietly. "You love this girl and there will be no other like her. You only have one love line written in your palm and it extends for your whole life. For this, you need a special ring." She reached under her table and pulled out a tray of rings like I'd never seen before. They didn't look like the $5 variety we previously had been grazing over. These were worth much more. She scanned her hand over the tray, feeling with her palms for the right ring to call to her. She stopped and pulled one out. It was silver, but it was a flower, a lily, wrapped completely around the ring from petals to stem, encircling it. "This, this is your ring," she said as she held the ring out to Ethan.

"But, I-I cannot afford..."

"Shhh. Nonsense," she said as she unfolded Ethan's other palm, the one that had held the $5 bill. In its place was $50 bill. Ethan looked in shock.

"Thank you. This will do just nicely," she smiled as she cleverly took the money. How it got there, Ethan didn't know. He seemed mystified and stared at the lily shaped ring. "You must give this ring to the woman you love, for it will protect her. It is a magical ring." She smiled and gave a wink to me.

Again, I had an odd feeling of recognition. Had we met? It couldn't be possible. This was my first faire.

She held out her hand to me and asked for mine. I quickly obliged. She unfolded my palm and looked deeply into the lines on my hand. She stood up from her chair. "I have seen this palm before. It is you! There is someone here who has been waiting for you." She leaned in. "Go now. He waits."

"Who?" I questioned.

She extended her long nailed finger in the direction of the chess board, and without a word I had an image enter into my mind of a knight.

"Thank you," I said to her and she nodded approvingly. Ethan looked at the ring, which he still held in between his fingers. "Yes, thank you."

"Let's go find Sara and Cam," I said to Ethan, focused on the chess board.

"But-," Ethan said and tried to stop me, but I quickly grabbed his hand and led him away from the fortune teller. We ducked into a shaded area, out of view from the gypsy.

"There. Can you believe her?" I said in amazement. "Do you think she was telling the truth?"

"I'm not sure. That was one clever trick she played with the money."

"Well, I don't believe her. I mean, how could she have seen my palm before? I've never even met her. I've never seen her before in my life!" I looked back at the gypsy. She looked down. I still felt her eyes staring at us. I pulled Ethan aside into a small alleyway and out of view. "And someone here has been waiting for me? Seriously. I think she's got me confused with someone else."

My intuitive feelings scared me. I did feel I knew her. She was very familiar to me.

"Maybe you're right. But it is a beautiful ring. And it looks magical, even if it isn't."

"Yeah."

I was anxious to try it on.

"May I?"

I held out my hand and he slipped it on my finger. There was a moment when my fingertip entered the circle of the ring. It felt like a tiny zap or an electrical charge when there is static in the air. It settled just as quickly as it happened and I wondered if it wasn't just my imagination. The ring fit stunningly, like it was meant to be there. I looked down at my hand. I *had* seen this ring before. I just didn't know where. A dream perhaps. Ethan's eyes were lit up and he looked like a puppy.

"Thank you. I love it!" I wrapped my arms around Ethan and kissed him.

"Hmm. That's funny. You look different somehow." Ethan scratched his chin.

"I do?"

"Yeah. Maybe the ring really is magical. You sort of – sparkle?"

A familiar voice interrupted us. "There you are. Where've you been? You have to come see this," Cameron said excitedly and Sara stood beside us anxiously eager to move on.

We walked as a group to the chess board, passing by the mead and mutton stand. It smelled good, but I didn't eat meat, especially not a gigantic turkey leg still on the bone. *How positively primal. I'm not a caveman. I'm a little more civilized than that.* Still, several ladies dressed in burlesque wench costumes walked around with a mug of mead in each hand, and roses tucked cleverly in their bosoms. Oddly enough, one of them also walked by snacking on a giant turkey leg. I wasn't sure if that was part of her character, or charm, or if she was just hungry. We all smiled at them and walked by, as the wenches flirted with the customers sitting at the picnic tables. We recognized a few students sitting at one of the tables. One of them was Holden Jeffries.

"Hey, Holden. Congrats on landing the part of Van Helsing," Ethan called over to Holden Jeffries. Holden looked appalled. He glanced across the table at the guy he was with, and let go of his hand. I don't think he had suspected he'd be recognized by anyone here.

Sara grabbed my arm. "Come on. Let's go. I'll tell you later."

I took Ethan's arm and we left.

Cameron looked as though he made his own revelations. "Ah-ha. That makes so much sense. Now I know why Principal Jeffries hid that photo he found in Jeremy's locker. He was Jeremy's boy-,"

"Could you just be quiet please Cam. Not everyone needs to know everything about everyone. I mean who cares anyways," Sara gave him a look that perhaps he should just drop it. He did. We arrived at a large opening in the trees, secluded by its own grove. In the center was painted on the ground a large chess board of red and black. It was surrounded by a stadium of wooden bleachers. A new game was about to begin. We took our seats. Out walked the Pawns first and they took their respective positions on the board, followed by the bigger pieces, including someone dressed as a castle turret to play the Rook. The Kings and Queens walked out, as did the Knights. No one seemed out of the ordinary.

Two announcers took turns calling out the position to which their chess pieces would move to. Instead of just sliding out of place on the board, the pieces battled for their position, usually involving some swordplay or fighting of some sort. It was towards the end of the game, and the black knight was fighting with the silver queen. He looked directly at me and paused, stopping his performance briefly before continuing and toppling the queen, thus the announcers declared the game to be won.

"Did you see that?" I asked Ethan, Sara and Cam.

"That was awesome!" Cam cheered.

"Whatever," Sara said as she filed her nails, bored out of her mind.

"I saw it," Ethan said quietly.

From behind us on the bleachers, we'd been approached by the black knight. He removed his helm. He was breathtakingly handsome.

"That dress!" he pointed to me. "That dress! That was Lily's wedding dress! Where did you get it?" The man almost seemed to the point of hysteria. He aroused the suspicion of several of the security crew and they walked over to our area on the bleachers. He calmed down and pretended to be signing autographs.

Ethan stepped in, "Look pal, I think you're confusing my girlfriend with someone else."

The knight spoke to Ethan, "Good sir, if I may be so obliged to speak to your lady in private please. There is a matter of utmost importance I have to discuss with her."

The sound of three bell chimes rang through the festival.

"I have to go. They're judging costumes now," I said trying to lure myself politely away from the knight.

Ethan once again interjected, "I don't think that's a good idea. I don't really want my girlfriend going anywhere with you alone!"

"Ethan, I think it's okay," I cupped my hand softly around his arm.

"Alyson, I don't trust him. I'm going to get security."

"No! Ethan, it's okay. Really. I'd like to listen to what he has to say."

Ethan leaned in close to me, "Are you sure?"

"Yes."

"I'm keeping my eyes on him."

"I'd appreciate it if you *just* kept your eyes on him. I don't think he wants to start a fight," I whispered back to Ethan.

Another set of three bell chimes rang through the air.

"We have to be quick," I said.

The man in the knight's suit led me aside, aware of everyone watching us both. "M'lady. Thank you for obliging me. Before I tell you my story, I must ask a question. Your dress, please, I beg of you to tell me where you found it."

"It was given to me to wear to this festival," I said as I looked down at the sleeves.

"Do you know by whom?"

"Well of course I know who gave it to me," I said surprised and offended. But really, I assumed it was Emelia that had left the dress on my bed. It just had appeared there. I didn't know for certain. "Well, I am almost positive it was given to me by a friend."

"May I?" He extended his hand towards one of the sleevelet cuffs. I assumed he wanted to feel the fabric. He turned the sleevelet cuff over and showed me an embroidered $\mathcal{L}$ on the sleeve. "That was for Lily." He knelt down before me on the ground and began to cry. "Please, who gave you this dress? Have you seen her? Have you seen my Lily?"

I saw Ethan hesitating to come over and rescue me. I shook my head not to. He frowned and stood his ground as sentry.

"I'm sorry. I don't think I can help you. I don't know who this Lily person is."

He stood and looked deeply into my eyes. "She was the only woman I ever loved. There was only one woman meant for me to marry and she was the one. She was so beautiful, like you are in that dress. But that is her dress. I'd give anything to feel her warmth inside of it again, to hold her, to be with her." He started to wrap his arms around me in the dress, unaware he was doing so, and pulled me close against him.

"Stop it!" I yelled, and Ethan ran over, as did security. They pulled the man in the knight costume away from me, but he would not let go of the dress.

"No!" he begged. "Please! You don't understand! I'm not from this time. I need your help!" he shouted as security pulled him away.

I realized I'd had a vision previously about a young girl, and heard a queen's voice shout the name "Lily." It was the day of my sixteenth birthday, just after Ethan had given me the lily flower.

"Wait!" I yelled. "Wait, please! It's a misunderstanding. I know him," I lied. Ethan nudged me and said quietly in a hushed voice, "No, you don't."

"Shhh," I told him. "It's okay. I'll tell you later."

Sara and Cameron just stood watching curiously.

The security let the man in the knight's costume go. "If you say so," they both said to me and walked off to attend to a drunken man falling over on the bleachers, obviously having had too much mead.

"Thank you. One thousand thank yous, M'lady. And to you good sir, you have nothing to fear. No harm shall come to her. I merely was mistaken by the dress she wears. It belonged to my fiancée, Lily."

"And you are?" Ethan asked very miffed.

"I beg your pardon for my rude introduction. My name is Ivan, noble son of King Peter."

"And so you are a Prince?" Ethan asked him.

"I am indeed. But that was not enough to marry Lily."

"A real royal Prince at a Renaissance Festival. Yes, that *is* believable," Ethan said sarcastically, and looked at me unconvincingly. "Alyson, I think I've heard enough. This guy's a nut."

"Shh, Ethan. Hear him out. I believe him."

A final three bells echoed through the festival. Seamus, the gentleman in tights that greeted us when we first arrived, ran up to me and spoke to me in character. "Oh heavens. I've found you. Please m'lady, you must come at once. I am faced with a horrendous horde of hags on the stage," he jested.

I looked at Ethan and to Prince Ivan. "I will be back," I said to Ivan, the prince in the knight's costume. I trusted he needed my help. The dress was my only clue. And the embroidered letter $\mathcal{L}$. How did he know it was there?

Respectfully, he nodded.

Ethan, Sara, Cameron and I followed Seamus to the arena, which wasn't far from the chess board area.

"I'm sorry, but you'll have to wait outside. The amphitheatre is full, except for those being judged for their costumes. You're not wearing costumes, are you?" Another judge, much less friendly than Seamus, and dressed as royalty, addressed Ethan and my friends.

They looked to each other and shook their heads.

"It's okay, Alyson, we'll just hang out here. Good luck!" Cameron said.

"Yeah, have fun and good luck," Ethan said and kissed my cheek lightly.

Seamus clapped and whispered, "You're a shoe-in with that dress," and the royal judge walked me into the amphitheatre and closed the wooden door behind him. The theatre was full, just as he said it was.

The arena was an outdoor amphitheatre, designed similarly to Shakespeare's Globe Theatre, right along the waterfront. It was beautiful and accurate! As a devoted Shakespearian, I was in awe to be on such a stage.

I walked in and the audience became abuzz with people talking. Even the other contestants on stage were pointing and smiling at my gown. "And like the moon shining brightly in the night's sky, she shines," Seamus said as I took my respective place amongst the other contestants. Two other judges were also noticing me, dressed as a royal King and Queen. I was overwhelmed by the attention. The King looked at me with the eyes of a predator. It gave me the creeps. I was eager for the contest to end so I could leave and stop him from watching me like a perverted old man.

After a few minutes of judging, Seamus came forward in front of the contestants. "It is with great pleasure that I introduce the winner of Woodhaven Renaissance Festival's costume challenge." He stood before me and presented me with a sash and a pair of passes. "The winner is the astonishingly lovely...," he said and leaned in to whisper, "What name do you go by sweetheart? Elisabeth?"

"Alyson."

"Oh, you look like an Elisabeth," he said hushed. He continued, "The lovely Lady Alyson, who has won a season pass to the Renaissance Festival for the remainder of the season and entrance to next years, and a complimentary jumbo turkey leg and flagon of witches brew. Let's give her a round of applause." Seamus cheered and applauded.

"Thanks Seamus," I smiled and gave him a kiss on the cheek, to which he made an exaggerated hand gesture of a pitter patter of his heart. Of course, my little kiss had also gotten the unwanted attention of the creepy judge dressed as King. He grinned and for a moment his eyes had an unwelcoming glow to them. He looked possessed. It scared me and my feet took tiny steps backward towards the edge of the stage and I almost lost my balance, but Seamus caught me.

"Oh be careful dear. There are steps to go down on the side here. Seamus assisted me to the stairs and then was snagged by another cast member. Be with you in a second dear," he whispered to me and walked across the stage to assist someone else.

The shadow of a giant bird was cast on the ground of the arena. Immediately I ducked low to the ground and looked up to see if it was I thought it was, or rather, who I thought it was. Terror ran through me. I'd only seen one bird before that was able to cast a shadow that large, and it was not a bird. Instead of applause from the crowd, there were gasps and fingers pointing up to the air. I glanced up to see what flew over us but it had already moved out of my line of sight. Tingles ran up my arms. I sensed it was him. I don't know how, but I feared he'd escaped the mirror, just like I predicted he would. I wanted to run to Ethan.

The crowd slowly began to applaud, but it was still soft and overshadowed by their whispers. Something was wrong. The air felt different. All I could think was to run. It echoed through my head as though it were a command. *Run.*

"Leaving us so soon?" the possessed King grabbed my arm too tightly. His voice didn't sound human.

I paused momentarily in shock. The King wasn't his usual self. Something evil had gotten a hold of him. "Let go of me!" I yelled at him and struggled to pry off his meat hooks.

"Is that any way to thank someone? I was expecting a little something… extra," he said as he leaned his body too close to mine. "Just a little kiss. Your boyfriend won't even know."

"Yuck! Get off me, you ape! I don't work that way. You can keep your sash and your --," I said angrily ripping at the sash and threw the passes in his face when the shadow swooped over us again, and the King backed off. His grimace across his face was all I needed to see to know that something was not quite right. "You are *so* getting fired mister!" I backed away from him, fled through the wooden door.

"Ugh, creepamillion!" I muttered under my breath.

Seamus ran after me and spoke to me out of character. "I apologize. I had no idea one of the judges would try something like that. I thought I knew him too. That seemed so very unusual for him. He's been King for years and never has anything like that ever happened. I saw the whole thing. I've already alerted security staff. Please don't let that experience keep you from returning here. Even at carnivals, there are some shady people. I just had no idea it would be one of our judges. I'm appalled as you are. Please accept my humble apologies, and these." He handed me the passes I'd thrown in the judge's face. "You dropped these. I feel you've earned them."

"Thank you Seamus. Why are you being so nice to me?"

"The world is filled with many types of people and it is a rarity to have someone like yourself walk into my faire. You have something very special within you and it radiates like pure love. It's so rare to find. But this morning, I felt very down. And just being in your company has helped me see my inner spark. I trust that you know that because of who you are, there are those that will seek you out to harm you, because they want what you have and will try to steal it. But you will be strong and succeed," his voice was not the playful and colourful character he had put on for us at the gate, but someone very deep and wise and spiritual.

"You're not just a wandering minstrel are you?" I asked him, aware of the possibility that he might be someone of great importance.

"No, I *am* just a wandering minstrel, like a pan seeking out his muses. You m'dear are one of my muses. You have given me great inspiration. I look forward to seeing you again," Seamus took off his hat and bowed to me and as he walked away, he played a few chords on his lute. I wondered momentarily if Seamus really was someone important, someone with a spark of magic in his heart.

Members of security, dressed in costume of royal guards, came barging into the theatre arena and restrained the King. He continued grinning madly at me as thunderous flapping of giant wings echoed throughout the park. As the King was led away, I looked at him one last time. He didn't take his eyes off mine until he went out of view. The sound of the wings flapping became much louder and swooped overhead. A familiar feeling swept over me. I'd felt the same way I did when I first encountered Sadie in her madness. Hremm Nevar had taken a piece of her soul and replaced it with something dark. Was it possible Hremm Nevar was back? Did he possess the King? Screams echoed through the faireground. A quick vision came to mind of Ivan and the chessboard. I sensed he was in danger and didn't know it. I took off running in the direction of the chessboard when Ethan caught up to me.

"Hey, where are you going? How'd the contest go?" Ethan tried to stall me. I looked into his eyes and he was completely oblivious to anything being out of place. The smell of danger was in the air. I felt it in every ounce of me.

"Ethan, I have to go," I said softly, pulling myself out of his arms. He looked confused, and I tried to hide my worry. "Order me a sandwich please. I'm famished. I won't be long," I said as I kissed him quickly and rushed off towards the chess board. I knew he watched me run away and I worried about what he thought. I wasn't hungry. My stomach was in knots. But at least Ethan would be inside of a building safely out of view from Hremm Nevar.

I entered the grove where the chess board was and frantically looked around. Prince Ivan was gone. I asked some members of the staff if they'd seen him, and no one had, but they also seemed abuzz about a giant bird. I looked around bewildered and confused, and down to the cuff of the sleevelet with the embroidered $\mathcal{L}$. How could he possibly have known that was there? Who was he? I regretted Seamus luring me away from Prince Ivan. He was gone and I still had many questions. I picked up a medallion off the ground. "Fortes Fortuna Juvat" was inscribed around the edges. It was similar to the one that rogue Duncan had worn. I had to get back to the tavern.

"We saved you a spot," Sara patted a place on the bench beside her. It was sheltered under an ivy covered pergola, which only allowed speckled rays of sunlight to enter through its canopy. I sat down and Ethan gave me a questioning look.

"You look disappointed," Ethan remarked.

"He wasn't there."

"Oh," Ethan said with his arms folded across his chest, "You went to go find *him*."

"Ethan, please. I believe him."

Ethan paused for a moment to look into my eyes and saw the hurt in them at his distrust. "I hope you are able to figure out what he wants. If you should run into him again." I leaned in to kiss Ethan to see if I could salvage the situation when I felt a hand on my shoulder. I turned around to see the gypsy woman hunched over me.

"Come," she spoke with her heavy accent. I wondered if she was Roma or one of the Irish travellers known as Tinkers.

Ethan stood up with me.

"No, it is alright. You must stay. She is strong. It is a lovely ring, no? You must trussst. Always have trust. Trust is equally as important as love," she said smiling at him. "Without trussst, you can have no love. Never, ever break it."

Ethan reluctantly sat back down on the bench.

"You must trussst," she said to Ethan as she led me away. Ethan looked curiously at the gypsy, but didn't say anything.

I looked at the gypsy with uncertainty. "Where are we going?" I wasn't sure who to trust. I felt as though I was part of some elaborate plot and I was the decoy. I stopped walking for a moment and spun the gypsy woman around angrily.

"Why should I trust you? I don't even know you. How is it you know me?" I confronted her, standing my ground.

The gypsy woman turned to me and looked into my eyes.

"Abigail?" I softly asked, almost disbelieving. But it was her. It was Abigail! Why was she disguised as a gypsy at a faire?

"You mussst trussst," she said, maintaining the gypsy voice. "I will take you to him."

Something was horribly wrong.

Chapter 6
INTO THE PAST

bigail amazed me with her disguise. How did I not recognize her before? She ushered me back to her tent where Prince Ivan crouched in a crowded corner.

"What's wrong? What happened to him?" Ivan sat in a corner with one arm resting on a propped up knee, still dressed in his knight's costume.

"We have to protect him, but he is very stubborn," Abigail said as she waved her hand and a circle of blue light surrounded Ivan. "He still has much to learn. Ivan wants to fight, but we mustn't let him. It is not his battle. He is powerless against him."

"Fight? Him? Fight who?"

"Hremm Nevar is here," Abigail said calmly.

"What?! But – how? He's trapped inside of a mirror! Isn't he?"

"Someone must've released him. Someone very careless. I'm glad it wasn't you, but only a powerful witch would know how to undo the spell we cast."

"Why? How? How did he get out?" I almost yelled at Abigail.

"Keep your voice quiet. We mustn't disclose our location. I will do my best to explain."

The sounds of a giant bird swooped over our tent. Screams filled the festival as waves of people panicked. I peeked out through a tiny slit in the gypsy caravan tent and pulled its curtains tightly together. A shadow of a giant raven cast a horrid, jagged image over the ground in front of us. His shadow was at least ten times the size of him. The shadow came closer to the ground as he landed and stood in the center of the main festival area, transforming before everyone's eyes into full human shape. He was no longer being subtle. This was no longer just a game of cat and mouse. I looked across to the mead and mutton stand and saw Ethan, Sara and Cameron. Hremm Nevar walked around menacingly sniffing the air and darting his eyes from side to side, looking, watching and waiting to find his prey. His eyes glanced at our tent and I quickly shut the slit that would've revealed us. I glanced back to Prince Ivan who was near breakdown, and Abigail who held him. I noticed in my mind's eye, a reflective white light, almost like a mirror, that shielded Prince Ivan. Abigail magically hid him from Hremm Nevar.

"I'm not sure how long I will have energy to keep him hidden. Hremm Nevar is strong," she whispered.

I peeked out through the slit, half expecting to see Hremm Nevar's eyes peering into our tent. But he was gone. Or so I thought. Amongst the flurry of panicking individuals, I caught glimpse of his black winged cape. He was at the mead and mutton stand. In one quick movement, he grabbed Sara beneath his wing and flew off with both

Cameron and Ethan trying desperately to pull her out of his grasp. They failed and Hremm Nevar was gone, taking Sara with him.

"Oh my goodness. Why? Why is he here? Why'd he take Sara?" I screamed.

Abigail rose from behind me and waved her hand towards the direction Ethan and Cameron stood in shock. Ethan and Cam found themselves walking towards our tent, as though we called them. They stepped inside.

"Alyson!" Ethan said, surprised.

Cameron was a mess of nerves and couldn't even speak.

"S-S-Sara... s-she," Cam tried to spit out an explanation.

"It's okay. I know. I saw. I know who he is," I reassured them.

Ethan put his arms around me and noticed Prince Ivan huddled in the corner. "What's going on?" he asked the gypsy woman.

Abigail outstretched her arms in the direction of Cameron and Ethan and said aloud in a voice that was not completely her own:

Into a field of poppies you shall sleep,

dreaming of blissful merriment.

For when you arise, you shall not keep,

any thoughts of discontent.

Restless you shall not be.

Sleep my children, sleep.

So mote it be.

Abigail waved her hand over Ethan and Cameron. Gently they fell to the ground inside the safety of the caravan, where they slept quietly and undisturbed.

"They are safe now. They are safe asleep, more than they would be helpful to us awake. They do not understand magic, and thus, it is better they do not know, lest they hurt themselves trying to rescue you."

"What's going on Abigail? How did Hremm Nevar escape?" I peeked outside of the gypsy tent through the slit into the open area and only saw crowds of people wandering around, wondering what happened. Some drunk fest goers clapped as though it was rehearsed and part of a show, cheering "More, more!"

"Fools," I muttered.

"Careful, Alyson. It is better they assume it was nothing magical. The less people know about this, the safer we will all be. We have a problem right here in this tent with us." She pointed to Prince Ivan, who slowly stood erect to speak to us, realizing the danger might be temporarily gone.

Prince Ivan stood up and thanked Abigail, and then turned to me. "M'lady, your dress, Lily's dress, you must tell how you acquired it."

I looked to Abigail. "Oh enough with the stupid dress already!" I paused. He looked hurt. "I thought it was Emily. I found it on my bed the other day. I thought she'd left it for me to wear."

"Emelia doesn't have a dress like that," Abigail said. She turned to Prince Ivan. "Tell us of Lily."

"Lily was to be my wife. We'd planned to be married, but her mother, the Queen, would not have it. You see, I am merely a mortal man. The Queen did not want her daughter to marry anyone other than another witch. Lily cast me through a mirror and into the future – your present – so the Queen could not find and kill me. Lily told me before she cast the spell, when the time was right, she'd come find me. She said to look for a sign, and I thought it was you."

"Lily created a portal through a mirror? But that's not possible. Lily is hidden inside – umm," Abigail stopped herself. "Are you certain it was Lily? How can that be?" she asked with concern. She looked to be in disbelief, as though something was very wrong with the Prince's story.

"Yes, it is how I traveled to this time, and where I've been hiding and waiting for someone to help me get back to her."

I quickly realized what Abigail thought. "Do you think the portal let out Hremm Nevar too?" I asked her.

"It is possible, if it was carelessly left open," Abigail said. "But Lily is not careless." Abigail paced the floor in deep distress. She spoke of Lily as though she knew of her. I was curious to know how.

"I arrived here, in the center of the chess board, within a blink of one's eye. It has been baffling trying to explain myself, but other citizens here are actors and assumed I took part in their play, and so I played the role. I am the part of the knight in a chess game, day after day, ceaselessly waiting to return to my own time. There are rumours this festival is coming to a close and it shall pack up and leave. When it leaves, so will the chess board. If it is a portal, I have no way to return to my own time. I'd hoped Lily would come for me by now, but she has not. Something or someone is keeping her. When you, m'lady, arrived in the crowd, I thought my Lily had come to me. I thought she had come to escort me back. Is it even possible?" Prince Ivan knelt down on one knee. "Ladies, I implore you; I know you are both witches, as Lily is. There must be a way you can converse with her?"

"Well, I am not a real witch, exactly," I said.

"Alyson, don't be modest. You *are* a real witch, but it takes time and lots of it to do it well. It is a craft, like many other crafts, that needs to be practiced in order to make your skills and spells potent. However, you were born with a natural gift of premonition, which will guide you on your journey. And my other two daughters, Emelia and Sadie, will help as well."

I let out a heavy sigh. "It still doesn't explain how Lily's dress appeared on my bed, especially if the portal is here, at the festival. You don't think Lily could've run into Hremm Nevar inside the mirror do you?" A look of panic waved across my face. "If Lily's a witch, Hremm Nevar might've charmed her into opening the portal for him."

"No, that is not possible. Lily is not easily charmed. Her heart is true and it beats for mine alone. We are destined to be together," Prince Ivan said convincingly.

"I am disbelieving it was the real Lily that sent you through time and opened the portal, Prince Ivan. Nor am I certain the chess board is the only portal that was opened. Alyson, the house – something evil has been stirred."

"What do you mean?" I asked.

She paused as though listening to the wind. "Emelia. Sadie," Abigail called into the air.

"Yes, mother?" they said in unison, standing behind her, arriving only by a mist. It was the first time I'd seen Sadie since her imprisonment. They stood side by side, as sisters, almost identical twins save for a few differences such as hair colour.

Prince Ivan fell to the floor overwhelmed by the presence of magical energy in the tent. "Help ground him properly girls."

"My daughters, Prince Ivan, Sadie and Emelia," she introduced them. They both curtsied towards him. He stood to his feet again.

Both girls immediately darted their eyes to Ethan in slumber and then darted their eyes quickly to Abigail questioningly. "The boys are alright. I've cast them into a slumber spell until I wake them, for their safety. It is a spell neither one of you can undo, so don't worry your pretty little heads or even *try* to undo it, Sadie. That is Ethan, and the other is Alyson's friend, Cameron. Now, I called you here to ask you some questions."

Sadie and Emelia looked to one another curiously, and as sisters. It was very unusual to me to see them interacting so cordially. *I still don't trust Sadie. She would probably have to spend her entire lifetime earning it back in my opinion for what she did to Ethan. She could've killed him. Even though she appears to be healthy and sane, she teeters. There is a look in her eyes that I cannot forget.*

"Have either of you re-opened the portal we cast Hremm Nevar into?"

Sadie shook her head. Emelia spoke. "No, I've just returned from the Elders, who were kind enough to allow Sadie's imprisonment sentence to be shortened on behalf of her good behavior. I came immediately here, and brought Sadie with me, from the painting."

"You were wise to come when I called. I sense there is danger at home?"

"The house has been ransacked. It has been turned completely inside out. Someone has been searching there very recently, someone I'm afraid to tell you who I saw. I don't want you to think I had anything to do with his return, because I didn't. I didn't do it, Mother, I promise you! It wasn't me!" Sadie pleaded. A look of recognition ran through all of us. She had seen Hremm Nevar.

"I watched him from the painting, shielding myself the best I could. I did not want him to see me or find me. I can't bear his torturous love a moment longer. I love him still, but it is not the happiness I've seen in the love of others. It is a lustful love, and I'm ashamed to succumb to it. He is a heartless murderer, with no soul of his own!"

"What did you see, Sadie?" I screamed at her, worried about my parents.

"Alyson, I'm sorry," Sadie whimpered.

"Tell me!" I screamed in panic. I was not prepared for anything she would say next. I willed my ears to stop listening, but they wouldn't. The words she spoke echoed through me with the force of one hundred daggers.

"Your parents are unharmed Alyson. It was just after they left for their holiday. I heard the door close behind them and there was a loud moaning coming from upstairs in your bedroom. Lots of sounds of shuffling about and glass breaking, as though burglars had intruded. This was no burglar. I saw *him*."

We paused and continued to listen to Sadie.

"I gasped when I saw him. Hremm Nevar came down the stairs and looked about in the foyer and living room. He looked straight as the crow flies into the painting and he saw me. His eyes narrowed and glared at me as he pulled the painting off the wall and tossed it aside, not knowing how to get me out of it. Frustrated, he ripped open the front door, pulling off its hinges and flew off. Hesitantly, I set one foot on the ground and peered out from underneath the painting. I thought the coast was clear. I stepped out and rehung the painting and as I turned around, the sound of a heavy footstep crunched on a broken mirror, and screaming. Emelia had returned and fled down the stairs and pushed me back into the painting, until just now when Mother summoned us. Mother, I had nothing to do with his return. I did not set him free. I promise you."

"I have to go home," I demanded.

"No," Abigail said calmly. "Home is one place you should not go. It will be alright for you to stay with your friend here, I will see to that," she pointed to Ethan. "But you must not go home. You must not enter your house. Alyson, if you take one step into your home, it will be your last. You may only enter when you have prepared for what you will find, and you will know when that is… but it is not now."

I knew she was sincere and not to doubt her.

"For now, work must be done. I must go consult with the Elders, and my daughters with me. Close your eyes and when you open them again, you and your friends will each be – right where you need to be."

I closed my eyes and felt the ground beneath my feet shift. I had been teleported.

Chapter 7

A FAMILIAR PLACE

than smiled at me as I opened my eyes, bewildered. We stood in front of his Grams' house at the door. *What just happened? How did we get here?* I felt disoriented and needed to sit down.

"Did you have a nice time?" he said, as though nothing had happened. I had to poke myself to remember that he had no recollection of the remainder of events that transpired in the tent. I glanced over to Grams' car, parked neatly in the driveway; as though we'd driven it home ourselves. I assumed Cameron was back at his house as well.

"Alyson?" Ethan asked me again, waiting for a response.

"Oh, yes, I'm sorry. The day just passed so quickly. I can't believe we're back… home again so soon," I said rather confused.

"I'm glad you're staying with us. It's really weird how the police came all the way to the festival to tell you your house had been broken into. I'm glad your parents were already gone for the weekend. Somebody must've been just waiting for them to leave to rob your house," Ethan said as he held the door open for me. "Well everyone knows it's full of antiques. You really should get an alarm system… or a dog," he jested.

The police? What is Ethan talking about? I remembered Abigail. I wished I knew what to do next.

"Ethan, please be a sweetheart and go get Alyson settled in the spare bedroom."

"Okay Grams," he said and kissed her cheek, winking at me.

"Come on," he said and motioned for me to follow him upstairs. It was familiar to me, but very different from the last time Sadie chased us inside.

I sat on the edge of the bed next to Ethan. The air between us got a little thicker.

"So. Did you have fun today? Do you remember the last time you and I were here in this room?" Ethan asked coyly as he brushed my bangs away from my face.

"How could I forget? It's etched in my mind forever."

Ethan leaned forward and brushed his lips lightly against mine. When we touched, a spark tingled between us.

"Want me to stay and hold you?"

It was an impossible temptation, but I shook my head.

He nodded gently. "Alright. Good night," he said as he pulled the door closed behind him. I fell back into the bed and wrapped a pillow between my arms and hugged it, reliving the moments of the day in my dreams.

※ ※ ※

The quiet sounds of night slipped in through a space in the window. An owl hooted three times. I sat up in bed as if I'd been summoned. I had been. I went to the window. Across from me was a tree, and perched on a lonely branch, a small black owl flashed its eyes at me.

Who are you? I wondered.

The black owl flew to a closer branch, almost adjacent to the window, and then flew inside. I waited for the owl to transform, but instead a woman slipped out from underneath an invisible cloak shielding her. She dusted herself off as she stood naked before me, her long hair cleverly keeping her modesty, and a tiny, sooty, black owl still perched on her now revealed arm. The owl mystified me. I'd seen it before that night in the tree; the night there was a noise in the attic.

"Take this and hang it up," she tossed the cloak in my direction, and in my surprise it hit me in the chest and fell to the floor. "Well, pick it up. Don't be sloppy," she scowled at me as she paraded the room fumbling her fingers over Grams' belongings, and making faces of unworthiness as she brushed invisible dust off her fingertips.

"You'd better not say one word, Henry," she threatened the owl. "I am Princess Lily. I am certain you were expecting me, although my name probably preceded me," she said with a confident smile. There was deceit in her eyes. I didn't trust her.

Lily set the owl down on the side of a long wooden desk made of walnut. The owl hopped up to the wooden slats on the back of the chair parked neatly at the desk. He watched over us and seemed uncomfortable being there. He tried to fly off several times when I noticed he wore a tiny shackle around his tiny owl leg. I felt sorry for him. She yelled at him as though he had done something wrong.

"Now behave yourself. No droppings. This isn't our home!" she barked at the owl so loudly, he briefly lost its balance before resetting its footing on the slats. "Ha! And you won't be escaping either! You belong to me now!"

Belongs to her now? Her slip of the tongue alerted me that something probably wasn't right with the princess. My instincts told me not to trust her.

Henry hooted to get my attention, but Lily shot him a glare that implied his doom would be imminent if he continued.

She turned to me. "So you stole my dress. I want it back."

"Your dress? I didn't steal your dress." I was miffed at the accusation. "I found it. So *you're* the one who put it on my bed."

"Not quite. You say you didn't steal it. Then just *how did* you acquire it? It was stolen from me! Quite literally, it was stolen *off* me. I had been wearing it at the time, and then it was gone, and I was left wearing no more than Lady Godiva herself!" she flung her hair aside briefly and then covered herself with it again. "It happened about the same time I was literally pushed out of my mirror portal and bowled over by this poor old man. At least he told me which time to find Prince Ivan. Alas, my poor Ivan," she let out a dreamy sigh. "I've been looking for him for centuries now. Have you – have you seen him?"

Her tone was innocent. I wanted to trust her. I recalled how menacing Hremm Nevar was at the faire, and how Abigail shielded

Prince Ivan. She wanted to keep him hidden. I didn't quite trust this princess. Something wasn't quite right. I didn't say anything. She watched me for answers and let out a huff when I didn't give her any.

"So, if you have my dress, I'll take it back now."

"The dress I found on my bed," I said more than annoyed.

"Yes. That dress. Do you have my dress?"

She waved her hand at the dresses on the floor and they magically shuffled and rehung themselves in the closet. "Well, it's not here." She let out a heavy huff of discontent.

"You know, I'd be stuck in that mirror eternally if it weren't for that old man letting me out."

"Which old man? What did he look like?"

But as she spoke, I already knew her answer.

"He had long white hair and a bad back, but I really remember his walking stick the most. It had the head of a raven on it, and the eyes of the raven appeared alive."

"Hremm Nevar," I muttered under my breath.

"Yes, yes that was it. Poor old man. So lost. He was so sweet and charming."

"Lily, you've been tricked," I told her.

"Tricked? What do you mean, tricked?" she looked at me with genuine uncertainty and I deliberated that perhaps she really was being honest with me.

"I mean, that old man disguised himself, so you'd take pity on him. He tricked you. My only question is why didn't he just kill you? He certainly wouldn't have any trouble doing so. He hates witches! We're the only ones who can overpower him. Hremm Nevar is a *very* dangerous creature."

She laughed maniacally. "Listen to yourself. Hremm Nevar is a very dangerous creature. He hates witches." Her face changed. A disguise. "Tell me, Alyson, do you scare easily?"

"I hadn't told you my name yet."

She smiled, but there was something evil in her eyes. A dark void. I hadn't noticed before. "Hremm Nevar is my son. He would never harm me. But you – you… he would."

I stumbled over my words and could barely spit them out. "Your son?! You're not the real Lily, are you?! Who are you?"

"Names have power. You will know soon enough who I am." She grimaced. "He will come for you. You have something he wants; something I need. I will return when you least expect it."

I pondered running, but she just disappeared into thin air leaving the owl behind.

My thoughts raced. *Hremm Nevar wants something from me? What do I have that she needs? Who is she?*

The owl in the corner stared at me before hooting three times softly. My attention diverted to Henry. His eyes widened. An unspoken voice filled the room with the words,

Thrice beckons the wise one, listen attentively, for it marks the moment of inspiration and change.

I knew I'd seen the owl. It had been Abigail's voice. This was not Lily's pet. Henry had been owl-napped. But why?

"Alyson, it is time," the voice said. It was Abigail.

Time? Uncertain what she meant, I felt summoned. Summoned to return home.

Henry would be safe. I looked at the tiny shackle, but had no key for it. However he wasn't bound to anything. I opened the window enough for him to fly out, but he did not move. Instead he watched me and kept guard.

"I have to go," I whispered to the owl. It didn't respond.

I tiptoed down the stairs and glanced over in the darkness of the living room to see Ethan's grandfather sleeping soundly in his rocking chair. I quietly slid out the front door unnoticed. It was unusually dark. My vision felt cut in half of what it normally was. The path home was familiar to me. I should be safe.

I needed to find Abigail.

Chapter 8
EVERYTHING IS NEVAR WHAT IT SEEMS

Strange how everything looks so abstract in the dark. Something as simple as a rock can become a distorted gargoyle, those grotesque statues of protection. I thought of Ethan's postcard from his Mom, as I passed a distorted rock with seemingly watchful eyes. *Maybe that's what a real gargoyle looks like. Maybe it's something unseen or something that can only be perceived.* Either way, it put me on edge. I picked up the pace on my walk home. Abigail had forewarned me not to go home, but it was time – whatever that meant.

Emily's night vision would be a blessed gift to have. Cats have excellent night vision. Ethan's house was behind me in the distance now, about half way down Colby Drive. My house hadn't been broken into by vandals, but by a soul stealing vampire! Would he be there? Is he waiting for me? What was it he wanted from me? Courage pulsed through me. I was ready for him. I'd fought him before and there was no way I'd let him harm a good friend of mine.

I paused briefly in the darkness. I knew my bearings. I'd walked this road one hundred times. Still, the ground felt different beneath my feet. It felt like sand falling through an hourglass, completely dissolving beneath me. My feet sank deeper into the ground and I closed my eyes as it connected to the Earth's core. Warmth radiated through me. I looked up at the half moon above me and was lost momentarily in its beautiful gaze down upon me. Particles of stardust floated upward from me and into the stars surrounding the moon. White light filled me. I opened my eyes and almost screamed as hands reached out to hold my own.

"Abigail!"

"Our family pet has been stolen. Recently, I returned to a secret area in the house to find that things inside were shuffled about and a window was not only carelessly left open, allowing Henry opportunity to fly out, but also the window sealed itself shut and disappeared altogether, so Henry could not get back in! He's in such a dilemma."

"Yes, I have seen him recently. He was around Grams' house. He's probably still near there. He was in the company of -," I started to tell her of the imposter princess, but she cut me off in her haste to find Henry.

"Oh no matter, dear. He'll find his way home. He always does. It's dangerous to be walking this path alone. I admire your perseverance in wanting to protect your family and friends. But beware... hidden dangers await you in your home. I shall escort you, along with the Lady's blessing."

"The Lady's blessing?"

"Our Mother is constantly watching out for us, guiding our steps. She changes everything she touches, as do you. I've cast a protection spell over you, or rather, you cast it on yourself."

"What do you mean? And who is *The Lady*?"

"I will tell you of her at a later time, but I shall teach you her gifts. After all, she has been with you all along but you have not noticed her. It has been recommended by the Elders that I become your teacher, and you my pupil. In time, you will understand our relationship more fully, and the gifts of the spirit will be bestowed upon you." She paused to reflect on the moonlight. When she looked back down at me, her eyes were silver. "You grounded yourself. Very wise. Keeping connected will keep you focused on your intent. Once you enter back into your home, it will appear differently to you. A portal was opened. I cannot close it. It can only be closed on a night when the night is moonless. There are other factors to closing the portal, but a moonless night is essential."

"Thank you Abigail. I can learn so much from you."

"In time, perhaps. You are only able to contain what you can handle and no more. Don't rush to learn everything; it will come. You will receive the help you need when you ask."

I reflected on her words and the moments I had quietly spent alone in the moonlight.

"There is a name you will come to know. That name is Elluna."

"Elluna," I repeated. She nodded only once. *Elluna. Why does that name feel so familiar to me?*

She softly glowed in the moonlight as we walked, as though her aura radiated a natural white light that followed her. My feet had disappeared and been swallowed into the darkness. Still, I knew the steps home. We were almost there.

The windows of the house came into view. Empty. The house was completely dark. I'd never felt so spooked. This was no longer just my home. It had been taken over by something dark.

The silhouettes of the trees looked bare and jagged against what little light the moonlight shone. The air was crisp. A few leaves crunched underneath my feet as we crossed the path towards the front door. As I turned to walk up the front steps, I caught glimpse of something moving around in the living room. An illuminated candle went from room to room, with seemingly no body to hold it mid-air. Its flames licked the air and danced shadows haphazardly as it passed the doorway into the next room and disappeared through a wall, leaving the room dark as though it had been extinguished. Abigail put her hand on the front door and looked back to me.

"Are you ready?"

"As I'll ever be," I said nervously.

She turned the knob and pushed the front door open wide. Just as we were about to pass through, it slammed shut in our faces. A thunderous "STAY OUT" screeched through the wind. A gust of wind rushed up behind us. It did not feel empty, but instead had a dark energy being propelled along with it. Abigail looked at me uncomfortably.

Sounds of shattering glass came from within. Windows slammed themselves shut from all sides of the house simultaneously. The front door heaved and bellowed as though it had breath. The house itself was alive with ghosts.

"You must pass through. This is your home. Show it you are in charge. Let no ghost *ever* have power over you."

"But that's not – that's not Hremm Nevar," I said with a rush of nerves.

Abigail stepped back and she motioned for me to approach the door. With a nod, I moved into place to open the door. I peered in through the etched oval glass window in the heavy wooden front door. The dancing light of the haunted candle returned and floated into the foyer. It stopped on the other side of the door. The door clicked and opened itself wide, emitting a heavy groan as the wood swung open and crashed against the door stopper at the base of the floor. There was nothing between me and the floating candle except for the threshold. I placed my foot in the doorway. The heavy door creaked lightly and for a moment I thought it might slam back at me, but it was held open. The air coming from inside my house no longer smelled of the familiar and comforting scents of home. It smelled like a cemetery full of dead, rotting bodies. My house had been taken over.

"No ghost will have power over me," I whispered to myself as I put another foot inside the doorway. I was over the threshold. It was time to retake my home.

Boldly, I entered completely and approached the floating candle. The area around it was ice cold and it was difficult to breathe. I heard a voice whisper "take the candle" simultaneously as the candle moved closer towards me. I couldn't. Scared, I turned to run out the door and ran into a force field instead, propelling myself backwards into the house and landing on my bum on the floor. Abigail continued to stay on the other side of the open door. I was inside now, and apparently trapped until I did as the ghost wanted.

"Abigail, help."

"This is something you must do on your own, my dear," she said. "Remember, you are protected. Stay grounded and you'll be fine."

My heart pounded. I looked back to the candle that floated in the darkness.

"Take the candle," the unseen girl's voice whispered again.

I couldn't feel my arms, let alone lift them, to grab at a haunted candle. I shook with nerves, my confidence in my new abilities wavering. I turned to look back to Abigail to ask for help, but she was gone. An empty black rectangle of a doorway stared back at me, and I looked into the darkness of the night just beyond.

"Abigail?" I called out frightened. *I can't believe she just left me here... with a ghost!* I wondered if the ghost could sense my fear.

The area surrounding the ghost in the foyer was ice cold. My breath was visible. Yet on the other side of the threshold in the doorway was a beautiful evening, warm and breezy. The warmth from the outside did not find its way to me. Exterior sounds were nonexistent. It was quiet. Too quiet.

The ghost waited patiently for my next move. I turned to face it, keeping my eyes lowered. In my current state of fear, I had to remind myself to breathe. I peeked out from the tiny slits of my squinting eyes down to the floor and looked at the ghost's black shoes. Ghosts don't wear shoes!? Then the ghost sneezed and part of a face became revealed from underneath an invisibility cloak.

"Lily?" I snagged the candle quickly out of the ghostly hand, hoping to reveal a hidden princess in hiding. "Is that you?"

I extended my hand to the area where her head would be hiding behind the cloak and caught a shimmer of pale blue eyes. In that moment, terror ran through me. The eyes revealed themselves more fully, along with the rest of the face. It was not Lily. It was Sara. I thought she would be smiling. She no longer resembled the best friend I'd sat next to in school. She looked petrified. Her eyes were fixed on something just behind me. Locked in a stare, hypnotized by the candle. As I opened my mouth to speak to her, a cold handprint locked onto my shoulder from just behind me. It rested there firmly and had the texture of an ice cold leather glove, placed very near to my neck. The cold hand swept the hair away from my neck. I was certain he or she … or it, stared directly into my veins and watched my warm blood pulse through them, perhaps in envy or desire for a life it no longer has.

The tiny hairs on the back of my neck stood on end and my feet locked to the ground. I could not move them or break away from the icy grip on my shoulder. My heart raced quickly, and then stopped. It was too frightened to beat. I looked into Sara's flickering eyes in front of me as she watched the shadow behind me. Her eyes told me a story. *She walks between the land of the living and the land of the dead, with one foot placed in each*. What had Hremm Nevar done with her? The same as he did with Sadie? Is he stealing her soul too? I had to pull her back into my world before death consumed her. The leather glove clamped down tighter on my shoulder. I glanced out of the corner of my eye at the glove. My knees buckled beneath me but I stayed grounded.

Sara stared at the ghost. She said no words, but a grimace appeared across her face, as she leaned forward and with a single blow took away the only source of light I had. The candle was extinguished, and I had a feeling I was about to become so too.

In the blackness of my foyer, I could not see, but heard Sara's feet take two steps forward towards me as the ghostly gloved hand continued to hold me in place. The glove emitted an icy chill radiating up my neck. Frostbite began to form on my skin. I cringed as it stung into me.

"We've been waiting for you," she whispered into my right ear. Her voice was no longer completely human. It had a familiar growl to it. She'd been put under one of Hremm Nevar's enchantments.

"Sara? How could you betray me like this?"

She didn't respond.

My fear turned to anger. Since when did I let ghosts, vampires and their minions get the better of me?

I closed my eyes and yelled "Silence!" and when I opened them again, the ghost and Sara were both gone. I looked to the unlit candle and focused on the wick. I thought if I focused hard enough I might be able to relight it, but it remained dark. A bolt of lightning shot through the sky outside as the silhouette of a raven passed through its trail. The raven landed in the doorway. It was a white raven. Abigail.

I ran to her, passing through the barrier and throwing my arms around her neck to give her a hug.

"I'm really scared, Abigail. Why did you leave me here?"

"You needed to see what you're up against. You passed the test. I stayed with you dear, but in the astral world. I flew to a window only I can see the entrance to. I'm always close by, even though you may not know it," she said with a clever smile. "I wear many hats and carry many purses, but you will always know me, and recognize me. You know where to look and it's not on the outside of someone," she touched the area where my heart would be and smiled. As she touched my heart, I felt it awaken. "You will always know who you are kin with, as your heartbeat connects with the same harmonious heartbeat in a friend, in ways we can only begin to understand. It is a beat familiar to us from the womb, a tribal beat of a drum. As long as we are living, we shall hear the beat of one another's drums, and drum along, or sing along, as we are intended to live in synchronicity."

I heard drums in the distance, long ancestral chants calling me to them. As I listened; I awakened. I looked down as a tiny frog hopped across my foot and back into the shrubs. Abigail's glowing skin reflected the blue tone of the night sky back on her beautiful face, where she smiled softly as we both watched the frog. I knew what it meant. Frogs are rather familiar to me.

"I silenced your ghosts temporarily," Abigail said, redirecting our attention to the matters that lie inside. "I cannot keep all of them at bay, more are appearing as we speak. A portal is open and it must be closed."

She motioned through the door and the candle I set on the mantle lit itself. "We must go back inside," she said nudging me. I looked to the area where she nudged and she stood at least a foot away from it. I must've looked very confused to Abigail. It was her aura that nudged me.

"You first," I said rather unsteadily.

"Shall we, then, together. Until you are ready. Then you must go alone. But always remember what I have said. Look within your heart. You are never alone. You are blessed my child. I am always with you, within you. Even in total darkness, light will always fight its way through."

She handed me a candle and lit it with her fingertip.

"The eternal flame resides within you and with it you will fight many battles. Be brave."

I let out a deep sigh. I looked at first to the candle, and then to the doorway. I felt empowered and confidently took the first step.

Chapter 9
BRUSH STROKES OF MIDNIGHT

 bigail and I passed the threshold into the foyer of the house. Many wisps whizzed past us. As they flew off, they appeared as bright orbs spiraling around in all directions, streaming trails of white light behind them like comets.

"Don't worry. Those ones are on our side," Abigail whispered as she held my left hand and directed me to the painting in the living room. "Come with me," she said, motioning to the painting.

"Into the painting?" I looked at her confused.

She didn't wait to give me a response. She pointed her finger at me and tossed me into the painting. I didn't feel the transformation, but when I looked at my skin, it was paint-covered. Ironically it was the painting my own mother, Claire, had painted after imprisoning Hremm Nevar and rescuing Sadie. I looked down to my shoes. They were covered in brown paint.

Sadie glided behind me and put her hands over my eyes. It terrified me.

"BOO!" she said and giggled. She removed her hands and came around to face me. She really was beautiful again. I had no reason to be scared. After all, she was Emily's sister, and the two were identical, save for their hair colour. "Hello Alyson."

I hesitated momentarily to respond. "Hello umm... Sadie."

"It's okay. Don't be afraid," Emelia said as she stood beside her sister. It was evident Emelia had given Sadie a second chance and forgave her for any wrongdoings, no matter how difficult. For the many years they fought, it was clear that the two were happy to be sisters again. Not fighting over suitors or clothes, but helping join to fight a battle against the enemy that harmed Sadie in the first place: Hremm Nevar.

"Beware, Alyson, if you leave the painting, you must be quick to either leave the house or go to a different room. The ghosts are frozen, but they can still move... just very, very slowly. If you stand still, they will find you, just as the man with the leather glove did. Let me see that frostbite," she came closer and put her hand on my shoulder blade where the icy ghost's glove rested.

"Who was that man?" I asked as Abigail healed my shoulder.

"There. All better. I don't know who it was. It most likely is one of them dear. The dark ones. Demons wear many faces. Or perhaps even a lost soul seeking revenge, or leaving its mark to remind those left behind that they once existed and not to be forgotten." She paused to contemplate something. "This situation might be more grim than anticipated. We imprisoned Hremm Nevar, so it was his prison that was let open. We might be looking at facing his fellow prisoners as houseguests. Not just any ghosts, but criminals, demons, villains of the worst kind."

Sadie looked at me with concern. She may have been a powerful witch, but she wasn't strong at controlling her own desires. There was a glimmer in her eye that whispered she still liked the bad boys. Emelia stood closer to Sadie and Sadie gave her a look of recognition and promise.

"I must go. Be wise in your choices girls." She transformed herself back into a white raven and flew forward directly out of the painting and through the front door. As she left, white paint spattered and then blended softly with the other surrounding colours, leaving no trace of her. It was as though she had been *un-painted*.

"Alyson, I am certain this is awkward for you. Be aware that I mean you no harm. You understand me. I only follow my heart. I feel with you, I am protected," Sadie stood face to face with me in the painting. She was very close to me in age, if only a few years older and a century before. Her raven hair fell upon her chest mirrored with mine. I felt drawn to her for some reason. It made me blush a little. She was intensely beautiful. I couldn't stop staring into her eyes. I was mesmerized by them.

"Alyson," Sadie's voice awoke me, as though I'd been under a spell. "It's okay. I have that effect on many of my acquaintances, be it male suitors, or their mistresses. You're very beautiful also." Her words made me smile. I found her very alluring when she was not in ghost form. Something that both confused me and amused me.

Emelia agreed. Sadie is a temptress. Seduction is one of her gifts. The two of them were enchanting and together they were a force not to be reckoned with. Sadie would break hearts and Emelia would mend them. They were like two halves of the same whole.

"You are wise, Alyson. I hear your thoughts," Emelia said smiling.

A crash came from upstairs.

"What was that?" I asked not expecting an answer, but I got one.

Tentacles of black wrapped themselves around the stair railing and as used them as hands. A black wraith floated down the stairs. Thick, heavy ankle shackles were chained to his feet, and dragging chains down each stair until reaching the bottom and coming into view. The hood turned in our direction and looked its silvery eyes directly into the painting. They glowed. It saw us. It started to approach us. Closer and closer it crept across the floor, chains dragging behind it. It stopped, hovering before us, moments before the painting. It peered in at us, like human child's eyes peering through doll house windows at the dolls. Sadie covered us in a cloak. I shivered.

"Crouch down," she whispered. It was the invisibility cloak that Sara must have dropped. The cloak that Lily wore. We were invisible to the wraith. His eyes darted around the painting looking for us. Beams of light passed left to right, like search lights. It did not find us. We heard a low growl and then the sound of the painting being ripped off the wall and thrown to the floor. We landed image side up. The wraith glided away angrily in search of something. Probably us.

From underneath the invisibility cloak, Sadie leaned in and kissed my cheek. "Thanks for keeping me protected."

Her kiss surprised me. "Umm... you're welcome?" I thought of Hremm Nevar, and how much Sadie was in love with Harding, only to be hurt so deeply she was driven to die for love. Her kiss lingered on my cheek. She loved Harding, but did she love Hremm Nevar? I needed to know.

"Sadie, tell me about Hremm Nevar."

She backed up quickly, loosening her grip on the strings holding the cloak around us and almost revealing our identities from underneath it. My question offended her, but she answered. "He is a murderous vampire. There is no love in him. And his soul is the soul of one thousand others. He is soulless himself. A person with no soul has no conscience. They believe they can do anything they want, as they were not created with life, but with death. It is neither his destiny to be alive nor dead. He just exists. I don't know how to get rid of him. But I am certain I do not want him back. It was a false love. I was tricked."

"Is there anything in your spellbook that might help us?"

"I've some very potent dark spells, Alyson. Many moons ago, my ancestors weaved some clever magic. I possess their knowledge. Although it is under lock and key, but still right under my nose."

A riddle from Sadie had me both eager and discontented. *Giving Sadie back any prior knowledge she possessed from her darker times might prove to be dangerous for anyone, including herself. It's been proven that Sadie is a little clumsy with her own spellcasting.*

I looked just under Sadie's chin. Her moonstone necklace glowed softly from its core deep within and radiated out as though looking into a star.

"Although it is under lock and key, but still right under my nose."

Her words rolled gently through my head like reading script. I stared at the necklace. How did she get it back?

"Sadie? I thought your necklace was taken from you by the Elders."

"Yes, well, they gave it back for good behavior. I've earned their trust. Do I have yours?" She stroked the back of my hair softly.

Unsteadily I said, "Yes." Whoever would have thought I'd have to trust my enemies.

She smiled, and a memory of her evil grimace painfully raced through my head hiding cunningly behind her seductive smile. There definitely were two sides to Sadie. Currently she behaved similarly to Emelia, and as twins, that is not uncommon. But her darker side... lays dormant inside of her, waiting to escape from the protective shelter of the Elders. I feared I would one day have to handle that person again... to face the demons inside Sadie. But for now, I had to put my faith in her, so that we could stop someone more powerful than herself.

"I will lead you to my spellbook and we can look together, alright? You have my word that no harm shall come to you from me, or may I take the punishment. Emelia, can you stay and keep the painting shielded?"

"Sadie, I've entrusted you with my faith that no harm will come to either of you. Be strong and resist the temptation of the darkness. Let Alyson be your light. She will guide you. She also can protect you. Yes, I will keep the painting protected. Make haste."

The chiming of three tiny bells rang through the house. I had no clue where they came from. Sadie smiled a sincere smile and waved for me to follow her. She lifted the edge of the painting as though lifting a trap door to peek out. The coast seemed to be clear momentarily.

We crawled out of the painting and I rehung it quickly on the wall.

"Be hasty, Alyson. We mustn't linger here outside of the painting," Sadie warned.

We ascended the stairwell together and took the hallway to the left. There was the door, the massive door that had my attention from the moment I walked into this house. And now, Sadie was about to lead me through it, where she would have access to her things, her powerful items, and spellbook, for the first time since being released from her imprisonment. I felt very unsteady. She pushed open the door and walked through while I remained in the hallway and looked in.

Sadie stood in place and looked around the room in each direction. She walked to her desk and placed her hand over several items on her desk. The items seemed to recognize her. She waved her hand over some cards and they flipped over. A ghost crept up behind me, and I jumped forward into Sadie's room. The ghost didn't follow me in. It stayed in the doorway, with its invisible nose pressed up against an invisible glass. Sadie's room must've had a ward against such things. *Maybe she's not such a clumsy witch after all.*

"Come in, please. Don't linger in doorways. It's bad luck and you never know where you'll end up if you stand too long in one," she said half serious and half mocking. "It's too dark. Just one moment." She walked to a row of candles and tapped her fingertip to each wick lighting each one. The room still was in shambles.

"Sadie? You didn't always live like this. I think I saw a photo," I said knowing full well that photo happened when I walked through a black scrying mirror and into Sadie's old memories. "A photo of what this room looked like before."

"Before what?" Sadie asked with the innocence of a child with no recollection of anything traumatic happening.

"Oh, just perhaps the way it was decorated when your family first built the house."

"Like this?" she said pointing her finger in the air and waving it in circles. The furniture of the room floated around us and landed themselves in former positions they once held before Hremm Nevar entered her life. Sheets and blankets folded themselves, a feather duster swept happily atop a bookshelf, a white face cloth held by an invisible hand carefully wiped off the mirror.

A tiny brown mouse stood up on its feet and addressed Sadie.

"Ahem. Over here," the little brown mouse cleared its throat and bobbed its head up and down motioning Sadie to come closer to it.

Sadie moved towards the mouse and held out her palm so it could crawl on top of it. It did and she brought it up to her eye level to look at it more closely. I didn't like mice. *Cartoon mice, but not real ones.*

"Father?"

Its tiny whiskers twitched. "Yes, Sarah, it is me."

Sadie's name is Sarah?

"If ever there was a moment I have waited for, it is this moment, and seeing my beautiful daughter before me." The chubby mouse clapped its little paws together. Apparently we had good snacks in the house. "Sarah, I am delighted to see you as yourself again my dear."

"Regretfully I cannot say the same to you, Father. I mean, what's happened to you?" Sadie took her unoccupied hand and stroked a single finger across the top of the tiny mouse's head. She overturned a bobbin of thread on its side, and she sat the tiny mouse on it, and it sat upright as though it were a chair.

"Well, not long after the accident, the Elders found me and asked if I'd keep watch over the two of you, and the house, as it needed to be protected and tended. I grew lettuce and other things in the gardens to stay fed. And thankfully Ms. Bell makes a mighty good pie too. The hardest part was avoiding getting caught by your sister, as you'd cursed her to stay a cat. Thankfully the time she did catch me, I didn't taste appealing to her. And so, I've lived here, all these years, waiting for you two to come back. But wait, Emelia is not with you?"

"She is here Papa. She is downstairs, shielding a safe haven for us in a painting. I can bring you to her after, but I needed Alyson's help."

"I never did get a chance to formally introduce myself. I did attempt to on the first day you moved in, but being stuck in Sarah's room, I couldn't get out that way. I had to crawl through a crack in the window and down the drainpipe to get in and out."

A flashback entered my mind, of being on my knees and peeking underneath the doorway to Sadie's room and seeing a mouse.

"Alyson, this is my father, Mr. George Augustus Finch."

I smiled at the tiny mouse as it held out a single paw. I took it between my two front fingertips and shook it gently. "Pleased to meet you, Sir... umm... mouse? Umm... Mr. Finch. Umm... how do you do?"

"I have something to show you Sarah. Come a little closer to your spellbook."

"One second, it's still a little too dark in here. Let me just light one more candle," she said smiling as her father sat perched on his thread bobbin. She struck a match and lifted it up to an empty brown candle next to a raven statue, while smiling innocently at him.

"Sarah, DON'T!" Mr. Finch squeaked loudly and scurried across the desk and jumped onto Sadie's arm, running up its length and extinguishing the candle flame just as the match licked it.

"Just in time, hopefully." The tiny mouse looked very worried. "Not *that* candle. I don't want to be dinner, if you know what I mean."

Sadie looked at him quizzically. I looked at the two brown candles and raven statue. It was an oddly placed altar left in what looked to be an ordinary teenage bedroom.

"I thought I'd cleaned everything up." She pointed her finger to the altar, attempting to make it disappear. It didn't. "How very odd. I can't remove it."

I recalled the way the cards flipped over when they recognized Sadie. The room went quiet. The tip of the candle wick still smoldered with a faint ember holding on to its rightful duty to ignite. Sadie leaned in to blow it out, but instead, her breath fueled the spark and the candle lit not with an ordinary orange fire licking the wick, but a black flame. She gasped. A familiar sensation of fear ran through me. She looked at the cast iron statue of the raven. Its eyes opened and turned its head at her. Sadie screamed.

"Grab the book," she yelled to me as she swiped the mouse into her hands and placed him into a pocket on her white gown. I grabbed the book and hesitantly followed her as she ran out of her room and into the haze of ghosts. "To the painting," she instructed as we fled down the stairs, the sounds of a hungry bird following the squeaking of a tiny helpless mouse.

Sadie's toe had caught on the tip of her gown and she fell on the bottom stair and lay on her stomach. I turned to help her when the raven swooped down over her and transformed as quickly as the blink of an eye. She rolled onto her back and crawled backwards like a crab across the floor as he hovered over her. She scooted right against a table leg and he pinned her to the floor with his hands.

"Did you miss me, my love?" Hremm Nevar sniffed her neck and kissed it lightly.

Tears streamed down Sadie's face. Clearly she still loved him and tried to resist his charms, but he overwhelmed her. She weakened beneath him. She thrashed her head from side to side, avoiding his deadly kiss.

"You will not have my soul!" Sadie screamed at him. "You do not love me! I saw you with another. I am no longer your bride!" She growled with every word.

"Quite the contrary. You will forever be my bride, even in your death," he hissed.

He leaned in to take a death kiss from Sadie. The tiny brown mouse crawled out of her pocket and ran up Hremm Nevar's cloak and bit him square on the ear.

Shrills of pain emitted through the air as the mouse would not relinquish his grip on Hremm Nevar. He shrieked in desperation, waving his arms and batting at his ears to remove the mouse's tiny grip. Sadie had crawled out from beneath him and grabbed me. She pulled me into the painting and covered me with the cloak. I clasped my hand over my mouth to keep from screaming.

"Don't watch, Alyson. Don't watch!"

Hremm Nevar gripped the tiny mouse in his hands, and when they clutched around its tiny body, they revealed talons.

"Alyson, Emelia, hold me. Keep me safe." Sadie quivered. Her fear was genuine. Emelia and I huddled close to her.

"You will be nothing more than a snack to me mouse!" Hremm Nevar growled and tossed the mouse across the floor. It did not move.

Hremm Nevar let out a powerful roar I'd never heard before. He transformed back into raven form and flew out the front door.

"Alyson. My father-- He killed my father. I will never forgive him!" Sadie spited him. "I will live out my every last breath finding every possible means to kill Hremm Nevar. He is Death, but in this case, Death doesn't deserve to live! He will pay for what he's done to my father, to my family. He will pay for what he's done to me, even if I have to summon an army of darkness to assist me."

Sadie's eyes possessed a familiar look of crazed wildness in them. She was back to her old self, but at least this time, she was on my side. Sadie thumbed the pages of her spellbook in hopes of finding a spell quickly.

"Mother, I need your assistance," she said as she slammed the book onto the floor and the pages flipped themselves over until settling upon an image of the grim reaper in the margin.

"Oh Sadie, I hope you know what you're doing," Emelia said with concern. "Brace yourself Alyson. I sense a storm brewing."

Sounds of thunder and lightning echoed throughout the sky, and shook the house. I braced myself against Emelia. Blue streaks of electrical charges danced all around Sadie, surrounding her with a circle of electric blue lightning. "Hremm Nevar is Death, at least a minion of him. You cannot hide from him if he seeks you. We must confuse him and call upon as many of his tormented souls as possible. I will only call upon the victims of Hremm Nevar. He holds a piece of their soul, like a lost puzzle piece, and they can never move on wholly without it."

I shook my head in astonishment of the impending spell to be cast.

"You're going to conjure DEATH to kill Hremm Nevar? Am I hearing you correctly?"

I felt the floor beneath my feet begin to vibrate. I looked down as the threshold cracked open and revealed the thick brown soil underneath the house. Thumping continued from underneath and all around. I looked down to the dirt of the floor. Dirt flung from side to side and a pale undead buried hand emerged from the soil. I jumped backwards and screamed as an arm attached to the hand began to unearth itself and feel around nearer and nearer the space within where I stood.

A spell for Death

Into one world you walked once and
now you shall walk again
Between the light and dark
worlds of the living and the dead
You shall walk among
the places you've never been
Seek the raven that bears the staff with its head
For his soul is not his own, he has none
Those who weep for love, he seeks
In a kiss of death, you and he become one
A sliver of your soul eternal, he keeps

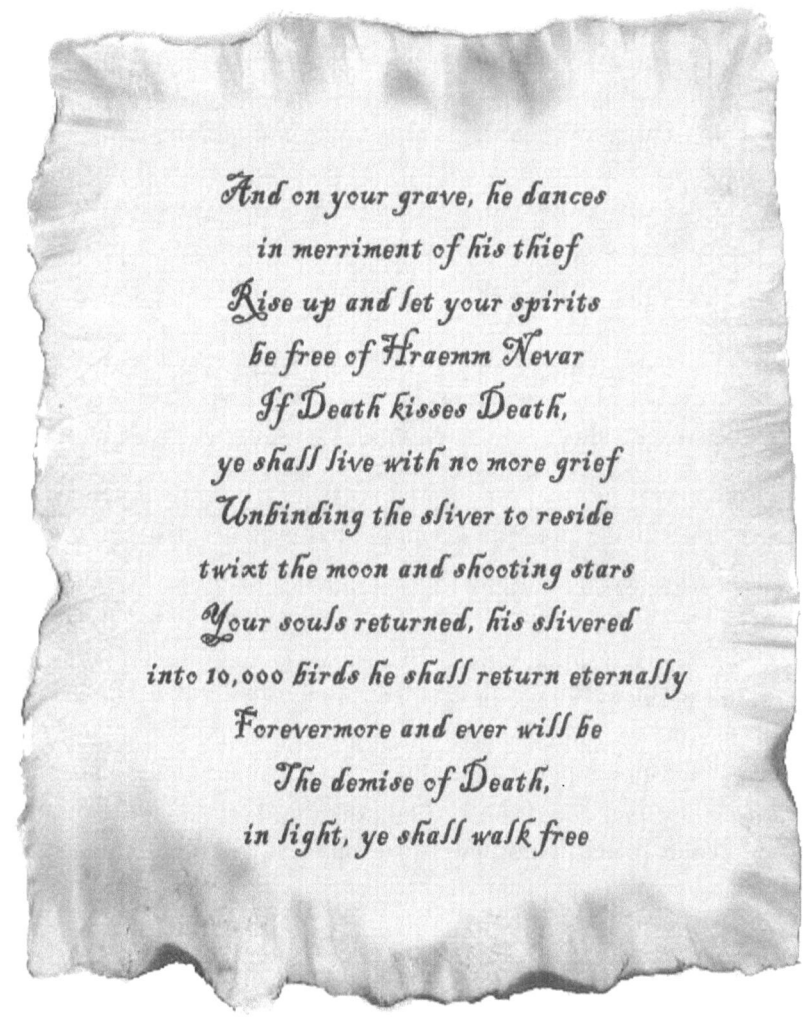

And on your grave, he dances
in merriment of his thief
Rise up and let your spirits
be free of Hraemm Nevar
If Death kisses Death,
ye shall live with no more grief
Unbinding the sliver to reside
twixt the moon and shooting stars
Your souls returned, his slivered
into 10,000 birds he shall return eternally
Forevermore and ever will be
The demise of Death,
in light, ye shall walk free

"I summon an army of death. Do not fear me, Alyson. No harm shall come to you. You have my word, remember? I promise to you, as you are like a sister to me now. Here. You must take this – for protection. Use the cloak, take the book and leave immediately." She yanked the moonstone pendant from her neck and placed it in the palm of my hand. "Take it. I hope to never be human again. My heart has gone black and therefore, it beats no more."

Its energy intensely radiated through me and felt hot to the touch as I closed my hand around it. A faint blue light shone through my fingers. She stepped out of the painting and as she did, she transformed herself into the ghost, only this time she was not alone. She was being backed by an incredible force. At the end of Colby Drive, an army of ghosts were being summoned to assist Sadie.

Emelia looked saddened. "Sadie, I've waited so long to have my sister back, but I know you must do this. I will keep watch over Alyson once again and aid her from any harm. I am safest and stealthiest in my both blessed and cursed form." Emelia transformed herself into a grey cat. "You have my protection should you need it."

Sadie could not speak. The transformation had already begun.

"Brace yourself, Alyson," Emily warned, as she hid behind me, covering her paws over her ears.

Before I could react, Sadie let out a blood curdling shriek. My ears feel like they could bleed. I quickly placed my hands over my ears and tried to block it out but the sound still crept in. I winced in agonizing pain.

I uncovered my ears. "What was that?" I asked Emily.

There was fear hidden in Emily's voice. "The cry of the Banshee. She has been heard. They will be coming quickly. We need to leave, Alyson." Emily jumped into my arms.

Sadie had changed completely now. A Banshee she was. The mesmerizing beauty she once had – left her. It was replaced by something very wicked and tormented, and unfortunately familiar to me. Mounds of earthen soil erupted all around her hair, and bugs of all types ran down the tendrils. Earthworms and slugs and beetles resembling scarabs, and dead leaves wrapped themselves around her. Her skin turned to bark and shattered, peeling off layer by layer and only leaving muscular tissue behind. It rebuilt itself in a ghostly, pale white, with black veins marking her like a tiger. But her eyes were what captured me the most. I felt so haunted, I wanted to look away, but felt powerless against the desire. She was beautiful. Her eyes were silver, just like Abigail's. I recognized her as the Sadie that stood outside my window and taunted me once before, only this time, she was not after me. Power emanated from her, but it was not the pure evil I'd felt before. She was on our side. She looked electrified and to touch her would prove fatal for anyone mortal.

Carefully I held Emily, as a cat once more, and tucked the spell book in the crook of my arm. I held the invisibility cloak over us. It appeared like a black cloak to everyone else, but ghosts could not see us in it. From every corner of my home, ghosts seeped in and stood next to Sadie, now their fearless leader. Scores of shadowy and wispy wraiths, imps, shadows, apparitions and orbs alike swam about her in an ethereal ghostly sea. Swarms of them arrived and flew about her, flying past Emily and me pausing briefly to wait for Sadie's command, like hungry sharks smelling for blood. I was bumped in all directions, but ghosts did not see me. Still, they sensed me.

She turned and addressed me. "Alyson, these are hungry souls seeking a home. They cannot harm me. I am a Bride of Death, eternally. The only one who can take my soul is Death himself. You must leave and not return unless I instruct you. Go. NOW!" she commanded as the shadows crept close to my exposed feet. "YOU MUST GO!" she demanded, and her growling voice was insistent.

I fled the house, with Emily under my shelter, knowing someday I'd return.

Chapter 10
A ROGUE ATTACK

I walked the road, shielded by my cloak, peeking over my shoulder for followers from the almighty army of darkness Sadie had summoned. There was no one. I walked alone, with Emily in tow. My stomach felt like an unbearable pit of painful knots. A wave of illness quelled inside. I stopped and doubled over. Something was horribly wrong.

A voice spoke from the darkness. "Alyson? Alyson, help me." It was a girl's voice, from within the forest. I passed over the kissing bridge and heard the voice again.

"Alyson. Help! I'm trapped," the voice said, this time more frightened. The voice came from all directions and echoed through my head. I looked down over the bridge and into the creek. The water became abnormally still for a creek. It halted and became mirror-like. My own reflection looked back at me until it shimmered away and was replaced by the face of a friend, the face of Sara.

She screamed as the scene from the RenFest repeated itself before me, only from Sara's eyes. Hremm Nevar swept her off the ground and flew her to the lake. It was the lake behind the Finch Estate.

"Please. Please don't do this," she pleaded with him.

"You called me," Hremm Nevar pinned her to the forest floor. "Your heart seeks to be loved. You shouldn't let a heart go hungry, m'dear. I have many brides, all whom were once like you. Scared, and alone, seeking the warmth of another, someone strong and powerful, someone in a position to take you away from your own pain and suffering. I can offer you a gift. A gift of immortality – in trade for a piece of your soul."

Sara continued to quiver beneath his grip upon her wrists. She thrashed wildly as she fought him. Her eyes locked with his. Her legs and arms went limp. She stopped fighting. He hypnotized her. He seduced her.

"There now. Shhh… be calm. You are like a little child to me. I would never cause you harm. You must trust me," he said with deceit. Sara didn't say anything in response. She just laid there catatonic, in a hypnotic stare into the sky above her. Hremm Nevar leaned in to kiss her and slowly began to unlace her corset she'd bought at the RenFest, her long brown hair spilling all around her. He ripped it open and flung off his own cloak to reveal the body of a man with large wings attached to his back. He opened his wings and closed them around her.

The current of the water lifted from its momentary pause and flowed as it normally would. The voice of Sara screaming carried throughout the forest and then disappeared.

"Sara!" I called into the vision in the water, but it had disappeared completely.

My heartbeat raced and I was filled with anger. Sara was in deep trouble – way too deep to save herself. I had to help her. She was innocent. *What a monster! Hremm Nevar doesn't deserve to live.*

"Sadie, I understand who you are and where you came from. I will be at your side to help you defeat this horrendous monstrous beast, this malicious seducer, this lustful thief, this callous murderer. Show me a way to help save Sara. Please help me save her," I cried out into the empty sky. "Please, I beg of you to send me help." I thought of the name Abigail had mentioned. "Elluna? Elluna, please, whoever you are, please help me. I need your help. Please show me where to go next."

A star shot out across the sky and fell just behind Grams' house.

Ethan.

I ran to Grams' house and stole back into the room where I'd left Henry earlier that night. Henry was gone. Lily had taken the dress and left, but not without a fight. There was a mess in the room, and loose feathers strewn about on the floor. Below it there was something that had fallen on the floor. It was a ticket stub, from the Renaissance Faire. It was Sara's.

I sat on the edge of the bed and cried quietly. Morning had already arrived and I'd hardly slept a wink. It didn't matter. I felt partially responsible for Sara's abduction at the RenFest and wondered if she was alright. Was the vision I had in the water of something in the past or the future? Had Hremm Nevar taken advantage of Sara? Was it too late? I knew in my heart that there would be a way to help her.

"There now," Emily nuzzled up against me. "I know your sadness. But you are not alone. There are many things you do not understand yet, even I do not understand them, but I trust they will be revealed to us in a timely manner when we are greater able to handle them. You must trust."

I thought of Abigail's words to me as a gypsy at the RenFest. "You must trussst," she had said.

"I do trust. I trust with all my heart."

"A perfect trust," Emily confirmed with a nod and in one swift move, transformed into her human self. She approached me and sat next to me.

"Everything will be alright. Your friend will be alright as well. She has not lost her innocence. But she has been made aware of what the consequences would be if she were to be so careless. She will retain her memory as a dream, a warning. A gift from Abigail."

I patiently waited for her to continue. "Alyson, you have seen firsthand what Hremm Nevar is capable of. Now, I will give you a gift." She moved forward and placed her fingertip to the area in my forehead just above the center of my eyes. As she touched it, an image of a flame filled my mind's eye. A blue light overwhelmed me. I felt the muscle relax in my forehead. It was an incredibly sensation of peacefulness and calm. "All of your eyes are opened now. You shall see more clearly from now on."

I rubbed my forehead. It burned. A vision of the iris of a cat's eye flashed in front of me and I passed through it into blinding white light. I could not see anything.

Ethan cracked open the door. I sat up from the bed, with Emily curled up at the bottom of the quilted blanket. I looked at her strangely and rubbed my forehead. It felt normal. I wondered what had just happened. Did I dream it?

"Ethan. It's good to see you!" I rushed to put my arms around him.

"Bad dream?" he asked naively.

"Yes, it was a very bad dream, I think. I'm not sure now." I wanted to believe it was all just a dream, but I hadn't even slept yet.

"Well I'm here now. You should've woken me. Come on, you can borrow one of my sweaters. Hey, how'd your cat get here?"

"She always finds me," I said. Emily purred.

Ethan made me smile. Still, it had not been a dream. I was very much awake. I felt more awake than normal. Something inside of me felt alive. I thought of Abigail and of Lily, and Sadie, and looked down at my fingertip and the ring recently adorning it. It still didn't look any different, but I felt it glow with an invisible band of energy. It felt alive.

"Thanks. I'm ready," I sighed and looked at myself in the mirror. I was a mess. What a night it had been and I felt as though I'd hardly slept. Ethan's house was up much earlier than mine would be on the weekends. It was only 8am. Still, I missed my parents. I missed my Dad poking me awake and the smell of Mom's cooking. I missed my home. At least they were safe. I tried not to imagine what would've happened to them if they stayed at home when Hremm Nevar stepped out through the portal.

Determination and exhaustion were both setting in. I tried to be subtle. After all, Ethan didn't know everything that had happened. He was safer not knowing. I stroked Emily's fur and she mewed contentedly. Ethan almost smiled, but still looked disgusted. It was a cat and he didn't like cats. Nothing I could do to change that.

Daylight brought with it very sleepy eyes. So much had happened in the course of one day and night, I couldn't make sense of it all. It was all a blur and I wondered if I hadn't dreamt part of it… but that would've meant that I had slept, and I know I hadn't.

"Maybe I'll just run a brush through my hair or something. You know, it's Sunday. Let's have a quiet and uneventful day, can we?"

Exhaustion took over as I attempted to step onto my feet. My world went black. I fainted and fell to the floor. I felt Ethan scoop me into his arms, but I could not wake up.

* * *

"Oh my stars Ethan. She must be overwhelmed with everything. Let's let her rest. She needs it," I heard Grams say, somewhere in my state of subconsciousness.

"I'll stay with her," I heard Ethan's voice. There was a pause, and the door closed behind Grams footsteps. Ethan lay down next to me. I was too exhausted to move. His fingers interlaced with mine and he held my hand. Sleep came easily. So did the dreams.

I dreamt of Sara and Lily. Sara entered into Gram's house, into the room where I had been and found Lily sitting there.

"I know where to find Ivan," Sara toyed with her and gave her instructions to the RenFest. Without even a thank you, Lily shot out of the window, taking the dress with her and headed for the RenFest.

At the RenFest, Lily searched the fairegrounds. She headed towards Abigail's caravan and opened the curtains revealing Ivan. She lifted her finger and pointed it at him.

"Wait," Ivan pleaded. "Let me explain. My dearest Lily, you wear the dress, such a beautiful dress. I've waited forever to see you in it. Please allow me the chance to explain."

"You don't need to explain my love. I know all. I see all. I was foolish to create you!" Lily scolded him.

"To create me? But it was the Queen who crea-," he said and paused. "Wait, no, you can't be!"

"How dare you try to muddle with my daughter's heart. If I can't have love, she can't either. How dare you love her and not me!" she raged. As the princess spat, she turned briefly and I could see her face. She was not the princess Lily at all, she was the Queen. Her face was not that of a young maiden, but of an old crone. Ivan fell to his knees.

"She's not your real daughter and you know it!" he barked.

"You dare talk to me? You're nothing but a little chess piece. I can turn you back into one." She raised her hand and pointed it at Ivan.

"I beg of you, please let me go. I will do whatever you ask of me," Ivan pleaded.

"Useless! I asked for a lover, not a servant! I created you to love me and you could not even do that right. You are not a real knight anyways."

"Yes, I am a real knight, and I shall show you just how real I am," Ivan stood and drew his sword and pointed it at the Queen.

"Ha! You think that metal blade can do anything to me? You don't know who you're messing with. No blade made of mortal men can pierce through me!" she scoffed and pulled back her gown revealing an hourglass.

Ivan lunged forward, aiming for her heart, but missed. His sword went right through her, as though she were a ghost, and had no effect. He pulled it out and she was unharmed and his blade had no blood on it. She laughed maliciously. Realizing he was powerless, he fell to the ground and backed into the corner.

"Coward. I thought so," the Queen let out a yawn.

"You can kill me, but you can never make me love you! Never!" he retorted and tore off the $\mathcal{L}$ on the sleevelet. "My heart is genuine to her alone. You will never know anything of true love."

"True love? Ha! You think Lily and you are true love? Do you think you'd be anything if I hadn't created you?"

"You only gave me a body. You didn't give me my soul! My soul is mine alone and no one can create that! Not even you! True love is something transcendent. Lily's soul and mine will find each other again. I will be with her whether you try to stop me or not!"

"I've grown tired of this game. It is time to find a new one," she uncoiled her finger and pointed her long fingernail at Ivan, and without hesitation, turned him back into a black knight chess piece. The little horse fell to the ground and the Queen stormed out of the caravan leaving it behind, alongside the torn piece of dress.

"Come on you fat and lazy bird," she barked at Henry the owl. "Now you must open a portal to the Black Hollow."

"The Black Hollow?" I said barely above a whisper to myself. It wasn't Lily who had opened the portal that released Hremm Nevar, it was this evil Queen, and I had talked face to face with her in Ethan's house!

I stirred briefly in my lucid dreaming to realize I was not having a dream at all. Nor was this a vision. I had astral traveled to the RenFest and observed events happening as though I were there, just a fly on the wall. Fascinated, I continued to dream.

I watched the Queen take Henry to the chess board at the RenFest and disappeared. Just before she did, she looked right at me and I wondered if she had seen me. I thought I was only dreaming, but maybe I really was here. Her eyes glowed a demonic red, just the same as the possessed King. I sensed that wasn't the last I'd see of her either.

Wendy the wench and Duncan the rogue tiptoed around the fairegrounds, giggling in their drunkenness and holding onto each other for stability as they staggered from one tent to another. What were they up to?

"Rich baubles and charms in this one here," Duncan said as he peeked through the curtain to one of the vending tents.

"Aye, but it is more than jewels I fancy. I seek something a wee bit more, special, maybe even magical? Care to find a ring for your lady?" Wendy flirted.

Duncan gave her a look that he knew of just the place. Duncan walked over to Abigail's gypsy caravan and opened the curtains.

"Tisk tisk, looks like a fool's mess in here. Hmm, what's this now?" He bent over and picked up the chess piece that lay softly in the middle of the straw floor and tossed it to Wendy. "Here lovey. A treasure." Wendy tucked the black knight chess piece in her cleavage, where she seemed to carry around most of her valuable things.

Duncan rummaged through the racks of rings in Abigail's tent. Nothing seemed to be what he wanted. He found a small trinket box under the table and lifted up into view. As he opened it, light shone from the box and he pulled the ring out and Wendy clapped her hands together with excitement. He slipped the ring on her finger. Wendy seemed disappointed that nothing magical happened. Yet.

"Maybe 'tis a broken one?" Wendy complained.

"No lovey. It was in a special box. It must be special, and it is lovely, just as you are," Duncan kissed her passionately.

"A feisty rogue are ye?" Wendy lowered her chin and batted her eyelashes at him. "Look at it, it's like a lil' lily flower, all the way round me finger."

I couldn't see closer to see the ring, but it sounded very much like the same ring Ethan had picked out for me.

Wendy and Duncan continued their thieving.

"Hide, here comes Seamus," Wendy tapped Duncan and they both concealed themselves into the shadows.

Seamus walked to the gypsy caravan to see that it had been ransacked.

"I'm going to have to get security on this one," he muttered. "What's this?" Seamus bent over and picked up the torn piece of Lily's dress, with the $\mathcal{L}$ on it. "Why, this is from the dress Alyson wore. Now why would she be here thieving up the place? Poor Abby's going to be furious. Her favourite trinket has also gone missing."

I realized I'd been framed inadvertently.

I awoke to see Ethan kissing my hand.

"It's time to wake up sleepyhead," he whispered. I looked down to my hand at the ring. "I'm glad you like it," Ethan commented.

I was still dazed from my dream and wondered if what I'd seen had already happened or about to happen or if my mind played tricks on me.

"I love it," I said to Ethan. "What time is it?"

"It's almost noon. You needed the sleep. Let's get up though and do something fun, like have a picnic."

I looked out Ethan's window. "But Ethan, it's raining."

"Wow, when did that start? It hasn't rained here in over a month! Not since we had all those bizarre storms and floods and stuff. Oh well, guess we'll find something to do indoors," Ethan said disappointed. We both craved being outdoors and stared at the window and the rain. After several hours of playing checkers and cards, we went downstairs to eat supper with Grams and Grandpa.

"You know what? We won't melt. Come with me. I know a playground not too far from here."

"Really?" I said surprised. I thought I'd already explored everything there was to know about Colby Drive. The thought of someplace new excited me, especially knowing Ethan would take me there.

"Yeah. I'd forgotten about it until just now. It's probably still there, but it may have closed down. It's just over a hill and across a small field. It has swings."

The rain lightened enough for us to walk without umbrellas and then it was just a mist. The sun broke out through the clouds.

"Look, something's up. I can feel it. I need you to tell me what it is," Ethan asked.

"It's nothing, really."

"No, it's something. You don't usually faint for no reason. And what happened last night? Are we okay?"

We passed across a small field, dodging puddles of mud and slippery spots. "Ethan, I can't go into it. There's just something I'm not ready to share with you – with anyone – yet. It doesn't mean we can't still have fun together. Promise me you won't stray because of that."

"Alyson," he stopped walking with me and stood me face to face. "You mean the world to me. I know that there will be many things between us and we don't have to rush into anything."

We made it to the playground. It was still slightly drizzling on us. It was surrounded by a small grove of trees, an open field where kids could play baseball. There was the usual metal slide, swing sets, a ragged tire swing and a rusty merry-go-round. Everything rusty, but still operable.

"Looks like this place could use some upkeep."

We each sat on a swing, side-by-side and slowly drifted as we talked. It felt like those same moments under the bridge. We didn't even need to say anything to understand each other, talking to one another… we were beyond words.

"I used to come here when I was a kid and my mom and dad visited Grams and Grandpa." Ethan got silent and stopped swinging. I had a feeling Ethan remembered his Dad.

"You know, he was a good man. Everyone loved and respected him. I still can't believe he's gone. I feel like he's still with me. He's like my guardian angel or something."

I didn't say anything. I only listened.

"It's weird being without my father. I worry about Mom. I feel I'm kind of obligated to protect her now that he's gone. But it's hard to protect her when she's across the ocean. She's found herself someone else. I worry he won't treat her as good as my dad. Dad treated her like royalty. 'Only the best' was his motto for us. He worked really hard to give us so much. I miss him. And Mom too. I want to go see her."

I didn't know what to say that would offer good advice. As soon as I went to speak, I hesitated and then closed my mouth. I had nothing good to say. I'd never been in Ethan's situation. I didn't know what it felt like.

"It's okay. I don't really want to talk about it anymore." Ethan threw a rock and it clanked off the metal pole of the swing set. "The sun is setting. Want to head back?" Ethan asked.

"Well the rain's stopped. I don't mind staying out a little longer. Just a little longer? I want to be with you. I don't want to go home yet."

"Sure, we can always come back here too. Judging by how unkempt it is, I doubt anyone even knows it is here anymore."

"How did you find out about it? Did you just walk here one day and find it? It's kind of hidden," I said, curious.

"Well actually, remember that girl you met the other day? Carly?"

I tried not to get jealous, but just the sound of her name made me wonder. My stomach went into a knot.

"Oh, mm'hmm. Does she live around here?"

"Well not anymore. She did when she was about 6 years old and she showed me this place once when I visited Grams. It was kind of a secret spot. We used to build tree forts, right over there." Ethan pointed to an overgrown area of the small park.

"Imagine my surprise when she turned up in my physics class this year. I didn't even recognize her until Professor Higgins said her last name. She was really a tomboy back then. It's kind of weird to see her as a, as a girl, you know."

I smiled. His humor untied at least one of the knots that had formed in my core. "That's cute. Tree forts. I can see that."

"Yeah. Anyways. She's really involved with her boyfriend Matt and they have plans to go to college next year together. It's cool."

The more Ethan talked about things like college and Carly and being a senior, the smaller I felt. I knew we had an age difference. It was only two years, but suddenly it felt like twenty. It was in that moment when I didn't want this year to move any faster. I didn't want Ethan to graduate and move away. Time passed too quickly. It was already mid-October and before long the months would fly by and then… would Ethan move away? What would happen?

"Ethan, I want to go home now. I'm getting cold."

He wrapped his jacket around me. "I'll show you the way back."

An owl hooted from deep within the forest.

"Henry," I whispered.

"What?"

"It's nothing. I just heard an owl."

"An owl," he said and paused to listen for it, but there were only the sounds of night. "That's cool."

"There. See it," I pointed right at Henry. It literally had landed just inches from Ethan's face. It hooted three times. "Of course you heard that. It's right in front of you," I said with a laugh.

Ethan hadn't. He looked at me oddly. "Are you seeing things? There is nothing there, Alyson."

"But it hooted." The owl turned its neck and looked at me and then back at Ethan. "It's right there!"

"Alyson, let's get you home. There's nothing there. You're colder than I thought." Ethan felt my hands. He was right. They were ice cold.

Ethan couldn't see Henry. It occurred to me that Henry was not an ordinary bird, but a magical one.

As we walked by, I looked directly at Henry. He still had the shackle around his ankle, but he was free. There was no one else around. Or was there?

Chapter 11

THE ILLUSION OF NIGHTMARES

Ethan walked me back to Grams' house. His talk about his mom and dad had me thinking about my own family. As comforting as it was to be with him, I wanted my own bed. I missed my room. I missed my things, my house, and my family. We entered the living room to see Grams rocking in a chair with Emily sitting quietly purring on her lap.

"She's just like I remembered her," Grams said. "Well, if she were *my Emily*. But that is not possible. Thank you for letting her come visit me. I think it is time I got another kitty." Grams stood and placed Emily in my arms.

"Grandpa already asleep?" Ethan asked.

"You know Grandpa stays up very late, too late for your old Grams. He's downstairs, having a pipe and reading one of his cowboy novels he likes so much. I'm sure he'd like it if you'd go down and wish him a good night. Then off to bed you two. School comes bright and early," Grams said with a smile. We went down to say good night.

"Well howdy you two." The entire room smelled of cherry tobacco pipe smoke.

"Hey Pops. How was your day?"

He smiled and continued to rock in his rocking chair. Ethan realized he hadn't heard him. He repeated himself louder, "How was your day today, Grandpa?"

"Oh, fine, fine. We had a good crop this year. We'll be eating pumpkin pie for a long while after this harvest." He turned to me. "Make sure you take a pumpkin or two home with you, sugar."

"Will do. Thanks."

Ethan and his Grandpa talked for a few while I looked around the room. Aside from the wood paneling and stuffed animal heads mounted on the wall, everything else seemed very country charm. One of the walls had a photographic mural on it of a forest.

"Josie took that photo. We had it enlarged to fit the wall. I can't get out much due to my health, so it was Josie's way of bringing the outside in. Now I can take walks whenever I want to, regardless of how bad the weather is on the outside," he said pointing to a treadmill he'd purchased upon doctor's orders.

"You know, I've seen some very magical things happen in the forests around Hollow Creek." He winked at me.

"Here you go. I brought you down some tea," Grams set a cup from Grandpa on his table. "When you kids are done, come back up and I'll have something for you too. Then it's off to bed with the both of you."

"Yes Ma'am," Ethan said. "Goodnight Pops." Ethan kissed him on the forehead and gave a hug. I wanted to ask Ethan's Grandpa about what magical things he's seen, but Ethan pulled me aside to go upstairs.

"Don't forget a pumpkin. Make a jack o'lantern with it," Grandpa added. "Need to scare off some of 'em old ghosts haunting around yer place."

I nodded and smiled. I said a goodnight as I left the room.

Upon returning upstairs, we found glasses of milk and cookies.

"Oh wow. You have the nicest Grams in the history of Grandmothers. These are sooooo good."

Ethan smiled, but didn't talk as he'd crammed his entire cookie in his mouth. He swallowed, took a sip of milk and agreed. "Yeah, Grams makes the best cookies I've ever tasted."

"Hmm. Sounds like competition," I teased him.

"Come on. I'll show you to your room, Miss."

Sleep was welcome, but it did not come. I fussed among the dusty old duvet cover that presented itself uncomfortably atop the bed in the spare bedroom. Its smell was unfamiliar. I stared out the window and looked into the darkness. It was a new moon and it was uncomfortably dark in Grams' unfamiliar house.

My head was full of questions. What happened to Lily? Was Abigail coming back soon? And Sara… school would come early tomorrow and Cameron would be wondering where she was. Would the school write her off just as they did Jeremy when he went missing?

Emily sat up on my bed. "Alyson, do not worry. Everything will be alright. You will see."

"Well, how do I know? And if I'm a witch, how come I can't just portal myself to visit the Elders and ask for their help? Teach me how you do it. How do I go see them? They can help me. I need to go ask for their help."

"Alyson, a moment of your time, please. There are many things I cannot teach you, not because I am not able, but because you are not ready and it is dangerous for you to possess such knowledge. There have been others, such as yourself, too eager to learn and hastily zapping open portals, and it got them nowhere. Some have portaled themselves into areas they weren't able to handle; some never came back. And some, such as Lily, opened a portal and forgot to close it and having a ghostly prison outbreak is difficult even for the most trained witch to handle."

"Well, can you go? Can you go see them? I need their help."

"Not necessarily. Undoubtedly the Elders are already aware of your situation and are doing everything in their powers to assist you. My mother is with them. I trust she will return soon with the news we need."

I didn't have any words. Emily was right. Everything takes time to grow, even learning. I didn't want to be responsible for unleashing another Hremm Nevar into the world, or worse – his mother.

"Emily. I just thought of something. The other night when I walked back, I had a vision in the water of Hremm Nevar and Sara. It was at the lake. We need to go to the lake."

"Oh. Alyson. Are you sure? It's very dark and dangerous." Emily looked out the window with concern.

My voice had urgency in it. "I have to do something. I trust Abigail will return, but I can't wait for anyone else to save my friend. I need to do it myself."

"And if I am here?" Abigail responded in the darkness and walked out of a shadow. "It is time. You are correct, Alyson. Hremm Nevar is with your friend, and they are at the lake. She is safe, but I fear for her continued safety as she is in the possession of such darkness. And to darkness we shall send him back. A new moon is a perfect time to banish something, and Hremm Nevar is most certainly in need of a good banishing!"

"Abigail!"

I looked at Emily and thought for a moment how long it would take us to walk there when Abigail snapped her fingers and teleported us there. Before I could get my sentence out, we were standing at the lake, and I only had on what I wore to bed… one of Ethan's mother's nightgowns. Abigail opened her arms and held them in front of her and magically, a shawl appeared. She wrapped it around me. It was very thin and made of only crocheted yarn, but it kept me warm as a parka.

A mist had formed on the lake. Somewhere, in the center of it was Hremm Nevar's lair. I didn't want to ask too many questions but I had no idea how we would get to them.

A boat appeared before us, led by an unseen captain. Abigail stepped in and ushered us to follow. Emelia was sharpest and stealthiest in cat form, so she chose to remain as a grey cat. Her night vision helped us to see. I scooped her into my arms and stepped carefully into the small boat. It teetered gently and I clung tight to Emily so she wouldn't fall out of my arms. Abigail waved her hand and the boat left the safety of the shore and traveled towards the center of the lake, all by itself.

Abigail leaned over the side of the boat and looked into the water. "Alyson, tell me what you see." I leaned over the side and looked at the water's surface. The waves from the boat made it difficult to see anything. I looked back to Abigail and shook my head.

"Look again," she requested.

Once more, I leaned over, only this time the surface was smooth as black glass. Images from Sadie's black scrying mirror came to mind. I recalled how easily it was to step through it and into the Land of Dreams on the other side.

"Now Alyson, listen to me. We have arrived at the center of the lake. Look around and tell me what you see."

There was no island as I had suspected. There was water on all sides of us. I gave Abigail a look of uncertainty.

"He is here. I see him, but he does not see us, as we are masked from him," Emily twitched her whiskers as she spoke.

I felt confused. Where was he?

"Just as in the Land of Dreams exists beyond the black scrying mirror, so does the realm of Hremm Nevar, the Illusion of Nightmares. There he sits, atop a giant nest," Abigail eluded.

I looked up to see nothing above us. "There is nothing up there. And no trees nearby. Where do you see him?" I asked with hesitation.

"Look at the water again," Abigail hinted.

I leaned over the boat once again. There, reflected faintly on the surface of the water, was a tree stemming from the water and a giant nest resting on a mangled limb. Hremm Nevar's wings were visible. And Sara. She lay resting next to him.

"Is this just a vision?" I asked.

"No. This is his lair," Abigail answered.

"How do we get to Sara?" I asked the obvious question. "Are they above us, or below us, in the water?"

"Open your eyes Alyson," Abigail said with a smile. "Are you good at climbing trees?"

My eyes had been opened. I knew last night when I saw the owl and Ethan didn't that I had stepped on a path with a second sight only I was supposed to possess. Abigail was very wise and I trusted her every word. She meant my mind's eye. I closed my physical eyes and there before me was a tree. I smiled and reopened them expecting to see it, but it was gone.

"It is there, Alyson. But you cannot see it with your physical eyes. It is in another dimension, another plane of this realm, but in the darkness of the new moon, our worlds collide. You must trust your intuition and go wake Sara without disturbing Hremm Nevar."

I didn't have a single ounce of bravery left in me, but I had to find some. My friend was in trouble and I was her only hope. *I have to climb an invisible tree?*

"*Yes, a tree in the astral. Ground yourself first,*" Abigail answered and instructed me telepathically.

I grounded. My eyes had been closed, but when I opened them, I saw the tree in my mind's eye. Outstretching my hand, I touched it. It was cold to the touch. Thankfully the tree was at such an angle, it wouldn't be too difficult to climb. I notched my foot into one of the trunk's grooves and ascended it. Periodically I looked down to the boat below me to see Abigail and Emily waiting. My hand fumbled for the first large limb and I pulled myself onto it and rested momentarily. He still was very high above me. As I ascended, the tree became colder and parts of it crumbled to the touch and fell off completely. The bark was grey. I pondered the possibility of the branch Sara was on falling into the water if I were to touch it. Still, I continued to climb until I was just below it. My heart raced quickly. I passed through what felt like a threshold and stepped on the limb that held Hremm Nevar's lair. My hands felt my neck to check my pulse, but there was none. I couldn't even hear myself breathe anymore. That's because I wasn't. I had passed into the land of the dead. This was Death's realm.

The threshold appeared as a misty grey, slightly transparent. I looked below to see the boat, but couldn't. It only shimmered, like light reflecting off a pond, just below me. I extended my arm out to touch Sara and rise her gently without startling her. She lifted her head slowly and looked at me. I thought everything would be fine. But it wasn't. Sara didn't want to leave. She laid back down next to him and he folded his wings around her even tighter, as if to claim his property as he slept.

"Sara?" I whispered to her. She ignored me.

I had no choice. If I wanted to save her, I was going to have to wake them both. I climbed in the nest and stood in front of Sara and Hremm Nevar.

"Sara, please," I whispered. "Come with me."

She didn't move.

"Fine." I muttered angry at her insistence to stay.

Hremm Nevar still slept. I felt a tap on my shoulder, something I hadn't expected. Behind me stood Sadie. She was not alone. Behind her swarmed all sorts of ghost-like spirits. Hremm Nevar sat up like a shot. He looked directly at Sadie, aware of the sea of spirits surrounding her. They were not interested in me. I saw fear in Hremm Nevar's eyes for the first time. Sadie played his game. We were in the world of the dead and she had an entire army behind her.

Sadie didn't even have to tell me what she had planned. I leaned forward and grabbed Sara's hand and yanked her out of Hremm Nevar's grip, thus disturbing him angrily.

"Oh my dearest, are we disturbing you?" Sadie mocked Hremm Nevar.

He rose and looked her in the eyes, trying to subdue her. "My bride. You have come to me. Why have you come to me? I have missed you," Hremm Nevar said as he extended his hand beneath his winged cloak to touch Sadie. For a moment, she looked at him sincerely. "I thought you'd left me, my Queen."

"We're doomed," I whispered to myself.

A bolt of lightning fired out of the sky and at Hremm Nevar. Sadie laughed. "Enchanted I'm sure. I am the Great Queen of Death herself, with a crown of ravens and dead souls and skulls to adorn my hair. Your eternal bride-to-be. Or have you forgotten? You cheating, murderous monster! You cannot miss what you never had in the first place!" Scorn and hatred filled Sadie's eyes and Hremm Nevar looked at her with great concern and awareness. Reflected in his soulless eyes, scores of ghosts, Sadie's army of darkness made their way to surround Hremm Nevar's lair. "But look, I have brought you visitors. Recognize them? You've killed them all! And they are wanting the shards of their souls returned to them," she taunted. "I am here to fulfill my bridal duties, and to deliver you an omen… until DEATH do us part! Let the battle begin!"

She let out another cry of the Banshee. I shuddered to hear its sound. Its wailing woke the dead and swarms of lost souls flew towards the tree, like storm clouds approaching swiftly.

She whispered to him enigmatically, "*I guard your death.*"

Hremm Nevar's eyes grew very large. Her words spoke to him in ways he understood.

Another bolt of lightning struck out towards Hremm Nevar as the army moved in closer to him. I held Sara close to me, believing she would fight me but she did not. She was aware that she had been fooled.

Sadie glanced at me and a bolt of lightning struck. Sara lost her footing and fell backwards into me, propelling me out of the nest and hurdling backwards. Time felt warped and distorted and the length we spent falling felt like an eternity. I clenched onto Sara as we fell through the threshold and back into the world of the living. The force of us passing through made me lose my grip on her and suddenly we both plunged through the water below. I struggled to swim to the top when I felt arms scoop underneath me and lift me to the surface. It was Sara. She had pulled me up.

Gasping for air, I took a gulp of it when I reached the top and placed a hand on the side of the boat. Abigail helped both of us inside.

"Alyson, I'm sorry," Sara wrapped her arms around my neck and hugged me. We both looked up as we hugged and I saw the army swoop over Hremm Nevar, but Sara saw nothing.

"It's okay," I said, comforting her.

"But I don't understand. We fell, but where did we fall from? Why am I all wet?" Sara asked confused and filled with anxiety.

"There, now child. Be still and sleep. When you wake, you will feel better," Abigail touched Sara's forehead gently to comfort her and Sara fell forward into my arms asleep. I laid her down gently in the boat.

"She'll be fine," Abigail confirmed. The boat started to move again on its own and headed back to shore. "You must have trust Alyson. Trust and believe."

I wanted to ask her about Sadie and what would happen to Hremm Nevar, but I didn't. Those questions would be answered in time.

We arrived at the shore. Abigail waved her hand levitating Sara out of the boat and hovering until she was safely on shore, lying on the grass. Emily hopped out and Abigail and I left the boat. I looked back at it, but it was gone. It had vanished back into the mists.

"She is home safely now," Abigail snapped her fingers and Sara vanished into thin air. "She will have no memory of this ever happening. However, she will remember certain emotions and desires… and fears. I cannot remove her feelings. She will not be the same ever again, but I feel that this incident has made her a stronger person," Abigail said wisely.

"How come you couldn't come up into the tree with me?" I asked Abigail.

"Because of this," she bent down and picked up a stem with a dead oak leaf and handed it to me. As I reached for it and held it, it was brand new again. Abigail was a healer and she also could awake the dead. "I would've woken him and perhaps done more harm by my healing. You were the one chosen for this task, and you've succeeded."

I smiled and thanked her. "It is time for you to go home now," Abigail said calmly. "All is well and your parents await."

"But how?" I started to ask, but then thought better of it. I knew she would just tell me to trust her. The Elders probably had a hand at closing the mistakenly opened portal and Sadie had led all of the ghosts out of it. I looked up at the trail that led to my house.

"Thank you Abigail," I hugged her and she transformed herself into a white raven and flew off. Emily pounced eagerly up the trail and I followed her.

I kept the oak leaf Abigail had handed to me; the one she brought to life again. It had sprouted acorns.

Chapter 12
ONE LAST GOODBYE

onday morning came with bright sunlight shining through my bedroom window. Emily lay curled at the end of my bed and a familiar knock on my door woke me.

"Time to get up, Peanut," Dad chimed through a crack in my open door.

Abigail was right. All was well again.

After brushing my hair and looking my outfit over, I ran downstairs.

Mom walked around the kitchen and had the phone cord entangled around her, something she was famous for doing. Apparently she'd been talking for awhile. "Thanks for everything Ginny. I'll be over soon with some bread. You take care now. Bye," Mom said and hung up the phone.

"Good morning," she said with one hand on the coffeepot and the other on the jug of juice, and with the skill of a diner waitress, poured each respectively and handed them to Dad and me.

"Morning," I said back. Nothing was out of the ordinary. It was almost like the past forty-eight hours had been just a dream. But I knew in my heart they weren't.

After breakfast I took a walk before school down to the lake. I had to see it with my own eyes. It was just as it was the first day we moved here. The sun reflected off the surface and the sounds of happy critters scurried about. A familiar meow had followed me. Emily changed into her human self.

"You didn't dream it, Alyson. It was real," Emelia said as she stood face to face with me, knowing my concerns. "But have faith. Hremm Nevar won't be bothering anyone for a very long time. And hopefully those lost souls that he stole life from will finally be able to move on."

"Is it still there?" I said pausing to look to the center of the lake. "The tree. His lair."

"Yes. I am quite certain his lair will always exist. But not on this dimension. There are countless places like it all around us as we move through our days. Great castles in the sky, tiny faery houses in the trees. One might even say that to reach the Elders is as simple as opening a closet door," she said smiling.

I thought briefly about running back and opening my closet to see if that's where it would take me, but then halted such thoughts. One portal had just been closed. I didn't need to open another.

"Better not to be late for school," she added.

"Bye Em," I gave her a quick hug and ran up the hill to my house to see Ethan waiting with Grams' car.

He got out of his car and rushed to give me a kiss. "I didn't even hear you leave last night. I went in this morning and you were gone. Grams told me your parents came and got you. That's cool, but say bye next time," Ethan said.

"Sorry. And hello to you too."

"How was their trip?" he added.

"Good," I made up. "Be right back." I ran inside to say bye and grab my backpack. "There, ready."

The drive with Ethan to school was quiet. My thoughts of the previous nights had consumed me, as had the lack of sleep. Desperately I fought off the urge to nod off. As we pulled into the parking lot of school, I saw Carly getting out of her car and walking towards school with her boyfriend Matt. Ethan parked and we both walked in together.

"See you after class," he said and kissed me. "Hurry, you're going to be late."

I waved and ran to Ms. Hildegarde-Snodgrass's homeroom. Opening the door, I wasn't sure what to expect. Jenny Fox was absent. Cameron sat in his usual desk, but not in his usual clothes. He had apparently changed his look to something "popular". And Sara. Sara was there. She turned to me and waved. I quickly scooched into my seat and threw my backpack beside it, hurriedly yanking my binder and pen out before my tardiness was noticed. Ms. Hildegarde-Snodgrass looked at me but didn't say anything. Perhaps she was just happy to see me and not Jenny Fox.

Desperately, I wanted to talk with Sara. I scribbled a note and folded it and slipped it to her unnoticed.

Hey, how's it going? She scribbled back her reply.

Not sure. Weird dreams. Breaking up with Cam today. He doesn't know. Talk after class.

Everything I wanted to talk about wouldn't fit on a normal piece of school notebook paper. It could probably fill a book, if not several. Class lingered on and on. The long awaited bell rang and Sara and I bolted for the door.

I let her speak first.

"I have a bad headache today. I think I ate something weird at the RenFest," she said holding her head. She didn't really look as good as she normally would, but then I suppose a weekend at Hremm Nevar's lofty nest in the underworld probably would take its toll on ones beauty.

"I thought you and Cam had made up? Why do you want to break up with him?" I said, unaware that Cam was just behind me.

"Oh, hi. Am I interrupting?" he asked. "I've got to get to my next class, but just wanted to give you this," he leaned in and kissed Sara's cheek. I thought it was sweet but she had little reaction to it. Cameron noticed. "Okay, well bye." He left.

A tear fell down Sara's cheek. "Alyson, I don't think I'm ready for a relationship. Cameron's really sweet… too sweet. I don't deserve a guy like him. I don't deserve anyone." I leaned in to give Sara a hug.

She carried on. "That's just it. I lied about Jeremy, because I really liked Jeremy. He hurt me and I still wanted to be with him. Why is that? Why Alyson? I don't understand it."

"I'm not sure. But why is it you want to sabotage your relationship with Cameron? He loves you. Can't you accept that?"

Sara paused like she wanted to say something important but couldn't.

"Sara, it's okay. You can tell me anything and I won't repeat it."

She looked ashamed.

"You know, Cameron's a good guy. I think you should give him a chance."

"I don't know, Alyson. We've been friends forever. I'm sure he'll understand that I just want to be alone right now. I can't be in a relationship… with anyone. I just want to be alone. Thanks for listening. I've got to go," she said and picked up her backpack and said bye with a wave as she walked down the hallway.

I waved back.

I bumped into Cameron later on at his locker.

"Hey Alyson."

"Hey Cam."

"Talked with Sara yet today?" he asked.

"Yeah. A little," I said.

"She just broke up with me," he said with great disbelief and shock. "She just wants to go back to being *friends*. Friends?! How can she do that? After I poured my heart out to her. How can we go back to just being friends?" He slammed his locker shut.

"She just needs some time Cam."

"Time for what? Time to find a better boyfriend?"

"I can't explain it Cam. She really needs your *friendship*," I said.

"Okay, if you say so. You're her best friend. I'm sure she tells you everything." He ran off, forgetting to take his backpack. Cameron deeply cared about Sara, and now above all, she needed him.

I closed my locker and went to the library. I wanted to be alone instead of doing the lunchroom table clique dance for a seat. I sat at one of the corner tables and ate my cheese and crackers. Ethan sat down across from me and stared at me.

"You okay?" he asked.

"No. I mean. I don't know. My friends are having some relationship troubles is all. How's your day?"

"It's going good, I suppose. I've been doing some research."

"Oh yeah? What about?"

"Lunar eclipses," Ethan said as he opened his pocket calendar and showed me the date for Halloween, also a night of a full moon.

"Really? That's less than two weeks away."

"I know," he said excitedly. "A full moon, a lunar eclipse, a school play all on Halloween night... I have a hunch it'll be interesting."

I smiled at him.

He read, "A lunar eclipse occurs when the moon passes through some portion of the Earth's shadow, thus giving it a ruddy colour, and is also known as 'blood on the moon'."

"Blood on the moon?" I repeated.

"Yeah. Spooky isn't it? And think about it. Halloween night, when all the ghosts are out to play, and the moon goes all red and stuff… you'd better come find me to hold onto." He smirked.

"Why? Are you going to be scared?" I teased him.

"No, I meant to protect you, silly."

I pursed my lips together. Ethan had done it. He'd made me smile, as always. "Oh, and I need a mighty protector do I? From what? The ghosties?" I said giggling.

A librarian walked by and shushed us.

"Oops. Glad the day's almost over at least. School play rehearsal after school again," Ethan said hushed.

"Yeah. Have a script with you?"

Ethan pulled out the script to Dracula and we each took turns reading through some lines. It was a lot of fun. The bell rang.

"See you after awhile," he said.

"K. Later." He gave me a quick peck and ran to his next class. I lingered behind. Warmth from the sun streamed through the window and fell on me as I sat. My eyes drifted out the window as I let out a big yawn. Before I knew it, I'd fallen asleep with my head on my backpack in the library. The second to last class bell rang loudly, waking me with a start. I sat up and several students walked by and laughed at me. "I can't be late again."

Last class of the day. Mr. Parker's Geometry class. I made it just in time to noisily shuffle and settle into my seat, disturbing the students which groaned about something written on the blackboard. It was only one word, but meant doom for me, as I hadn't studied at all over the weekend. "Quiz."

I may as well accept my fate and hand in a blank paper. But I decided I'd at least try. Surprisingly the answers came quickly to me and as I handed my paper to Mr. Parker, he said, "Well done Miss Bell."

Smiling, I took my seat again. Jenny Fox leaned over and whispered, "Suck up," at me before raising her hand.

"Yes, Miss Fox?"

Jenny excused herself from her seat, taking her test with her and glaring at me as she sashayed her way to the front of the class. Cameron looked at me. I smelled trouble.

"Miss Bell. May I see you for a moment after class please?"

Moans and ooos and ahhhs filled the classroom.

"Quiet please," Mr. Parker said softly.

After class, I stayed as Mr. Parker had directed me to. "Are you aware Alyson that Jenny witnessed you copying your answers? Recognize this?" He held out a piece of cleverly folded paper with answers to today's quiz written on the sides. It was in my handwriting, but I hadn't written it.

"No. That's not mine. I mean. I wrote my name at the top and some of it is in my handwriting, but that's not mine."

Jenny Fox smirked as I tried to weasel my way out of her trick.

"So you admit this is your handwriting?" Mr. Parker paused. "I've no choice but to give you a failing grade on today's quiz and a day of detention."

My jaw dropped. "What? But I didn't cheat! She's lying!" I spat at Jenny's direction.

Jenny looked at Mr. Parker with eyes of an innocent puppy, and flirty as Lolita. She dragged her fingertip over his desk and across his hand. "Oops," she said coyly. Mr. Parker grinned as she played her charms, and handed me back my test with an F written in red pen with a circle around it at the top.

"What?!"

I gasped in shock and disgust. My mind raged with all sorts of treacherous scenarios for Jenny's demise and misfortune. *Why should she get away with lying? Girl's like Jenny Fox could get away with anything.*

"Thank you. That'll be all," he said. He handed Jenny her paper. A. A?! She got top marks. I fumed inside at her. "Miss Bell, return this to me tomorrow with your parents signature, thank you."

My parents signature? I wanted to scream.

The final bell rang of the day. School was over. Students sped out the classroom doors as though they fled from a fire.

Jenny stayed behind to talk with Mr. Parker.

I overheard her conversation. "You know, if there is anything you can suggest for some extra credit, please let me know. I'm really good at sharpening pencils." She flirted and demonstrated the improper 'how-to' with the electric sharpener and blew on the tip. "See?"

Mr. Parker coughed. "Thank you Jenny, umm... Miss Fox, but that won't be necessary. You're doing just fine in your coursework. And I can sharpen my own pencils, thank you. Perhaps you could tutor Alyson, your friend. She's waiting for you."

Jenny looked at me with a glare.

"Uhh... thanks." Jenny grabbed her backpack and made sure to extend her leg beyond the dust ruffle of her miniskirt so Mr. Parker got more than an eyeful.

"Ugh, you're so disgusting," I said under my breath as she walked by me. She attempted to avoid me, but I wouldn't have it.

Outside the classroom, I spun Jenny around by her shoulders and gripped into them.

"Why? Why'd you do it?" I spat at her. I wanted so badly to slap her, but I didn't.

"I don't know what you're talking about. You're the one who cheated," she said cockily.

"I didn't cheat and you know it." My anger raged inside of me. I felt the tip of my finger tingle.

"Maybe it's because all you ever do is hang around with nerds. Maybe you are a nerd yourself? Too bad you're not as smart as one. Resorting to cheating. Well that's just not smart Alyson, is it?" she belittled me. "Maybe you'll have to spend less time on the school play and more time studying." She smiled a malicious smile. I clued into what she wanted. She was jealous she didn't get chosen for the school play.

"Lucky for you, I know all of your lines by heart," she taunted. Her words echoed in my head as the realization that I'd been duped sunk in. "Hope you don't mind I'll be kissing your boyfriend either, but the scene calls for it, LOTS of it."

"Why, you slut!" I raged.

She laughed. "Jealous much?"

Rreaow. A student walked by making cat noises. "Cat fight!" he jeered.

"Oh yeah? Bring it on," Jenny taunted. "You're a nobody, Alyson. No one will even remember you at this school."

As if it happened in slow motion, my index finger lifted before me and pointed right at her face.

"What? Are you going to punch me with your little finger? Ha!" she taunted.

"No Jenny. I want you to have everything you deserve, and if you deserve to take my place in the school play, and kissing my boyfriend, well then, as they say in showbiz, *BREAK A LEG!*"

As soon as I felt the words leave my mouth, I knew I could expect a great punishment from the magical world. I wasn't wishing her good luck as with usual showbiz intentions. I really wanted her to break a leg. With power comes responsibility, and misusing it on the likes of

Jenny Fox was wrong. Jenny Fox looked at me baffled as to what had just happened.

"Oh sure. Runaway. Go cry little girl. See if anyone cares." I couldn't stand her anymore. Why had she singled me out to be so mean?

I fled to the girl's bathroom on the second floor and locked the stall door behind me and cried in frustration. Ironically I was more concerned with the curse I'd spat at Jenny than my math grade. I stepped out of the stall and walked to the sinks, splashing cold water on my face. I already was feeling uneasy, but more so when I looked in the mirror. I went cold. Standing behind me to the right was Jeremy Fox. Only he wasn't the ghostly apparition he'd appeared to be just days before. He appeared human – at least an undead version of himself. His skin resembled that of Sadie, pale and bluish. His life had been drained out of him by Hremm Nevar. As he stood there, I felt myself get weaker. The smell of stale cigarette smoke filled the bathroom, although there was no one smoking.

"Got a light?" he asked as he propped one foot up against the long since jammed closed door of a stall appropriately still with a sign stating "out of order" on it. His eyes reflecting in the mirror were black. I wondered for a moment if he knew I could see him. I turned around to talk with him.

"You see me?" he asked.

"Yes. I can see and hear you Jeremy. Why are you here? Why haven't you moved on?"

"I can't," he reached out to touch my arm but it went right through me. I jumped. He felt like ice. He looked at his hand and wiggled his blue fingertips curious as to what had happened. He lunged at me right into my face and stared at me with his black, empty eyes. His head twitched. "Something really strange is happening."

I tried not to let him scare me. He probably wasn't even doing it intentionally. But he's a *ghost*; he's bound to scare someone. I wondered if Sadie was successful in overpowering Hremm Nevar into releasing the soul shards that were stolen from his victims. If Jeremy had his back, how come he wasn't moving on?

"There are others here. I don't belong here. What's happening to me?" Jeremy's voice echoed in the girl's bathroom. "Please! You have to help me!" he pleaded and attempted to grab at me again. I ducked and moved away. The longer I stood near him, the more I felt my happiness being sapped from me. Jeremy's presence drained me.

"Where is Sara?" his voice was stronger now. I looked in the mirror at myself. Part of my energy visibly was being drawn out of me and going into Jeremy's spirit. I felt incredibly weakened. I guess part of Hremm Nevar's talents got transferred to Jeremy when he killed him. He's the type of ghost that drains flashlight batteries cold.

Energy vamp!

I severed the link he'd formed with me and ran out of the bathroom, swinging the door wide open behind me so strongly that it slammed against the wall. The second floor hallway was empty. I looked both directions and then straight across at the lockers. Opposite me was Jeremy's locker. The locker flung itself open. With a rush from behind me, Jeremy's spirit passed through me and into his locker, slamming it behind him. I fell to the floor unconscious. No one saw. No one except for one…

Sara lifted my head up off the floor.

"Alyson? Alyson, talk to me."

I stirred to consciousness and looked at Sara. "What are you doing here?"

"Thinking. Are you okay?" she said.

"Yeah. I think so."

"That was Jeremy, wasn't it?"

"You saw him?" I said stunned. "But you don't believe in ghosts. How did you –You saw Jeremy?"

"I didn't see him. I felt him, and I smelled his, ... cologne," she said.

"Oh? How?"

"I'm not sure how. I've never really had ghost encounters like you have before. But I know Jeremy's cologne and that was it. It's still lingering in the air," Sara looked around to his locker.

"Why are you here all alone?" I asked her.

"Cam came to see me. I just felt so sad and I couldn't stop crying. Remember that day up here? Remember that voice you heard from over by the window? That voice haunts me. I wanted it so badly. I begged for it. And look where it's gotten me. I'm alone now." She sat and cried. "Alyson, my life,... my life is so not easy. Everyone always looks up to me, the popular girl, the pretty girl, the rich girl. They have such high expectations. I'm not used to people looking down on me. Especially Cam. I've lost his trust. You were right, Alyson. Everything you said was right. I do love Cam. I do. But I can't be with him right now. I can't be with *anyone* right now. Something inside of me has changed."

I gave her a hug. "I know."

"We've been best friends forever. You'd think getting together as a couple would be awesome, but it's totally awkward! Cam acts really nervous around me, more so than usual, and gets jealous easily. And there's this pressure between us, this tension... we can't just be ourselves anymore. I mean, you've seen us changing our clothes and hair. It's like we have to be this cool perfect boyfriend/girlfriend couple. I swear, we were better off as friends."

"It'll work out. I think you're nervous because you don't want your relationship to jeopardize the friendship you've been building all these years. But you guys like each other a lot and it shows. There are a lot of people that don't know what it's like to fall for their best friend. I say, just relax and try to have fun with him, just like you always have. Nothing's changed, really, if you think about it."

"I know you're right. He thinks it's his fault and he has to change. And it's not even totally about him. He thinks it's because of how he dresses and his hair, but it's not. It's not about him. It's about me. Look at me." Sara stood up. "There isn't anyone at this school who doesn't know my name. I'm the most desired *and* the most hated girl here. The guys want to sleep with me and the girls want to be just like me. Just like me... *"Oh look at her, her hair's perfect, her clothes are perfect, even her boyfriend Jeremy... is perfect,"* Sara mocked herself and then stopped.

"Jeremy! I said Jeremy. I meant to say Cam!"

"You're not okay, are you? I mean, about Jeremy. You haven't moved on from him fully, that's why. You need time to heal. He really hurt you."

Sara nodded through tears.

"It was a huge secret, Alyson. But he didn't tell everyone, just me! Just me, like it was my cross to bear. I had to pretend I didn't know. I had to pretend it was because we had sex. I've been living a huge lie and hurting so many people to save my own skin." She sobbed. "And now, even Cam is hurting. Hurting because of me – hurting because of Jeremy. I can't get over him. He's still in my heart." She couldn't finish her sentence, but I knew what she felt. Her heart screamed in pain of heartbreak.

"Even his scent lingering in the air torments me. I swear, I wish he'd just go away. Why does he haunt me still?"

"Because you loved him. And when you love someone, you give a piece of your heart to them. And Jeremy took it, but didn't give it back."

She sobbed quietly, thinking silent thoughts.

"Alyson, I don't want to talk about Jeremy anymore. In fact, I don't want to ever talk about Jeremy again!" she wiped away tears and shred the note she held in her hands into tiny pieces. "Jeremy's gone. I'm over him," she said to me satisfied.

"Do you hear me Jeremy? I'm over you. You don't exist anymore! You can't hurt me, because you don't exist. You have no power over my heart, and you have no right to keep something that doesn't belong to you!" she shouted down the empty hallway, hoping Jeremy's ghost would hear.

The thickness of the air shifted. I stood up and looked around for any sign that Jeremy was nearby. The fluorescent bulbs above us in the hallway began to flicker. The light directly above Jeremy's locker went on full beam.

Sara shielded her eyes from the bright light. The ballast flickered and then burst. I knew Jeremy was nearby. He'd taken the energy from the fluorescent light.

"Jeremy?" I called out in a whisper.

Jeremy's locker opened wide and Jeremy stepped out of it. I saw him. Sara did not. She continued to look around.

Sara shouted into the air of the hallway, "Give me back my heart you stole from me all those years ago. Give me back the love you took, but never gave in return. Give it back. You can't keep it. It's not yours! I love Cameron now and he loves me back. Do you hear me Jeremy? I don't belong to you anymore!"

"Sara," I whispered to get her attention. "Sara, he's here."

Sara got quiet and a little scared.

Jeremy's spirit rushed towards Sara and I hugged her to protect her. He rushed through both of us, spinning us around and knocking us both to the floor onto our stomachs. We looked up towards the end of the hallway at the open window. A trail of rose petals led from it to us.

Sara sat up and looked overwhelmed. "He gave it back," she said in shock. "I don't believe it. He gave it back!"

"Did you mean it?" a voice from the stairwell spoke to us. "Did you mean what you said? About Cameron?" The figure walked towards us. "Do you love him?"

Sara smiled and took the outstretched hand that lifted her from the floor.

"I do."

Cameron smiled.

Jeremy's spirit was gone. He'd given us both back what he'd stolen. It was love that helped him move on. Love. A feeling Jeremy was unfamiliar with, so much so that he was desperate to keep it. *Love*.

Chapter 13
DISTURBED GRAVES

A week and a half had passed since the last day we'd seen or felt the ghost of Jeremy Fox, the day I'd sent a curse after his conniving sister, Jenny. School rehearsals went on as continued, and with only one more week, we were ahead of schedule. I managed to avoid a day of detention, but instead, ended up losing my position in the play to none other than Jenny Fox and was put in charge of set decorations in its place.

Working tediously and covered in paint, Jenny Fox rattled off her lines opposite Ethan, who shot me helpless eyes and mouthed the words "help me" after every scene with her. She hung all over him and blamed it as part of the script. Even Principal Jeffries apparently regretted his choice at the casting replacement.

"Okay, from the top again. Jenny, try to be a little less pep rally, Dear. This is Dracula. It's not a cheery play," Ms. Hildegarde-Snodgrass consulted her.

"Like *she* knows how to act!" Jenny said just under her breath to one of her cheerleading peers. "Besides, Ethan's a good stage kisser," she taunted me. "Otherwise these scenes would be very tedious, say… especially if I had to watch *you* do them?"

I tried my best not to get angry and just ignored her. Ethan wasn't enjoying himself, and I knew he probably wasn't kissing her with the same *oomph* that he kissed me with. It was just a school play, not Broadway. Still, I fumed inside with each scene they painfully rehearsed. She made sure I watched and really laid a kiss on Ethan. Even he looked shocked.

"I just don't know if your little Ethan will be so eager to go back to mediocre after he's kissed the best? Hmm… tough choice. Fruit juice or champagne? Me," she smiled and did a curtsey followed by a gesture I'd rather not imitate.

"Whatever," I gunned back at her and walked off.

The set was flustered with tired actors and stage props. "We need more headstones," the prop master shouted at me.

"Headstones, right. Got it," I confirmed back. "Where are the extra theatre props?" I shouted.

"Second floor. There's an office there. Should be some extra props in there left from last year's play," the set director shouted back. "Be right back. Smoke break."

Second floor. I'd been there recently. All too recently, and for different reasons.

"I'll help," Cameron said. "I don't really need to practice too much. I'm narrator… I just read from the script. And anything to get away from Dracula's minion over there – ugh!"

"Trust me, Cam. I sympathize. I have a feeling she'll get what's coming to her real soon. What goes around, comes around," I ranted.

Cameron and I rushed the stairs to the second floor. "The only office I know of up here that holds props is the one in the Janitor's office. Come on, let's go. It's probably fine now," Cameron reassured me. Even if there were a few ghosts lurking about, I had my own curse being lived out by losing my role to Jenny Fox!

We knocked on the door to the Janitor's office. The janitor opened it and it swung outwards.

"Hey, if it isn't my two new friends. What can I help you with today?" he said sarcastically.

"We need theatre props," Cameron said, "you know, from down there."

"I'm busy. You don't need an escort. I know you're down there, so go ahead. Just watch your step," he said and grabbed his mop and left.

Cameron and I slid open the metal grate across the elevator and stepped inside, closing it behind us. "Let's hope this works this time," he said pressing the button to the basement. Without problems, it descended. Arriving at the basement, we stepped out of the elevator and into the vast room.

"Well, he knows we're down here this time. I suppose we can at least do this," I said flicking the switch near the elevator, setting a series of bright fluorescents aglow across the room. One across from us on the far end flickered uncontrollably. Below it appeared to be just what we came for, theatre props.

"Over here. Give me a hand. These things are heavy," Cam yelled. "They're real stone! Look – this one even has dirt on it."

"Grab that dolly. We can use it to carry them."

As we stacked the realistic stone markers onto the dolly, I read off some of the names and dates.

"Wow, these things are authentic looking, aren't they?" Cam suggested.

"Yeah. Betcha these were the ones with typos. You know, like printed the wrong date or misspelled the name."

"Maybe they're just some old ones that a cemetery wasn't using or something," I said naively and nervously.

"Yeah, prolly."

We took about four of them, from a stack appearing to have ten times as many. Cumulatively, they weighed about a hundred pounds on the dolly.

"These'll be great." Cameron wheeled the dolly to the elevator and slid open the grate. It hadn't left from the basement floor.

"I'll grab the light." I flicked the switch and the lights all flicked off again. "Well that was easy." I laughed as I stepped into the elevator and closed the grate. I leaned forward to press the button to go back up to the second floor. "Wonder where 'G' goes to anyways?" I asked rhetorically.

"Press it," Cameron dared me.

I did. The elevator began to move. I looked out through to the empty dark room, and the lights flicked themselves back on over the area where we'd retrieved the headstones. Then they flicked back off again before we went out of view.

Ding.

"It says we're at 'G' but there's only a brick wall in front of us."

"Bricked up. Wonder what's on the other side of it. Got a map of the school?"

"Well not on me obviously," Cameron said laughing at the idea, and pressed the button to go up.

Arriving back on the second floor, we slid open the grate and wheeled the dolly back out into the office.

"A lot less jumpy that time at least," Cameron commented on the elevator.

"I don't like them to begin with. That basement is really creepy. Did you see the way the light came on by itself?"

"Yeah. But at least the dog wasn't there, or if it was, at least it was, ummm… sleeping or something."

"Yeah."

We both hushed simultaneously. I looked at Cam. He looked at the headstones and then back at me.

"The gravedigger's dog," he noted.

"Graves."

"Do you think-?"

"These are real headstones? Nah, they couldn't be real. Why would they be?" I let out an uncomfortable laugh. "I mean, that would imply there's a cemetery around here missing a bunch of headstones." I laughed again uncomfortably, but Cameron wasn't laughing with me.

A chill ran up my spine.

"Let's take these to the theatre and get out of here," Cameron suggested as he wheeled the dolly towards the door. "I've got something else I want to check out later."

"What are you thinking?"

"I'm thinking these are real headstones, Alyson. I mean, look at the dates! You heard them say this place was used as a morgue. Where do you think they put the bodies? There's a cemetery close by, I just know it. I've got some research to do."

"Do you think-? Do you think there's a cemetery around here… missing a bunch of headstones?!"

"That is precisely what I think."

"Well this is a Sherlock Holmes moment if I ever had one!"

"I mean, it all makes sense. Why else would there be a gravedigger's doggie ghost lingering around in the basement? One of these stones or one still down there might belong to the gravedigger! His master."

"We should go back down there," I said. As soon as the words left my mouth, even I couldn't believe them.

"What?!"

"The dog. It wasn't mean to us. Maybe it knows where the cemetery is. Didn't you ever watch Lassie? Dogs are good at finding stuff, and people and places."

"It's a dead dog, Alyson. I imagine its sense of smell is a little, umm... gone."

"Then we'll have to find out ourselves," I said with confidence.

"Are you crazy?" Cameron jested.

"A little bit. Hope that doesn't bother you." I gave him a slight maniacal laugh and googly eyes.

"Come on."

"Here, let me help you." I took over wheeling the dolly as we walked the stones carefully down the wheelchair ramp and towards the theatre.

"I'll grab the door."

Cameron pulled open the door as Jenny clumsily rushed out of it, spilling over several stones and cracking several in half.

Cam appeared unscathed, but something had happened. Something more than coincidental. Jenny wailed in pain.

"I'm so sorry! I didn't see you Jenny." I attempted to help her up, but she couldn't move.

"You! Get me help. You broke my leg. My leg is broke!" she yelped at me. "Like oh my God! You ruined my new nail job too! You're so dead meat!"

"What?" I didn't believe her.

"Ha ha, Alyson. Break a leg! Remember? Next time don't bother to wish me luck. You probably put a bad luck curse on me, you WITCH!" she spat at me.

I couldn't deny it. I had. The crowd of students in the gym had pooled closer to see what all the commotion was about.

"Witch!" she yelled at me. "You're a witch, aren't you? I knew it all along," she said snidely. *So what if I was?* The accusations normally wouldn't have even bothered me, but it was the way she had said it, so accusatory. Granted, I had cursed her, which felt wrong but I hadn't learned how to undo curses yet.

Feeling empowered by her attempts to overthrow me, she yelled it into the gym. "Hey, Alyson's a witch! Everybody better run! She'll put a hex on you too!"

There were only a few gasps and finger pointing, and even some raised eyebrows, but the label and how it was attached to me felt all wrong. It was *how* she said it. She was mean about it. I'm not evil. Not any more so than Jenny Fox!

"Watch out, Alyson. They'll burn you at the stake!" she said and laughed sinisterly. "I'll even light the match," she said as she narrowed her eyes into tiny, anger-filled slits. Her words struck at my core, but I did not shake.

"I'll go get you some help," was all I could muster and I dropped the handle to the dolly and ran towards the principal.

Not like I needed to run far. He was right behind us. Jenny's wailing and the sounds of crashing headstones made a ton of noise.

"Help. I don't need help. Think I needed help when Jeremy died? Ha!" Jenny whined. "She did this on purpose!"

"Miss Fox. Enough already with the accusations. There's no reason for Miss Bell to attempt to harm you, now is there?" Ms. Hildegarde-Snodgrass tried to reassure her, but Jenny became livid.

"She's vengeful! This is revenge, for what Jeremy did. My brother, poor Jeremy, is the victim of this mean witch. She probably put a curse on him too!" Jenny rampaged.

"Enough with the name calling please, Jenny. This is madness," Principal Jeffries tried to calm her down.

"Name calling? Principal Jeffries, you of all people should know about name calling. After all, my brother was secretly dating your son. You knew your son was gay didn't you?" Jenny looked smugly satisfied. She'd accomplished knocking down at least two if not three of her peers to below her, or so she thought. Holden gasped. First he looked mortified, and then he looked hurt.

Principal Jeffries looked too upset for words. He marched out of the gym and into his office. Watching his father walk away, Jenny looked smugly at Holden. Just another life she ruined. Holden ran out of the room.

Why Jenny Fox decided to out Holden Jeffries was beyond me. Her rampant venting was fueled at everyone at this point. Obviously, I wasn't the only one who pointed fingers in this school, and it was Jenny Fox's words that were doing far more damage than my silly curse could ever do.

"Escort her away," Ms. Hildegarde-Snodgrass commanded the paramedics, who strapped her onto a gurney and wheeled her out of school. This was the second time in just a short while that we'd witnessed Jenny Fox escorted out of the school for her outbursts. Psychologically, I wondered what she was capable of if left alone with her temper for too long.

Ms. Hildegarde-Snodgrass walked into the gym and looked at the mess on stage and back at the headstones. "Rehearsals are over for today. You're all excused. Go home," he announced and disappeared to his office.

I looked to the cracked headstones and picked one piece up. Deep within the property of the school, a dog howled mournfully. Something inside my core stirred.

"Let's go see Mr. Jeffries. I've had some experience with school counselors," Ethan said as he directed us to follow him.

"What are you going to say to him?" I inquired.

"I'm not sure. But you saw Holden's face. I don't have to like him, but I don't want him to end up like Jeremy did either." Ethan grabbed my hand.

"This school has enough ghosts as it is," Cam added.

Through the foggy glass of his principal's office door, Principal Jeffries silhouette showed his head held in his hands and hunched over his desk. I knocked politely on the office door.

There was silence and then finally a "come in" shouted through the door. I peeked through the door and then entered, and behind me followed in Sara and Cam, and Ethan.

"Yes students, I must say, this is not a good time. You all should head home now."

"Look, we didn't really know Jeremy Fox as a person, or probably quite the same way that say, umm, Holden did," I started. "He's dealing with Jeremy's death on a whole different level than the rest of the school."

"Holden's probably just as upset right now, and needs a parent, not a principal. He needs a friend. This is a big deal to him. Unfortunately, I know this first hand, as I was one of the few people who knew about Jeremy's secret." Sara's words seemed to strike a chord within Principal Jeffries.

He slid open his drawer and pulled out the photograph. He showed it to Sara and we all peeked. Sara gave a look of indifference as she peeked at the photo. She was no longer hurt by the choices Jeremy had made, as she no longer would allow herself to be affected by them. The photo only showed Jeremy and Holden sharing a kiss.

"This is how I have to find out?" Principal Jeffries said back to us. "Why couldn't he just tell me? I'm not mad, but as his father, I felt I'd earned his trust."

"Why does it matter who your son is dating?" Cameron interjected.

"It matters." Principal Jeffries lowered his head. "Students, there are topics which are difficult for anyone to talk about with their parents, including this one."

"Which is probably why it makes it harder for Holden to come talk to you. You're his father, and his principal too," Ethan said to Principal Jeffries. "You know what that photo says to me? It says 'I just want to be loved, not judged, not ridiculed, not pressured, just loved. But now, the whole school knows, and Holden is probably feeling exposed. But he didn't have a chance to talk to you, because you're not giving him one. Hiding in your office is the last place you should be."

I didn't know why Ethan stood up for Holden the way he did. He just did. He was great at speaking man-to-man, even to adults, and Principal Jeffries just needed a little reminder of what it's like to be human.

Principal Jeffries set the photo down and looked at Ethan with discernment. He opened his mouth, about to yell at us to get out, when Holden peeked his head inside the office and Ethan ushered him inside.

He looked at Holden with concern. It was time for us to leave. "Everyone out!" he commanded. "Except for you, son."

We left promptly. We knew inside the office, the conversation was a difficult one, but at least they were talking. Holden would live on to see another day and not end up a statistic.

I probably had the most difficult time with Ethan's words. I, too, felt very exposed. Jenny had called me a witch, in front of the whole school. True – I was one. I've felt this way since I was a child. I've always felt ... different. But the looks everyone gave me, made me very uncomfortable, like I had potential to harm them or something. *Nonsense. I suppose I could, but why would I? Anyone has that kind of potential really.* But it's about choices. I had a responsibility to help defend my friends against evil, *not towards it.* I thought of Abigail, the wisest woman of all. She had only ever used her gifts to help others, to heal, to protect, to give life to and guidance to those that needed it. She did it unconditionally. Abigail was pure light. I slowly began to realize, that being a witch wasn't always black or white, and certainly not green and warty like the storybooks and movies had shown.

I felt as called-out as Holden. Ethan looked at me, but didn't say anything. I wondered if he already knew, or was afraid to ask.

In the course of fifteen minutes, everything changed. So many lives changed by one person. I wondered why Jenny Fox was so spiteful, and why she felt the need to attack others and put them down. Perhaps she was only taking over where Jeremy had left off. The school bully. Afraid of those who go against her beliefs – whatever they are. Jenny's eyes had revenge lurking in them. Her wrath wasn't over. My heart told me she'd only just begun.

"Let me take you home," Ethan said.

Home. Someplace I was desperate to return to, but I still needed a distraction. After watching Jenny all afternoon snog with my boyfriend, I only wanted to spend time with Ethan.

"I don't want to go home yet," I said to Ethan.

He smiled. "Follow me."

Chapter 14
MEMORY LANE

"Thanks Ethan," I said, closing the car door behind me as we parked at Grams' house. Soft piano music played from inside, and through the front window we saw Grams and Grandpa sitting side by side on the bench. Ethan got out of the car and held my hand.

"They look so cute together." I smiled as I looked through the window into the living room. It felt like I'd looked into a portal of the past. Romance that lasted through the ages was hard to find. They looked so happy and still so in love with each other. Occasionally they shot each other glances and then joyfully continued their music. "To be so in love still, after all those years." I sighed hopelessly.

"Come on, dreamer. Let's not disturb them – they look happy. We don't have to be at your house for another hour." Ethan gave me a curious smile, and he looked down at his watch and then towards my house. "That should be enough time," he muttered under his breath.

"Time? What? Where're we going?"

Ethan just smiled and led me the same path as we had gone a week ago to the playground. The moon was at first quarter. Only one week away until Halloween and the night of the lunar eclipse. It excited me to think about how special that night would be. I've been told that eclipses in general bring times of change.

We made it to the clearing with the playground and sat on the swings. The rusty chains looked like they would break at any moment and the squeals of the swing set as we swayed back and forth mimicked that of a frog inhaling and exhaling wheezily. Ethan stopped swinging and looked at me like he'd just had an idea.

"I just remembered something."

"Oh?"

"Yeah. Come with me."

We left the swings and walked to the area where he built his tree forts with Carly all those years ago. Ethan rummaged the ground for something blunt. He grabbed a sharp flat rock resembling shale and started digging with it at the base of a tree near his fort.

"What are you doing?"

"Hang on. You'll see. I hope it's still here."

"You hope *what* is still here?"

The rock hit something in the ground and made a chink sound. "This," he said as he scooped around it and pulled it out. "I buried this here when I was ten, just before my Dad died. I meant to come back for it but I forgot about it." Ethan had his own buried treasure. He unwrapped several layers of foil and plastic from the mystery item. It was a cigar box. "I stole it. It was my Grandpa's box."

"You smoked when you were ten?"

"No silly. Don't be ridiculous. It was empty." He lifted the lid and peeked inside. His fingers fondled over all sorts of trinkets. There were old photographs, bottle caps, dice, a yoyo, a broken butterfly barrette, and other 'treasures' inside that made Ethan's eyes gleam to see again. He reached inside the box and pulled out a gold pocket watch and held it to his ear. "It's still ticking!" he said in amazement.

"Let me see?"

Ethan handed me the pocket watch and I opened it. The face was unusual. It had Roman Numerals instead of the usual clock numbers I've become accustomed to. I, II, III, IIII, V, VI, VII, VIII, IX, X, XI, XII

"That's strange," I said.

"What?"

"The number 4. It's four lines. Shouldn't it be IV?"

"Yeah. That is strange. I don't think I realized that before. I wonder why they made a watch like this?"

"Where'd you get it? Steal this from Grandpa too?"

Ethan gave me a look of distaste. "I was a kid Alyson. Not a thief."

"Ouch. Sorry. I didn't mean that."

"It's okay. I know you were just kidding."

I bit my lip. Ethan opened and closed the pocket watch and wrapped his hand around it. He choked back a tear.

"I bought it from a pawn shop. It sort of called to me and I knew it was the right gift. I was going to give it to my Dad for his birthday, but I never got the chance. He died. I didn't want to look at it anymore, so I buried it the day they buried him. I can't believe it's still here!"

I didn't know what to say so I said nothing.

"He meant the world to me," Ethan paused briefly. "He still does."

"Ethan, I think he would be proud of who you have become. He probably knows. He probably watches over you."

"Yeah, I hope so. I hope he's proud of what he sees." He smiled. His tone shifted abruptly. "Hey. Did you feel that?"

"What?" I said just as a tiny snowflake fell upon my nose.

We both looked up to the sky to see more of them descending upon us and giggled. "It's snowing!" I spun around in a circle. One snowflake turned into ten and then it fell in thicker clumps resembling potato flakes. It melted as it hit the ground.

"Want to head back?" he suggested.

"Well I don't really *want* to," I said and got to chest-to-chest with Ethan. The snow fell on us and melted instantly. It felt like tiny fairy kisses as it hit my face.

"Alyson?"

I smiled and giggled. "Yes, Ethan?"

"Do you believe in magic?" he asked.

My eyes must've been filled with wonder and delight. "Undeniably."

I couldn't tell Ethan just how much I believed in magic, as I was bound by oath to Emily not to tell him, or anyone.

Ethan paused and looked into my eyes deeply. I felt like I looked back into his, only beyond them, into his soul. He had such compassionate eyes, so much love behind them. I would never tire of looking into them.

"Wow," Ethan commented and giggled. "I could really get lost in you. I don't want to head back, but we should. I don't want Grams to get worried, and you should get home too. Let me just grab the box." He collected the various items we'd been looking over and put them carefully back into the box.

"Would you hold onto the pocket watch for me?" he asked and I nodded.

I felt my ring finger tingle as a snowflake hit it just right. My hand fumbled over the silver lily shaped ring. Even it felt magical. Unusual. The ring glimmered under the light of the moon. *Could it be? Is there magic hiding in this little ring?*

"All set. Let's go. We need to get you home." Ethan smiled at me as though he had a secret. I wondered what it could be.

We walked back through the path and cut through to Colby Drive. Snow continued to fall on us and the temperature had dropped significantly.

"It's really getting cold," I said.

"Yeah. Let's walk faster." Ethan and I made it to my front porch.

"I can't stay unfortunately. I have to head back to my home. I had a lot of fun with you though. Wish I could take you with me."

Ethan grinned. "Yeah. Me too." Snow had collected on the shoulders of Ethan's black jacket and I looked to his feet. The snow stuck. His eyes looked like they held a secret. He bit his lip. "You should get home now."

"What are you playing at?" I tried to pry the information out of him.

"Oh – nothing," he said with a smile in his voice. I knew he hid a secret, but what was it? He didn't divulge.

"I know you're hiding something. I can see it in your smirk. Maybe we'll have a snow day tomorrow," I said with high hopes.

"Maybe," he said as he kissed me lightly, laughed and walked away giving a wave as he looked back.

I walked the path home quickly, enjoying the snow, but not the cold.

I closed the front door, which had recently been fixed. There was also a new lock, but no alarm. Still, I felt the presence of something just behind me. I hesitated to turn around, but the sound of it breathing became more and more noticeable. It wasn't just breathing, it was panting. I turned and it came over and sniffed me curiously, wagging its frisky black tail. It had a small, blue ribbon on its collar with what appeared to be a folded-up note.

"I think it likes you. It's been sniffing everything around up in your room. Must be lots of good smells up there," Dad teased.

"You got a dog?"

"Well, I didn't. Ethan came and asked me if it would be okay. It's from Ethan. A gift, to you. And Mom really likes him too. I thought perhaps it would make you and Mom feel safer. We can't really afford an expensive alarm system, and well… your cat… well let's just say that a dog has more bark. So I went to the store with Ethan and he picked this little one out. He dropped it off this morning before school and I kept him hidden. Happy you're home! He needs a walk."

I crouched down and rubbed the puppy's head. It cocked its head and let out a deep "woof" sound, almost on cue. The black dog was a beautiful mix between a Labrador and a collie, and probably part wolf, and only had white patches around its nose and feet.

"Does it have a name?"

"Well, not yet. We were waiting for you to come back so you could help us think of something."

"I'll think about it."

"Oh, and there's a note for you. Check the collar," Dad said as he casually smiled and walked off.

I bent down and untied the tiny ribbon on the collar. The note was cleverly folded and slipped through the ribbon. I unfolded it.

"He's adorable! I can't believe Ethan gave me a puppy!" I took him for a quick walk and play in the snow. I was cold and eager to come inside, and feeling altogether just a little bit lazier than usual after spending such a romantic time with Ethan.

I hung up my jacket and walked through the house. The puppy curiously followed me and stayed on my heels. From room to room, it followed me. I didn't know what I'd done to deserve to have my own shadow. That was it.

"You're a shadow, aren't you? Shadow."

"Woof!"

"Very well then. Let's hope you and Emily get along. A cat and a puppy dog, this should be interesting."

I walked into the living room and Mom sat in her chair. She seemed upset. "I can't believe they would take my painting. Why would anyone want to steal a painting?" she vented. I looked to the wall where the magical painting had been hung. It was gone. I assumed maybe it was Abigail that hid it.

"I'm sorry Mom. Maybe you can paint another one like it?"

"We'll see. It was a very special painting. I'm very disappointed someone would do something like this. It was the only one they took. It doesn't even make sense to me. Nothing else got stolen. They just came in here, tore up the place, and stole my painting!"

Shadow came and sat next to me. I didn't really know what to tell Mom. I wasn't sure where the painting had gone either.

"They left all the antiques. They left the jewelry belonging to my Grandmother. They left even the artwork that hung here for much longer and is probably worth much, much more. I just don't understand it."

"Umm... maybe you have some really big fans of your work Mom?" I said trying to make humor.

She noted it and it gave her a giggle too.

"I guess we should just count our blessings that nothing else was stolen."

Shadow let out a woof.

"It's snowing outside," I commented.

"Really?" Mom ran to the window. "You're right. Beautiful! I feel inspired to paint. Perhaps tomorrow. I'm tired."

"Okay, Mom. Nite." I gave her a kiss.

I took Shadow up to my bedroom and he sat down near the side of the bed. "Alright. Talk to me. Who are you?"

"*Woof!*"

"No seriously. You're not just a dog. Come on. Out with it. You must do something magical. Can't you?"

"*Woof?*"

Emily lifted her head from her cozy spot on the reading nook by the window. "I am certain he is just an ordinary dog. He does not sparkle."

"Sparkle?"

"Yes. On the astral. Magic can be seen on the astral plane, even when it is not visible in your realm. He does not sparkle. But he does seem sweet, and apparently likes you. And, he was a gift from Ethan. This means Ethan really likes you. A dog is a commitment, and Ethan must want to be in your life pretty seriously if he gave you a puppy. He reminds me of Harding, so much. That would've been something Harding would've done," Emily said sentimentally.

"*Woof!*"

I scratched Shadow on the top of his head. "*Woof...* silly dog. Is that all you can say?"

Emily preened herself. Shadow hadn't really paid too much attention to her, which was unusual considering she was a cat.

"How come Shadow isn't chasing you around the house?" I asked Emily.

"Because, it knows that I'm human. Dogs don't usually chase humans unless they're up to no good and stealing your mother's good pearls," she said with a smile. "He doesn't see me as a cat. He sees me on the astral, and on the astral plane, I am human... always."

I scratched my head confused.

"It will make sense to you. Try not to put too much thought into it. You only think you are a new witch, Alyson, but on the astral...

you are to a certain extent very old. As is your mother, but she hasn't realized it yet."

"My mom's a witch too?"

"Why yes, Alyson, although it is her clumsiness that gets her into trouble. I thought you knew. How else could she have painted the painting that was the safe haven to Sadie and our Mother, Abigail? Alyson… your mother is our mother's sister. She's an aunt to us. You are part of our family. Come with me. I need to show you something. It is time you knew who we are."

Emily hopped down from her perch and stood patiently at the door waiting for me to open it.

"Shadow, stay," Emily commanded.

"*Woof!*"

I opened the door and Emily led me to a table in the hallway between the bathroom and my room. "Have you ever looked closely at this table, Alyson?"

"Not really. I was always more concerned with Sadie's room, the previously locked door at the end of the hallway. I never really noticed the table before."

"You must look underneath it."

I got on my hands and looked below the table. There didn't appear to be anything out of the ordinary. It had four post legs and a single drawer. It was upon noticing the drawer that the line in the wall behind it caught my eye.

"It is well hidden for a reason, Alyson. Put your hand into the depression on the wall."

I pushed gently and a tiny door opened, and upon releasing my hand, it shut itself again and blended with the wood paneling on the wall.

"Astonishing!"

"I shall show you inside," Emily pressed her paw against it and the door opened. She easily pounced inside. I had to crawl and squeeze into what felt like too tiny of a door. We were inside a tiny room, with a set of stairs leading up to an attic. She pounced her way to the top of them and stood at the landing.

"Well come on. Don't dilly dally." She twitched her whiskers at me.

I walked to the top of the tiny attic stairwell and stood on the landing with her. There were two rooms, one on each side. These were the rooms with the tiny windows I'd seen from the outside, but hadn't figured out how to find them on the inside. Amazing. Emily led me to the room on the right.

It looked like a child's room, with very old dolls, a rocking chair, a doll house with porcelain dolls inside, and toys I'd only seen in museums. Things like jacks and marbles and simple toys handcrafted by patient hands and not modern machines. On the walls, there were painted murals of animals, and of a treehouse. And there was a mural of seven dancing girls, holding hands in a circle. Emily changed into her human self.

"We are the seven sisters, Alyson. You're the last to be born. You're the one we've waited for."

"But I don't understand. How is it you can be my sister if you were born so long ago? And wouldn't you be my cousin, if my mother is your Aunt?"

"You're thinking too hard. On the astral, we are all the same age. It is on the astral that we are… the daughters of the greatest Elder."

"Who is the greatest Elder?"

"I cannot speak the name, for it is not made of words you know, but rather a symbol and a sound. No one has ever been able to look directly at the greatest Elder without having gone blind. There is only one who has seen him. Abigail."

"Abigail is blind?"

"Yes, but not always. And she does not speak of 'the moment' nor should you ask her of it."

"Because it upsets her right?"

"No, not at all. She is not upset. She considers her blindness a rare gift. She feels very blessed. She has seen the Divine. She is now an Oracle."

I recalled how Abigail looked at me at the RenFest. If she was blind, she'd have had to have relied on my aura and Ethan's aura, and our voices alone to know it was us. I was speechless. How could she know who we were? *Of course! She told us to trust. She trusts herself to know! She trusts her intuition. Amazing!*

I looked curiously to the room on the left. The door was unusually skinny, and could've easily been mistaken for a closet or cupboard. It wasn't even at full height to be for a real room. "What is in that room?"

Emelia smiled. "Go ahead. But beware... from this moment forth, you cannot unlearn what you have learned. You cannot forget knowledge that is buried deep within you. Not even in death, can that knowledge be destroyed. For the knowledge you possess is not of this world, and does not live in your head. You have a secret knowledge passed down by ancestors of old. I cannot teach you something, because you already know it."

I shook with nerves. The Elders may have closed the portal, but something... something else had been opened. A seal had been broken. Somewhere on the astral, a seventh candle had been lit.

I reached my hand for the doorknob to the room on the left and opened the tiny slender door in the cupboard.

Chapter 15
THE SECRET ROOM

The doorknob turned easily and the closet door opened. What was beyond it felt familiar to me, like I'd opened that door sometime before. I stepped inside. The room was vast. It was as large as the living room downstairs, which is impossible considering its location in the house. I'd have easily seen it from the outside, but had not. How could a hidden room be so large and yet unseen? *This couldn't possibly have been the room with the window, the window that disappeared from above my bedroom. Could it have?*

Stained glass windows adorned the room. And at the ceiling, there was an observatory. I looked up through the window in the ceiling and it aligned with a tiny cluster of stars coming into view. It made no sense to me. Certainly I would've seen this from the outside.

There was someone already in the room. Abigail waved for us to enter fully.

"Come in. Good. I see now that you are beginning to understand what we're all about, Dear."

"But I don't, really. I still don't understand."

Abigail put her arm around me and led me to a wooden pedestal in the center of the room. Her long, silvery-white hair draped over my shoulder. As I looked down at it, it blended with my own hair. Abigail and I felt like we were the same person in that moment. It took me by surprise and I jumped back, breaking our connection.

"Don't be so surprised, Alyson. You would be wise to listen so as not to be ill-prepared for the destiny that awaits you. This room is such as the lair of Hremm Nevar. It does not exist to the mortal eye, nor does it exist on this plane. But you can see it, and you can feel it, and it will always remain… as it is a room protected by the Elders themselves. No element can destroy it. Even if the entire house was consumed with fire, or flooded with water, or buried deep into the ground, or even swept away by a tornado… nothing can destroy this room. It just is and always will be."

"So why didn't you just run here when all the ghosts and demons were being set loose in the house? Why hide in a painting where they can see us? Why didn't you tell me about this room?"

"Alyson, I am forbidden. This room is being in the epi-center of the star. It is the eye. No one but us can enter it, however, we don't need anyone to stumble upon it either. It is possible for outsiders to find this room. Especially if foreign objects attributed to outsiders are brought in. Be careful with the items that you bring here. They will take on magical properties." Abigail waved her hand over me and it hovered just over my pocket, where I concealed Ethan's stopwatch inside of it. She glanced at me. Her eyes were silver.

I heeded her caution and looked at the pedestal. A very large book rested on top of it.

"Go ahead. You are free to look inside."

I opened the cover hesitantly. Inside the cover page were seven ovals, each with a portrait. I looked over the portraits, and although younger or older, I recognized each of them. Abigail, Emelia and Sadie were easy enough to recognize, as was a portrait of my mother, Claire. Beside her in the picture, stood a horse.

"My mother?"

Abigail nodded.

"But this horse has wings," I said in disbelief.

"As does your mother," Abigail added.

Then there were two portraits I didn't recognize.

I scanned to the seventh portrait. I knew the face all too well. It was a portrait of me, although it was no portrait of me in the present time. It couldn't have been. In the present, I was much younger than the girl in the photograph, but yet clearly this was a photo taken a long time ago by how faded it was. I looked to be about twenty five in the photograph, which was faded and sepia in colour. Each portrait had a gilded frame. I ran my fingertip over the gold leaf of the fifth portrait and my ring finger with the lily shaped ring tingled.

"Lily?"

Abigail nodded, but didn't speak.

"Is this the princess I met?"

"You've not met the real Lily. No. The real Lily is safely hidden and cannot be revealed to anyone unless I reveal her. The imposter you met was the Queen of Sands; she who wears a red hourglass on her gown. It is the hourglass that she uses to manipulate time. Or end it suddenly to those unsuspecting or who meddle too closely in her life. She is the Black Widow, forever seeking a mate, only to kill him. She is no one to rival with. Her powers are great, but ours are greater. Still, she uses disguises and trickery to her advantage and should never be trusted."

I rubbed my forehead. It felt like it had cracked in half. My dream came to me. I'd seen the Queen. She was disguised as Lily. "The ring. They stole the ring! I saw them at the RenFest. And the Queen." I explained my dream to Abigail and Emelia listened on.

Abigail laughed. "They are fools. But nonetheless, I do not take thievery lightly. Especially when it is not done out of necessity, but out of greed!"

Emelia nodded in agreement with Abigail.

Abigail waved her hand over her gown and her long white flowing hair turned raven black and the garments of a gypsy robed her once again. She smiled and sprinkled stardust into the air and stepped inside of it.

"I have matters to attend to girls. Keep watch. Be mindful of the time. Remember that it does not exist here." Abigail vanished into the air on a portal of shimmering light.

I pulled Ethan's stopwatch from my pocket. I still had it. I'd forgotten to give it back. It wasn't ticking anymore.

"It's not broken Alyson," Emelia noted. "Time does not exist here. Time is a measurement, and here… nothing is measured. We just *are*. Items in this room become enchanted. Your watch is, if you will, under a spell."

I nodded as though I understood, but I didn't. How could time not exist? I slipped the pocket watch back into my pocket to remember to give back to Ethan.

"Alyson. Let me explain a little more. Time does not exist here, but it does exist for those we've left behind. It is still moving forward and we must return to it. There are matters for us to attend to as well."

I looked back to the portraits of the seven sisters. The sixth one was blank, but I sensed something there. I couldn't see a face, but there definitely was a sister's portrait hiding in that dark, black space of the gilded frame.

"Who is this one? Who is the sixth sister?"

"She is known only as Rowen. She has not been found yet. Legend has it she weaves between the trees, like a dryad, searching for her home. She sings constantly, waiting for her tree to call to her. Other legend says that she has already found her tree, and is one with it already." Emelia leaned in closely. "I believe it is *she* who writes these pages. She is a scribe of wisdom."

"The pages in this book?"

"Yes," Emelia confirmed.

"But how? Where is she?"

"She… lives in the book."

"The book?"

"She, once a tree, now paper… do you follow me? Her essence flows through the pages, as she too was once a tree and on the paper she if free to live again. Her spirit is free."

I looked at the empty sixth portrait frame one last time before closing the cover of the large book. The cover of it tingled underneath my fingers. *Rowen. Why is it you seem so familiar?*

We walked to the door and turned the knob and left. I felt time returning to me instantly, as though I'd received a jolt to the heart. We descended the stairs and passed through the tiny door under the table and back into the hallway that separated the two bedrooms.

"I should tell my Mom about this."

"No Alyson. She will not be able to open it. It requires a certain enlightenment and celestial attunement to open. Your mother, although she is one of us, is still unaware. To openly tell her will make her lose her own mind, and her faith in what she knows and trusts. She needs to come into this knowledge on her own, and in time, she will. After all, we've had centuries to come into our own."

I entered my bedroom and Shadow faithfully waited at the foot of my bed, on the floor, sleeping. He lifted his head and simply said, "*Woof.*" His presence humored me, but on another level, perhaps a spiritual level, I felt protected by him.

In bed, I thought about the broom closet that wasn't, the missing face of the sixth sister's portrait, and of Ethan. Ethan gave me Shadow. Shadow was more than just a gift. Shadow was protection.

Chapter 16
A TRICK OR TWO

Dreams filled my head ceaselessly. Dreams of places I'd been or places others had been to. Somehow, my link to the secret room let me see into Abigail's mind. I watched the scene unfold as though they happened before my very own eyes – but they were Abigail's. Perhaps she wanted me to see.

Shimmers of light beamed and shone from the stained glass windows of the gypsy caravan wagon. Abigail arrived. It wasn't completely disheveled, but evidence of greedy thieves had made themselves known. Spilt booze and crumbs from a pastry tart littered the floor, as trays of disturbed jewelry lay scattered. One box in particular caught Abigail's eye. It was open, and its contents were missing.

Seamus knocked on the caravan.

"Come in Seamus."

"My dear Abby. I thought I'd sensed you return."

"Thieves. Common ones no less. Nothing magical here."

"'Twas Duncan and Wendy. They're the thieves you're searching for."

Abigail waved her hand and summoned them. Duncan and Wendy arrived on the floor of the wagon as they had previously been engaged in flirtatious activities. Wendy quickly assembled herself and drunkenly attempted to retie her corset as Duncan adjusted himself proudly, ruffling his shirt and fluffing his chest hair so it peeked out of it.

"You see. You see. I knew there be magic here," Wendy squealed. "She's one of them... those dark arts folk. Beware Duncan. She's got 'er eyes on you. Don't look into 'er eyes. She's like a Medusa, that one. 'Tis like 'er sister Belladonna. A friend 'til she betrays you."

Seamus rolled his eyes and gave Abby a look of trust.

"If you want to be thieving gutter mice, so you shall be. You shall learn to not steal from me!"

Duncan's eyes got big as Abigail pointed her finger at him. Wendy squealed like a pig and tried to run away, but the invisible rope that Abigail slung to catch her, had caught Wendy in her place. She looked at Abigail with full awareness of her crime.

Thieves and pirates you are
And wicked your punishment shall be
Live as proof of your true identity
In its form, you bodily shall acquire
Scuttering about in the gutters
Forever, until your debt is paid

Abigail pointed her finger at Duncan and as he tried to flee, he transformed into a ferret. Duncan scurried about the floor of the wagon and tried to run up Wendy's fishnet stocking. Wendy squealed. "Get it off me!"

Abigail lifted her finger in Wendy's direction and pointed. Wendy screamed in horror and begged with Abigail not to kill her. She looked at Abigail's eyes and awaited her fate. Abigail changed Wendy into a shrew. The two of them scurried about each other and then wandered out of the tent making a ruckus and heading towards the nearest trash receptacle.

"That should take care of them. Don't need a bunch of thieves wandering about, do we?" Abigail reassured Seamus.

"Lookie here. The old wench had something." Seamus bent over and picked up the black chess piece.

"May I see it Seamus?"

"Certainly," he said as he handed it to her. As Abigail took it, she saw a vision of her own of Prince Ivan and the Queen.

"Thank you, Seamus. I think I'll hold onto this one, for safe keeping."

"Faire thee well, my lovely Abby – forever my Bella." He smiled.

"And to you Seamus. Until we meet again, as we always do and always will." He kissed the top of her hand. "And I'll hold onto this one too, for safe keeping." She smiled as she closed her hand over the kiss. Seamus was gone.

Abigail fumbled the chess piece around in her palm with her fingertips. "Hmm. Curious. This is no ordinary chess piece. *Reveal yourself.*"

The black chess piece spoke to Abigail. "You can hear me?"

"Prince Ivan?"

"Yes. The Queen herself tricked me. She is gone now, but left me like this. This is an awful predicament to be in. How am I ever going to get back to myself?" the tiny mouth of the black horse spoke.

"For now, you are safer like this. I sense dangers still await you."

"And my dearest Lily?"

Abigail smiled. "She is not far or near, but will be here when you least expect it and need her to be the most."

The chess piece didn't say anything else.

"I will keep you with me. I cannot change you back into your human self. You have a curse placed upon you, and I cannot undo it. There is only one night that you can return. A moonless night. The night of the lunar eclipse on All Hallows Eve. But, in order for the curse to be lifted, you will have to receive a kiss. Not just an ordinary kiss, but one from your truest love. If it is Lily, then her kiss will break the curse."

"But what if the Queen finds Lily before it's time? What if she kills Lily? I'll be cursed like this forever?"

"Perhaps it's wise not to worry about events you have little control over. Lily will remain safely hidden. True love is keeping watch over her."

"True love?"

"What better guardians than the lovers themselves? I cannot tell you where Lily is hidden, for if the Queen questions you, she for certain would get it out of you. Unless you want to stay a chess piece forever, it is best to just trust … trust in things you believe in … trust in love."

"Abby, I don't understand."

"You don't need to. Things will happen, in due time."

"Time. Seems like I have too much of it these days. I can only wait."

"Time passes all too quickly for those who are not being mindful. Be aware. Opportunity is easily missed. You might even say that an opportunity like this one requires the assistance of the stars. In one week's time, all will be revealed. For now, you will stay with me."

Abigail sprinkled stardust into the air and stepped into the portal, once again returning her to the secret room. She set the chess piece on a table and opened the curtains. Moonlight shone through into the room.

"Count the moons. On the night of the seventh moon, the night when it is fullest, at its peak, you shall be summoned."

"But – I don't,"

"Trust. You are safe here. I promise you no harm shall come to you here."

Abigail sprinkled stardust into the air and teleported herself away.

Prince Ivan, immobilized in his stone chess piece form, could only wait for the night of the seventh moon, the night when the moon will disappear… a moonless night.

I awoke to see Henry the owl looking back at me from the tree. He was only there briefly, long enough for me to acknowledge him. Abigail had wanted me to see something in my dreams – and I had.

Chapter 17

The Day That Time Jumped

Shadow lifted his head and looked around the room before settling down again. I sat up to see what he'd heard. Shadow's eyes had closed again, resting his head on his paw. I was comforted knowing he was close by. He was like an old friend, a protective old friend, and one I had believed would keep me safe and alert me to danger. Shadow may not have been a magical dog, one with powers or the ability to talk, but his presence with me was one of kinship. I knew he could be trusted.

Snowflakes fell past my window as I drifted off to sleep. I slipped into a dream rather easily. I ran on a staircase that had no ending and as I looked back to the top, I could see no beginning. Shadow was at the little door in the hallway and pawing at it, sniffing at the base of the table. Shadow revealed something hid behind it. I reached a landing on the never ending stairwell. I heard a dog howling in my dream and then saw Shadow running towards me, only Shadow was a black wolf. It wasn't Shadow anymore. It was a spirit of a wolf. I woke.

I awoke to find a set of eyes staring at me. Shadow cocked his head and panted with his tongue hanging out to the side. *How charming.*

Dad poked his head through my doorway and tossed a leash my direction. "One thing about dogs is they need to go for walks kiddo. Rise and shine." Shadow caught it and gave me an impatient look.

"Fine. I'll walk him," I said grudgingly. I still had to get ready for the day for school. "Why can't they walk him? When did Shadow become *my* dog?" I muttered knowing full well Shadow was my dog. Ethan had given him to me. I zipped up my jacket and opened the front door. To my surprise, snow had covered the ground.

"Snow! It snowed!" I yelled through the house. Shadow bolted outside bounding with energy and ran to the nearest tree to attend to things.

"There's only an inch on the ground. School is delayed by an hour, but you still have to go," Mom said.

"Still… no Algebra!" I said with a huge smile. Anything to get out of math.

I drove to school with Ethan and ran to class. Cameron poked me in the back with something. It was a scroll.

"What's this?" I asked.

"Blueprints." He smiled at his rather clever presentation.

"Blueprints? For what?"

"The school."

"What? How?"

"Let's just say, I made an arrangement with the janitor," Cameron smirked.

"What did you do?"

"I didn't do anything. I asked him about it and he handed them to me. It was kinda weird actually. He just pulled them out from a filing cabinet, and handed them over, as though he expected me to ask him for them."

"Well go on. Roll it out."

Jenny Fox leaned in and eavesdropped.

Cameron glared at her and whispered to me. "Not here. Meet me in the library at lunch. The west, near the microfilm room. There's long tables and we can look at it there, undisturbed." As he said his last word, he gave Jenny a look of annoyance. She smiled at him innocently. I'd wondered if she heard our plan.

"Good morning students," an unfamiliar man's voice said. "Ms. Snodgrass-Hildegarde … err or is it Hildegarde-Snodgrass has been delayed and I'm subbing in her place. He turned to write his name on the blackboard. My name is… Professor Dhur, but you can all just call me Rick."

"Oh great. A substitute. Looks like we can fluff this class," I muttered quietly.

Overhearing my comment, he interjected, "Actually, I am well informed of what you are currently studying and since it is Friday and you've had all week to prepare, perhaps we'll have a small quiz to test your knowledge?"

I scoffed and sulked in my chair. I loathed quizzes.

Cameron poked me. "What's the big deal? It's just a quiz."

I knew it was just a quiz. Quizzes seemed trivial though in comparison to the grand scheme of things. Still, as mundane as it was, I would still have to pass math class. As our substitute teacher wrote questions for us to answer on the blackboard, I looked out the window, and got lost in a daydream. The secret room. There were so many mysteries inside of it. I wanted to go back. Its very presence intrigued me.

I snapped out of my daydream long enough to read the questions on the board.

"Huh?"

"They are riddles. In honour of Halloween being one week away, I thought it might be fun to do some brain teasers. Do your best. There are correct answers, but no one will receive a pass or fail, but you must at least try to answer each question. Give it your best."

"Riddles?"

"And there will be no talking for the remainder of class. You must solve these on your own. Good luck. When you are finished, please wait for the bell to ring and you may be excused." He sat in the teacher's chair, pulled up behind the desk and grinned as he delved into a science fiction novel.

1. You use a knife to slice my head and weep beside me when I am dead. What am I?

2. A word I know, six letters it contains, subtract one, and twelve remains. What am I?

3. can spell
yet i have no mouth
i can speak to animals
but can't speak to humans
i am fierce but small
What am I?

4. A horse is tied to a five meter rope in front of an old saloon. Six meters behind the horse is a bale of hay. Without breaking his rope, the horse is able to eat the hay whenever he chooses. How is this possible?

5. With thieves I consort, With the vilest, in short, I'm quite at ease in depravity;
Yet all divines use me, And savants can't lose me, For I am the center of gravity.

6. You are in a room that is completely bricked in on all four sides, including the ceiling and floor. You have nothing but a mirror and a wooden table in the room with you.
How do you get out?

7. Duels of good and evil,
A fighter of good am I,
Revealed beside watched words,
King of the black night sky. What am I?

8. No sooner spoken, than broken. What am I?

9. What row of numbers comes next in this series?
1
11
21
1211
111221
312211
13112221

I couldn't have been more filled with delight. It wasn't quite math, not even Algebra or Geometry or word problems, but a test of wit. *Amusing.* I wrote my answers down quickly, guessing at a few and when the bell rang, passed in my quiz to the teacher before dodging off to the library to meet with Cam.

The library was a quiet place and the back room was hardly ever used. More students opted to use the newer computer systems than the old fashioned microfilm, so it was relatively a safe spot for us to hide in.

Cameron rolled out the blueprints. The school grounds were huge. There was much more on the map than we'd known about.

"What do you suppose is this black square over here on the map?" I asked.

"I'm not sure. It looks like it's been scratched out. Guess they couldn't afford erasers when they made this? Maybe we'll check it out. Maybe it's the cemetery. Maybe it's *The Boneyard*!"

"Cemetery?" A voice came from behind a nearby book shelf. Jenny Fox emerged, hobbling on a crutch. She giggled. "Couldn't help but overhear what you nerds are plotting. You're going to seek out the Boneyard? You're brave or stupid. I heard they murdered people there and then threw their bodies in with the coffins, never to be discovered unless someone dug them up."

"Go away Jenny," Cameron spat at her.

"Testy. This is a public library, for all students, correct? I have every right to be here, and probably more so than you do considering who owns this section."

"We are in the Clifford R. Fox library. Oh bother. Your dad owns this too?"

She nodded snidely. "So, what are you two possibly up to? Planning a séance at the school, Witch? That would be fun. Summon up all your demons to help you out?"

"I don't conjure up demons. I would never have a séance. I don't even like Ouija boards," I retorted.

"Ooooo, I hadn't thought of a Ouija. Thanks, Witch. Maybe I'll have my own séance. I'm sure there's more than one eager student here that isn't afraid of their own shadow."

Her cockiness really annoyed me. "I'm not afraid!" I spat at her, resuming my confidence. "I just don't like them."

"You're afraid," she poked.

"I am not. I just don't want to do it, okay? I've heard bad things can happen to people who mess around with them. Especially people that don't know what they're doing, and Jenny, I think you fall into that category!"

Jenny Fox got up abruptly and shoved her chair in underneath the table. "Well, never mind then. I don't want to waste any more of my time with you… you… nerds!" She gave me a mean look followed by a "hrmph" sound and hobbled off with her pink cast on her leg.

"Ugh, she drives me nuts. I wish she'd -," I stopped myself before continuing. I remembered that sometimes, unknowingly, my words had more power than I knew. "Oh, never mind. She's not worth talking about."

"Who's not worth talking about? I'm not talking about anyone. Jenny Fox doesn't exist to me. She's just a speck of lint marring up my otherwise perfect day," Cameron rambled on, ignoring her.

I giggled.

A school librarian wheeled her large, heavy book cart out of the way and a row of tables came into our view. The squeaking of the cart, desperately in need of oil, grabbed our attention. The tables all had sunlight streaming in over them. Sara sat at one of them, alone and illuminated by a sun ray. Her brown hair had streams of gold shining through it. She looked angelic, but something still was wrong with her. Cameron looked at me with uncertainty.

"You should go talk to her."

"But she doesn't want to talk with me. She said she just wants to be left alone."

"Yes, but she doesn't... really. She needs to talk with someone, and you've always been the friend she trusts. You've always been there for her... as a friend."

"I get it. Okay, I'll go talk with her."

Cameron walked over with soft footsteps to Sara's table. Sara defensively lifted her head from her blank paper and looked at Cam. He pulled his chair out and sat across from her and they started talking... just talking... like old friends.

I packed up my books and left. After school, I didn't want to stay for rehearsals. I faked a period cramp and went home. Ethan was nowhere in sight, so had to take the bus, which only drops off at the corner of Colby Drive, so I still had to walk the mile home.

The walk down Colby wasn't as exciting as it previously had been. The snow had all melted during the time I went to school and there weren't even any remnants that it had ever been there, save for a few tiny rocks this and there, with small mounds of unmelted snow leaning against them.

I pushed open my front door.

"Hello? Anyone home?" I yelled throughout the house. I was alone. Guess Mom went out shopping and Dad's still at work. Shadow ran down the stairs and greeted me with a tail wag.

"Come on. Let's go upstairs." I climbed each stair as I normally would, however something felt very unusual. The stairwell seemed to go on and on, more so than usual. So I ran up them faster. Still, the top of the stairs seemed to be still out of reach. I stopped and looked behind me. I'd only stepped up the first stair. I was still at the bottom. Perhaps I wasn't supposed to be going to my room. Discouraged, I turned to walk back down the one step and found myself at the top of the landing.

"Okay, that was just weird. What's happening?"

A giggle came from behind me. Emily came out from my bedroom. "Having trouble?" she said with a laugh.

"Emily, what's going on? The stairs…,"

"It's not the stairs, Alyson. It's you."

I looked at her confused.

"There's a part of your subconscious that is attempting to portal, or to learn how to portal rather. It's amusing to watch your attempts."

"But I wasn't trying to do magic. I just wanted to get up the stairs."

"Sometimes, though you may not realize you're trying, your heart does magic automatically. It is something that is within us, Alyson. It's not always about spellbooks and wands and ABRACADABRA. Did you not know that true magic comes from within?"

"Yes, Abigail told me."

"Well, if our Mother told you, then you know it is true." She smiled.

"Emily. I want to go back. I want to go back into the secret room."

"There's nothing stopping you. You have as much power as I do to enter. You're attuned to the door. Go ahead."

I bowed down underneath the table and pressed my hand upon the wall. The tiny door opened. I stepped inside and found myself already at the top of the landing of stairs. I'd skipped over them completely.

"Strange."

The cupboard door looked as it did before. Small and unimpressive. Still, I knew the magic that lurked within. I turned the knob and entered.

The room was full of potent magic. Light shone through the stained glass windows and illuminated the floor with a vast array of colours. I took my time exploring every inch of the room. The tome in the center of the pedestal caught my eye. I'd only just opened the cover and looked at the portraits. What other secrets lurked inside?

I lifted open the cover of the book and flipped the pages.

Blank. How odd. I could've sworn these pages had writing on them when Abigail flipped through it.

A loose page flew out of the book as I flipped it. It had a picture of a star cluster. The Pleiades. I looked above me through the observatory. It was still daytime. *I wonder.* I read the torn page and the notes within.

They are the stars, and together, they are THE star.
The star that guides us.
When the seven become one, we shall all have wisdom.

The seven sisters.

Unusual. I wonder. I wondered if this observatory had anything to do with this book. I remembered seeing a star cluster through it last night. I looked upon the portraits of the seven sisters at the front of the book. I especially looked upon my own.

"This is how I will look ten years from now," I said softly, thinking I'd only spoken to myself. "Not too shabby," I boasted.

"Hello?" a voice came from beside the book, on the table.

I paused to look around for a possible talking mouse or other magical creature, but saw nothing.

"Hmm... curious. Oh well. Back to the book," I said as I browsed over the gilded frames. As I passed over Lily's portrait, my ring tingled again. "That's strange. It did it again, and over Lily's picture."

"Lily. Did you say Lily?" the tiny voice spoke again. I was certain I heard it clearly that time around.

"Hello? Yes, who are you? Are you in the book?" I looked into the book and flipped the pages. Nothing seemed too unusual for me these days. I've learned the hard way. Part of perceiving the world of magic, is understanding how it is incorporated into our world. It doesn't happen in some far off land in fairy tales. Magic happens when you least expect it.

"Down here. I'm beside the book," the tiny voice spoke again.

I looked beside the book and only saw a chess piece. *A chess piece!*

"Prince Ivan?"

"Yes! Hello!"

I attempted to pick him off the table, but he was being held down with a magical sort of glue.

"I'm sorry. I can't move you."

"Yes, I suppose Abigail did that for my own protection. So I couldn't fall off and break or something."

"What are you doing in here?"

Ivan explained his story. "... And then on the seventh moon, the night of the eclipse is when it should happen. Lily will finally come for me."

"I see. Well then I suppose for your sake, I hope time moves a little faster. Less time to wait!" I giggled slightly, but then felt unsettled. The pocket watch in my pocked began to tick. I pulled it out. It didn't tick at a normal speed, and as I looked at it, the hands on the dial spun wildly. Ivan looked out the window and he counted aloud, "One, two, three, four, five, six." With each number he spoke, the ground beneath my feet shook hard. The moon appeared and replaced itself with the sun before reappearing. With each reappearance, the moon became more and more full. I realized unknowingly, I'd cast a spell. As the ground shook harder and harder, I fell to the floor.

"No more! STOP!" I yelled with force. I intended for time to hear me. And like a lucky lotto spin, it had landed on the moon. It was nearly full, and as I looked at its presence before me through the window, realization of what just happened sank in.

The pocket watch stopped ticking. I was afraid to speak. I stared at the pocket watch. The hands were stuck at eleven minutes after eleven. Time did not progress further.

"Did you just speed up time?" Ivan asked, breaking the silence and scaring me. I jumped.

"I… um. I'm not positive, but I umm… I think so."

"Less time to wait, just like you said."

"I guess so. For you that's a good thing, but not so sure what it's done for me on the outside world."

"Maybe you'd better go see," Ivan advised. I sensed he was right. Just as I was about to leave, something familiar caught my eye. It was my mother's painting. I grabbed it and took it with me. She'd be happy to see it rehung.

I left the room and crawled back through underneath the table into the hallway. Things were different. The house had been decorated for Halloween. There were skull streamers down the stairwell handrail and pumpkins on the walls. I walked into the foyer and Mom sat on the couch.

"Hey sweetie. How's the homework coming along? Oh my gosh… is that?" she sat up from her spot and rushed the painting.

"Yes, I found it hiding behind a door. Guess the thieves must've hid it."

I smiled to see how happy having her painting made her. As soon as she hung it back up on the wall though, I noticed a problem. Sadie was back inside of it. Abigail wasn't there. Just a smudge of paint where she should be.

"Oh, would you look at that. I'll have to fix that. Paint must've gotten chipped off or something. The bird is gone. Oh well. Happy to have it back. Thanks for finding it. Come on. Let's go bake more cupcakes for your play tomorrow."

"The play's tomorrow?"

"Yes honey. You've been practicing your lines all week. You'll do just fine. How many cupcakes did we need to bring? Was that one hundred or two? Almost done. Let's see if we can wrap this up by midnight. You should really get to bed. I didn't expect you'd be up so late."

I *had* sped up time. And Sadie was back in the painting.

What have I done?

Chapter 18
ELDERQUAKE

ny quiet expectations of having a good night's rest were gone. This wasn't just cursing a broken leg. This was altering time. No doubt the Elders would have something to say about this.

I entered my room anxiously awaiting the punishment I was certain would be thrown at me. Especially considering tomorrow was now Halloween, thanks to my time slip, and who knows what awaited me at school. I closed the door behind me and Emily greeted me nervously.

"What did you do?" she scolded me like a big sister.

"What?"

"Look!" she pointed to the window. I walked hesitantly to the window and looked outside. It was difficult to see anything under only the light of the full moon, but some things were unmistakable. Hundreds of black birds littered the lawn and sat perched silhouetted in trees.

We watched through the window as one of them dive-bombed straight for us as though it were shot out of a gun. It hit the glass hard, cracking the window with the force of its beak. Both Emily and I screamed. It slid off and fell to the ground.

"Don't open that window," Emily shouted at me.

Another one flew at the window, cracking it further. *Was it their intent to get inside?* We moved from the view of the window.

"Ravens. Hundreds of them. Where'd they all come from?"

"Don't you know? Didn't you do this?" she spat at me furiously.

"No. I didn't do this."

"You meddled with time didn't you?"

"I didn't mean any harm by it. I only wanted to help the Prince!"

"Admirable as that may be, you inadvertently may have harmed many more. It is not wise to time warp, at least until you know what you're doing." She looked back to the window. "Those birds. All of those birds. *Those are* Hremm Nevar. He is now scattered into a million birds, like a million broken souls. He is no longer whole and although not as powerful, he will be harder for us to defeat being scattered."

"Sadie! Sadie is back in the painting! I – I rehung the painting. It was in the secret room!"

"It was in the room for a reason. The room is safe from time. Time does not exist. Once you brought the painting back, everything that was inside of it had to return to it. So Sadie is back, and I trust Abigail is too?"

"No. She wasn't there."

"She wasn't?"

Both of us looked at each other mystified. Another raven rushed the window and fell to the ground similarly to the others. The window cracked fully and it would only take one more raven to break the glass barrier that separated my room from the outside world. The sounds of the squawking birds shook the house. Emily and I carefully went closer to the window and looked outside. A blast of white light illuminated the entire area, radiating from a wispy sprite that hovered in the yard. The black birds were blasted out of the area and sent strewn into the atmosphere. The wispy sprite became into full form. It was Abigail.

Abigail teleported into my bedroom.

"We haven't much time before he'll be back. For now, he is aware he is defenseless against us. Sadie and her army destroyed Hremm Nevar's lair. His nest is no longer there. He has nowhere to return to. But he is quite irritated, and hunting. Alyson, it's not safe to be outside." Abigail did not scold me for making a time warp. I was certain she knew about it, but realized I'd recognized the error and had already learned from it. Even good witches make bad mistakes out of good intentions.

Exhaustion set in.

"Alyson, rest. I will keep watch over the house. Hremm Nevar has gone elsewhere for this evening, I assure you. Rest. You'll need your strength tomorrow."

I felt myself wanting to argue that I wouldn't be able to sleep, just as my eyelids fell shut and without choice of my own, I was cast into a land of slumber.

I awoke refreshed, feeling like I'd had the best sleep ever. I'd only slept for about 4 hours. Time for school already. I ran down the stairs, completely oblivious to the previous day's activities and ran into the cupcake queen herself, my mother. They were perfectly decorated like spider webs and Frankensteins. I wondered if she even went to bed. I thought for a moment... *unless she just used magic. My mom... the kitchen witch.*

Of course! It's Halloween! Yikes.

It finally clicked and visions of yesterday came pouring into my head. Tonight was the school play. Already. *Did I even know my lines? I have to kiss Ethan! I've never done that on stage before! I've never kissed Ethan in front of anybody.* I had a slight panic moment. Not only did I get horrible stage fright, but the thought of kissing Ethan on stage, in front of everyone, with a spotlight on us, and probably microphones, and watching us. I fainted right there in front of Mom.

Shadow was quick on the ready to wake me up. A big slobbery tongue came at me and licked my cheek.

"Ewww yuck!" I squealed. "Dog slobber. Thanks Shadow." At least kissing Ethan wouldn't be *that* bad.

All day at school I felt nervous. My palms wouldn't stop sweating. I had my lines tucked into my biology book and practiced reading them inside my head while we learned about cellular transport and splitting atoms and genetic yadda yadda. The teacher's voice faded in the background somewhere lost in my subconscious mind.

"During metaphase, the chromosomes move to the equator of the spindle. Which of these illustrations shows metaphase?" he asked. "Alyson?"

"Huh?" I snapped out of my daydream and play rehearsal to summon an answer. I looked at the diagrams on the board. Centromeres. Sister chromatids. Spindle fibers. I pointed to the answer I thought was correct.

"Wrong."

Ouch.

"What is the correct order of the phases of mitosis?" he drilled me again, clearly making an example of me for daydreaming. I felt like the whole room stared at me waiting. The whole world waited for me to speak. I looked out into the classroom and only saw the stage. The audience. The parents watching me kiss Ethan. My heart went THUD in my chest when the chalk snapped back into the grooves at the base of the blackboard.

"Oh umm... let's see.... Mitosis starts when the chromatin coils to form visible chromosomes. Prophase-Metaphase-Anaphase-Telophase is the correct order."

"Right. Very good."

I smiled. The cute guy I once had a crush on smiled at me. How could I force myself to get over my stage fright when I couldn't even answer a simple biology question correctly?

A note passed to me. I looked around the classroom to see who passed it. The cute guy made a smiling gesture and a nod for me to read the note. *Are you for real?* It read:

Want a tutor? ;)

I smiled at him. He made me blush. He was really cute. A different kind of cute. A smart cute. He blushed back and his blonde bangs fell into his puppy dog eyes as he waited for my reply. I liked him. There was no doubt about that. But I was in love with Ethan. I scribbled back on the note.

Thanks. I'm okay.

He shrugged with a "well if you're sure" gesture and I smiled back.

"Yeah, maybe next time," I said to myself. I stared at the back of his head for the rest of class. My palms went sweaty. As I wiped them on my jeans, I thought about Ethan, and the school play tonight. The hours passed quickly and it would soon be here.

* * *

Students came pouring in from all directions and entrances into the school gym. They filled each carefully planned and placed folding chair and choir bleachers they could find. *I bet some of those students brought both sets of parents. Why are there so many parents? Wow. That's a lot of people who are going to be watching me kiss Ethan.*

I quickly pulled the curtains shut and looked around at the cramped backstage. It was almost show time.

"Ethan. I'm really nervous."

"Why're you nervous babe?"

I wanted to spit out… "Because I have to kiss you" but instead I just shrugged and said, "Oh, you know… stage fright. Just the jitters. They'll pass in time for when I have to … oh never mind." I ran back behind the backstage and into the girl's bathroom.

I didn't think I could blot all the shine off my nose. *Where'd that zit come from? I am going to scream!* I covered my palm over my mouth. Breath check. *Why am I so nervous? It's just Ethan.* I popped a tic-tac and almost gagged on it as I walked back to the backstage.

Principal Jeffries came out and tapped the microphone a few times.

"Thank you for coming. We'll begin our presentation shortly."

Silence. A hush passed over the audience, catching my attention. Why'd they all stop talking? What's going on?

I peeked out through the curtains and saw the parents all staring towards the door at the long end of the hallway adjacent to the gym. The door had swung open and a tall figure stood in its doorway, shovel in hand. It was the gravedigger. A light flicked on in the hallway. Our eyes had played tricks on us. It wasn't the ghostly gravedigger. It was just the school janitor. And the shovel had been a mop. A sigh of relief passed through the crowd. Many were on edge simply because it was Halloween. Many were on edge because they were unaware of what their evening held.

I looked at Ethan and stormed over to him and grabbed him behind the neck and pulled him into a kiss. He completely was caught off guard and attempted to fall backwards. He landed on the floor and I knelt down to help him up.

"Sorry," I said blushing and feeling a bit stupid for trying such a thing.

"No. Don't be. It was great." He turned me towards him. "No, I take that back. It wasn't great. It was awesome." He scooped his hand behind my neck and pulled me into a kiss with him. The curtains opened. I couldn't stop kissing him. But I heard the parents making comments when it set in that they'd opened. Stunned, I stopped kissing long enough to pull away slowly and surprised from Ethan to look into the crowds. Stage fright set in and immobilized me like a deer caught in headlights.

"Alyson?" Ethan whispered and then corrected himself, and spoke loudly, as though in character. "Lucie, you have come to me," Ethan said in a vampire accent mimicking Count Chocula more than Dracula, but he improvised, so it worked. I still couldn't make words come out of my mouth. I waited for him to just take me there. *Just do the vampire kiss and get on with it, Ethan. Just do it, so they can close the curtains.* Ethan kept smiling into the crowd, lost in the gazes of the lovelies staring back at him. He was a looker, for any woman, regardless of age. Old women especially seemed attracted to Ethan. He had a boyish charm they all missed, or had lost in their husbands. Still, I looked at him and knew he was mine. I lifted my hand to his cheek and turned it towards me. My eyes locked with his. There was a moment between us where the crowd faded away. It was only the two of us, and once again, we were surrounded by stars and gazing into each other's eyes in the moonlight outdoors on a blanket. That moment captured us. It forever etched itself into my memory. My first kiss with Ethan. One interrupted by Sadie herself. Still, this was another moment and the people waited for Dracula to give his famous blood sucking kiss to Lucie, so it was time to give them what they wanted.

I pulled Ethan to my neck and he bit me. Not hard, but I did wince. While faking death, Ethan nudged me that I don't die – that I'm now one of them. The curtains closed around us.

"Are you okay? You're lost for words. It's okay if you've got stage fright." He must've known I had stage fright. Yes. That was it. That, and perhaps that I skipped ahead in time about a week and he had more time to prepare the scene. But that was probably inconsequential.

After the play, everyone pigged out on the cupcakes and assorted baked treats the parents had made the night before. I walked into the sea of chaperones and headed to get my own cupcake. Jenny Fox bumped into me.

"Hey, watch it!" she snapped at me.

"Whoa. Take it easy, Jenny. Hey, what is that?"

"I swiped it. Want some? Just kidding. Too bad you're such a loser," she said making an L on her forehead. She curled her finger grip tightly around the bottle and giggled as she walked away, with it stashed under her coat pelt.

"She's going to get it for sure," Cameron said as he brought me a cupcake.

"Hey thanks. Umm.. yeah. I was thinking," I paused and pulled Ethan closer to our group. "We should definitely keep an eye on Jenny Fox tonight. Remember what she mentioned she wanted to try doing?"

Cameron gasped exaggeratedly. "So what. It's just a Ouija."

"And a gun is just a gun. Doesn't matter. Once you put power behind something, you may have well just pulled the trigger and fired.

Jenny's not in any condition to be communicating with the dead, or the living. Come on, let's go."

Ethan and Cameron ran out with me towards the hallway where the janitor had been standing, and similarly where Jenny Fox had ran to. We ran out the doors into an area of the school we'd not really been to before. These were the senior classrooms, and this hallway lead to a courtyard. We walked to the double doors and pushed them open.

The courtyard had four pathways, one leading to each direction and marked with a N-E-S-W direction marker at each doorway. In the center was a fountain, with roses on all sides, dried up and frozen for the winter. Hedges were neatly planted in unusual rows. It seemed oddly out of place. It was quite elaborate considering it was only a high school courtyard. We had entered from the door to the South. As we moved in closer, intense vibes shook through me.

The full moon pierced the courtyard's darkness.

"This should make a good spot to watch the eclipse," Ethan noted.

"The eclipse. I'd forgotten." I sniffed the air. "Anyone else notice that – that smell?"

"What smell?"

"It's an odd smell. Kind of like mildew or mold, or like rotting trees. It's musty to breathe here. It's chilly." I rubbed my arms.

Cameron looked at me, sniffed the air and shrugged. "I don't smell anything. Look, there's Jenny," Cameron said in a loud whisper and pointed.

She sat near some bushes, in a huddle with some other girls from her cheerleading team, and passing around a bottle.

"She makes me sick. Just because she's rich, she thinks she can do whatever she wants. I hope she gets caught. I hope she gets in trouble," Cameron said angrily. "I wish she would just…"

"Be careful what you wish for, Cam," I reminded him. He fell silent.

Sara walked into the courtyard. "Hey. Here you guys are."

"Hey, yourself. Glad you found us," Cameron said in a completely different tune as he turned and faced his whole body towards Sara.

She leaned in and gave Cameron a kiss on the cheek.

"Thanks for earlier," she whispered to him. Cameron instantly turned a shade of pink only a watermelon could compete with.

"Um, don't mention it," he said smiling.

"What's Jenny doing?" Sara took note of the activities lurking in the corner.

"She's being stupid, is what she's doing," Cameron commented.

"Let's go see what she's up to." Sara went to crash Jenny's little board game drinking party.

We followed, but I stayed out of the group and just watched from the outskirts. Sara sat down next to Jenny. Jenny passed her the bottle. Sara looked at me.

"A little won't hurt," she said as she swigged, giving a hiccup after.

"Sara," I quietly scolded her, but folded my arms and looked away mad. It was her life. I didn't want to see her mess it up by attempting to be a Jenny wannabee.

"Is that a –, what I think it is? How do you pronounce it?" Sara commented on the box.

"Yep. It's for our séance. I told Alyson about it, but she was too afraid to play. It's just a game, Alyson. If it wasn't just a game, why would they sell it in toy stores next to checkers and other board games? It's just *a harmless little game.*" Jenny mocked my fear. I felt it wasn't completely irrational. Her point did make sense. Perhaps they aren't as harmful as I thought. They did sell them in toy stores. She had a point. At least for once she got my name right.

"Besides, we have goodies," she uncovered another fancy shaped bottle. "I'm not even sure what this one is," she said with a naïve laugh. "Look – it's green."

"It smells disgusting. I'm not drinking that," one of the gals spat at Jenny. Jenny glared at her for refusing her sacrificial offering as though she were a Queen Bee of a popularity cult or something. "Okay, okay – I'll drink it," she said as she caved. The gagging sounds that followed were all I needed to confirm I wasn't going to partake in any of Jenny Fox's little reindeer games.

Hesitantly, I sat in the small circle that formed. I wasn't particularly interested in joining Jenny's bra-snap clique but since Sara was here, I felt obligated to keep her safe. She'd already had a rough month. Jenny leaned in and passed me the bottle. "Come on. To sisterhood. You want to be one of us, don't you?" she taunted. Sara nudged me to just try it, or at least fake it. I faked it. I should've just left, but I had to stay. There was a part of me that knew I had to stay. I tilted the bottle back, and put it to my closed lips. My hand covered everything. No one saw that I didn't sip. I smiled and let out a burp I summoned from somewhere deep within. They were right – it did smell disgusting.

Jenny looked satisfied. The other two girls with us were cheerleaders, but not very bright ones. The both of them put together might have had an IQ value of as high as Shadow's, but that was being generous.

"There. Let's begin," she said in a deep voice, lifting the cover off the Ouija board box, with the famous brown cover, hands touching the planchette. There it was, in the box. The planchette. I didn't even want my hands to touch it. I sensed great danger from being in the area.

"Umm... shouldn't we put up a protective circle or something," I said, looking at Jenny who didn't have a clue.

Cameron rushed to our little circle. "Alyson, can I see you for a moment?" he said while grabbing my arm tightly and pulling me up off the ground.

"You didn't really drink did you?" he muttered.

"No, of course not. Let go of me."

"Good. Anyways, look." Cameron rolled out the map and showed me the blacked part of the map that had the word cemetery written across it. With a flashlight behind the map shining through, the words 'prospective' appeared above it. He moved his flashlight to the area on the map that was relative to the courtyard that we stood in the center of. The blueprints revealed the words, 'old cemetery' and 'moved to new location at Eastlawn' scribbled over it.

"Cameron. But the headstones…"

"Yes. Do you think? Yes, of course I'm thinking that too. They didn't want messy headstones dirtying up the school courtyard, so they moved them. The school moved them!" Cameron said furiously, but with some fear in his words. We both shared the thought of the possibility that we stood on top of buried bodies below us.

The Boneyard!

My eyes caught Jenny Fox out of their corner. She already had one hand on the planchette hand others had placed theirs. Her head was tilted back and she whispered into the air as though attempting to call upon a spirit.

"Stop pushing it," she yelled at one of her groupies.

"I'm not!" they complained back in unison.

Jenny looked spooked as their hands moved over the board. "You did that. I know you pushed it there," the groupie yelled at Jenny.

She retorted with a sharp, "Shhh. You'll scare off the spirit. Look, the pointer thingy is moving on its own."

They leaned in and followed it with their hands. T – I – M. "The first name is Tim."

"Maybe it wasn't finished yet," Jenny spat.

"Maybe it's spelling out a code or something."

"Well shut up already," Jenny barked.

"I hope she gets ectoplasm coming out of her perfect little nose-job nose," Cam said snidely in a whisper.

Everyone in the courtyard became overwhelmingly and spontaneously quiet. It was a disturbing quiet. The kind of quiet that only comes before a big storm. The silence broke when the sounds of a howling dog entered the Boneyard. The gravedigger appeared once again in the doorway with his shovel, but then left. I felt my shoulder get frostbitten, the same way it did that night I fought the ghost in my house. *The ghost with the black glove.* Sara had been there!

I felt the urge to close my eyes just then, so I did. What I saw before me amazed me. I saw the headstones, as they were, stuck in the ground. I mentally walked myself through them. I could read the names on them distinctly. I saw a little room over in the corner of the courtyard, so I approached it in my vision. It was a doghouse. There was still a chain tied to the doghouse, and adjacent to that was a headstone. I read the name.

I snapped out of it. "Hey Cameron. What's the janitor's name?" As Cam whispered it to me I knew.

"He's a ghost."

"What?"

"The janitor. He's a ghost. His grave is just over there, next to the doghouse. I'm staring at a headstone – a headstone that isn't really there. I can't explain it, just trust me!"

"I do… but, Alyson, there's nothing over there but Jenny Fox and her boozing girlfriends."

"I haven't lost my mind, okay. Just trust me. The janitor is the gravedigger. Who gave you that map?"

"The janitor."

"I rest my case. He wanted you to find this place. He probably can't put his soul to rest, because no one can find him. His headstone is missing. We need to tell someone about this and get them to rest in peace."

I expected Cameron to at least say something, but his gaze fixed on something else completely. Jenny had made contact with something. It wasn't good either. Penelope the ghost dog came barreling through the door and straight at Jenny. There was a moment and I pulled Ethan's pocket watch from my coat and yelled "Stop!" and so it did. I looked to the pocket watch and it had stopped ticking. But more noticeable was everything in that courtyard, except for Penelope the ghost dog and myself, had frozen. Not literally, but figuratively. Time was frozen. My time stop had not gone unnoticed.

Abigail teleported in around me, arriving on a mist. She grabbed the Ouija board and planchette out of Jenny's hand and shattered them into tiny pieces and flung them into the atmosphere like bits of burnt up comets. Penelope cowered and hid behind the doghouse.

"What's with that dog?" I mumbled.

"You cannot stop time for everyone. The eclipse needs to happen. But maybe we can put them … on hold." Abigail snapped her fingers and time ticked on the pocket watch again. Simultaneously, she'd cast a magic circle around the courtyard and made the space sacred. We were protected on all sides, by the elements, and their guardians. Everyone else remained motionless, except for Abigail and myself, and a ghost lurking too near Jenny Fox.

"Abigail. There's a ghost here."

"Oh, I'm well aware. He's more of a prankster really. You've met him before. He's the ghost with the black gloves. You see I have come to know who he was," she began to tell me. "He worked out here late in the cold many winters long ago, and deep in the snow, he was instructed to remove the headstones so they might continue building this courtyard. The walls had been constructed already. The doors were in place, as the original idea was to leave the headstones in the courtyard, as a memorial. But the original architect died, and a new one took their place. This person wanted the headstones removed. Well, late at night, working with a very thin coat and only black gloves to keep warm, he decided he was going to take a break and go in to get warm. Snow had fallen very deeply by then, as clearly above us there is nothing but the night sky. The headstones were all stacked up neatly, but the owners they belonged to were not happy about the new arrangement. The man went to open the doors to get in and found them locked. He tried all four doors surrounding the square courtyard and each was locked. He yelled for help, but no one heard him, so he crawled in the doghouse to keep warm. He died alongside Penelope. They both froze to death in the cold that night. That ghost is the gravedigger, Tim Harbinson."

"You knew all of this?"

"Not exactly. When I returned to see the Elders about all of the demons attacking your house, I was informed to whom each one was. It's really a formality dear, in case any of them are family. I've had several warlocks in my family that have gone bad really. I've only one relative that is still alive. I believe you've met him. A past life love. My late husband, Seamus," she said with a smile. "Shall we go give him a visit? The eclipse awaits as does the moonless night. A spell has been cast and there is magic in the air. Look there Alyson. The star."

In the center of the courtyard was a star etched out of mosaic on the cement. The area above it became illuminated and shimmered with a welcoming light. Above us, the eclipse of the moon had begun.

"It is time," Abigail instructed as she grabbed my hand.

Chapter 19
THE GRAVEDIGGER'S SECRET

We stepped into the center of the courtyard, affectionately known as 'the Boneyard' by the students, and the many undead residents still haunting the high school. I was in the center of the star again. I knew what it meant this time. Abigail waved her hand and I stepped into the portal of light and stepped out on the other side. I'd set foot on the grounds of the Medieval Royal Faire. We had portaled.

"I wish I knew how to do that," I whispered to Abigail.

"Do you?" she replied and only gave me a smile. I wondered if this was a hint of things to come.

The RenFest hadn't changed much, except it was dark. Very dark, save for the lamp posts that selectively were placed throughout the faire grounds. It gave the place a much different feel. Additionally, I wasn't here with Ethan and that bothered me.

If only Ethan knew magic, I thought.

He does, Abigail spoke back to me in my head. She smiled. *But not the sort of magic you know.*

You can hear me?

Yes. But only because you're letting me hear you.

Abigail spoke aloud. "Ethan's magic is all his very own. He helped me seal Lily by giving you that ring. He didn't know it, but his power lies in true love. That ring you wear is very special; more than you know."

"What? What are we doing here?" I asked her, fiddling with the ring on my finger. It shimmered and almost looked alive. The ring had an unseen energy. I hadn't noticed as much before, but something about the eclipse made everything seem different.

"It's time. Did you not see the eclipse changing above you? We have to be hasty." I looked above to the moon. It was a strange colour and the normal glow of the full moon was swallowed into the darkness.

"Hasty?" I said with uncertainty. The ring pulsated. The silver lily flower petals on the ring shimmered and came to life. It was a tiny lily, but the soft petals were real to the touch. I had no idea the ring was magical. Images of Ethan buying the ring at the gypsy tent came into my mind. It was Abigail that had made sure I wore the ring.

"Alyson, would you please be so kind as to remove your ring and place it into my palm?" Abigail requested, holding out her hand.

I removed the ring and delicately placed it into her palm. As soon as my fingers let go, I felt it tingle at me, as though a tiny silver thread still connected us before it broke free.

"You are much more than sisters," she said with a clever smile.

"Sisters?"

I wasn't sure what she referred to until I looked more closely at the ring. I stared at the flower. The lily flower. And then it struck me. … Lily.

Abigail waved her hand over the ring three times and spoke:

As true love freely gives,

you are free to give true love.

As the dove is released from its cage,

Open your wings,

you are set free.

The ring sparkled and shimmered and fell to the ground, expanding itself into the diameter of a pizza. Shimmering from this round circle stepped forward a girl, a girl I'd not met before. She had dark brown hair and fair porcelain skin. Her features were striking. She was dressed in rags and I would've easily mistaken her for a peasant. Her rags were dirty and torn, and she had been scuffed around. She had a smile of sincerity, and when she smiled, her pale eyes glanced at me with kindness. She had the heart of a princess. Now her identity was unmistakable.

"Alyson. I'd like you to meet, the real Princess Lily."

"Pleased to make your acquaintance," Lily greeted me with a curtsy and held out her hand. I didn't know how to act in Medieval times, but I knew she was royalty, so I kissed the top of her hand. She looked at me very surprised, and let out a giggle. I guess only the men did that.

"Lily. There is someone who has waited a long while for this moment, for this moon, and to see you again. I fear we must make haste. There are still forces trying to stop you two."

"Trying to stop whom?" Lily questioned.

"You and Prince Ivan," I alerted her. "He's in the chess piece," I blurted out.

"The chess piece?" Lily retorted with a questionable look on her face.

Seamus entered the area. "My dear Abby. You've come back," he said rejoicing and holding open his arms to pull her in for an embrace. They hugged. For a split moment, I saw them both having angelic type wings and then they disappeared.

"Of course. Have everything ready and in place?"

"Just as requested."

"Good," Abigail walked to the center of the chess board and drew a similar magic circle as she'd cast in the courtyard. As she drew it, I sensed colour coming from her fingertip, like a light. Once she sealed the area, I looked around and had difficulty seeing outside of the chess area. We were in our own separate space. Light shimmered in the center of the board. Abigail was in happy spirits and excited tonight would be the night the curse would be lifted off Prince Ivan, and he and Lily could return to their own time.

"Ivan? Ivan is here?"

"Yes," Abigail said. She held out her palm with the chess piece in hand. "He only can be awakened by true love. Go ahead."

Lily took the black knight chess piece gently from Abigail's palm and held it in front of her. She closed her eyes and with the grace of a Princess kissing a frog, leaned in and placed a tiny kiss atop the head of the black horse-shaped chess piece. The chess piece quivered in her hand and she dropped it to the ground. She covered her mouth in surprise. A tear fell from her cheek. There sitting before her, was Prince Ivan. He wore his knight's suit of armor, with the helm off. She held out her hand to help him off the ground. As she stood, light shimmered through translucent wings seemingly attached to her back. They were barely noticeable, much like a damselfly, unless she moved quickly and their rogue shimmer was revealed. Unmistakably, Lily had wings.

"Lily?" Ivan looked her in the eyes.

"No Ivan. I'm over here," a voice called from behind. I knew instantly that this was the imposter Lily. This was the Queen of Sands. Only she stepped out before us wearing the wedding dress, Lily's former wedding dress, which now missed a very important letter $\mathcal{L}$ from the sleevelet.

"That is the dress! You were there the night the thieves broke into Abby's tent. You were one of them," Seamus pointed his finger at the Queen.

"You must be mistaken. I've been trapped inside of a ring all this time. How is that even possible?"

"Lily?" Prince Ivan looked to the Queen. His eyes were focused on the outside, the dress, the hair, her alluring smile.

"Prince Ivan. Don't step any closer to her. That's not Lily," I yelled to him. The Queen of Sands grinned at me, realizing how easy it was to confuse this love sick boy.

"You just need to kiss me to prove it. I am your true love," she boasted with tempting lies. She moved closer to Ivan. I saw her just as I saw Sadie as a threat long ago. I saw right through her. Her red hourglass glowed from within her cape.

"No!" I yelled at him.

He was allured by her beauty and her deceitful charm. It had been so long since he'd seen her. The real princess Lily, quiet and shy, felt ashamed by her rags and raw beauty. She fell to her knees and wept gently. "How could he not see me? How could he not see the real me?" she said weeping through tears.

Prince Ivan stopped and looked at the weeping girl. She lifted her head. He gazed into her eyes... and he knew. He ran to her and lifted her off the ground. He brushed the fallen hair from her face and looked deeply into her eyes.

"It *is* you!"

Ivan placed his hands behind her neck and pulled her in for a kiss. In that moment, the Queen of Sands pulled her hourglass from inside her cloak and aimed it at the kissing couple. The hourglass suspended itself in front of her and began to spin wildly. As it spun, the sands were flung to the ends of the hourglass.

The hourglass spun continually, connecting the ends visually so it appeared to be a globe. Spinning fast, it formed a circle of red with a glass center. I stared into the spiral that formed into the center. Abigail held my arm and pulled a silver hourglass from her gown.

"Don't look into it!" she commanded to me.

Abigail's eyes glowed silver and the pupils filled with moonlight. She held it in the air and confronted the Queen. Two Queens of time, weavers of fate, deciding for each other where the other should go.

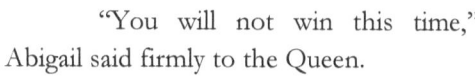

"You will not win this time," Abigail said firmly to the Queen.

"I already have." The Queen revealed her true self. Her eyes glowed an intense crimson blood red and she let out a malicious laugh, one echoing my mind with memories of Sadie in her worst madness. She pointed her finger at Lily and Ivan.

"Say good-bye to your daughter, Doña Bella!" The Queen yelled at Abigail, as she cast her spell.

Doña Bella?

Abigail looked mortified.

Through time and space, I send you from this place...

Cast to and fro into the eye you will go.

Distance fades and approaches, you shall wait no more,

Matter not – do not – aaagghhh! STOP!

Seamus yelled at the Queen. "No! You will not harm Bella or Lily! I will see to it that you never harm anyone again!"

"No, Seamus!" Abigail yelled at him to stop, but it was too late.

A thunderous sound came from behind as Seamus let out a roar and the spirit of the lion took over him. He attacked the Queen with such velocity, she barely had time to react. He was swift and powerful.

He lunged at her, but he was no longer human. His feet had grown into giant, golden paws and his face turned into that of a lion. Golden yellow aura was surrounding his mane, like the gold that shines from the sun on a summer's day. On his back, he had grown vast wings belonging to an eagle. Majestic. His keen eyes narrowed and targeted the Queen's hourglass and he sprung forward. His wings opened, and he leapt through the air and flew briefly, carried by shimmers of white light trailing below his wings. He shimmered as he jumped. His landing was near fatal, powerfully pouncing on her hourglass, shattering it and bursting red sand everywhere that turned instantaneously to blood seeping into the soft ground. The blood pooled and extended to my feet. I stepped back, but noticed it still had been splattered on my skin. I wiped it clean, hoping no magical bloody side effects left their residue on me, but it stung like acid.

Seamus lay covered in red sand and blood. Abigail ran to him and quickly healed him, blasting away the impurities with light.

The young couple pulled away from their kiss gently to look at what just took place. Lily shielded her eyes as Seamus lay atop the fallen Queen. The Queen lay with her glowing red eyes open, as they went to black. She was dead.

"Is he dead?" she asked Abigail worriedly.

Seamus lifted himself up and smiled at Lily. "Child, it would take a lot more than that to hurt your old man." He stood up and limped away to stand by Abigail. His right front paw still hurt. Abigail took into her hands and closed her eyes, focusing white light into it and healing him. He changed back into his human form.

"Thank you, Abigail. Forever my Bella, I am in your debt."

"Seamus," she caressed his cheek. "You must take care. That took all of your energy. I shall lend you some of mine. Do take time to recharge yourself, lest I need to call upon you again. Someday, you will be able to keep your true form. You cannot deny your royal lineage. It is not of your concern or nature to worry. The sisters and I shall keep safe watch over you until it is time."

Seamus nodded and she stroked his cheek.

The Queen of Sands lay in a pool of her own blood, spilt red sand and broken glass. Like acid, it ate away at her flesh, leaving nothing more behind other than the dress.

"She is dead, only of this time, as she was not from the present. She still exists in the past and it is uncertain if she remains in the future. Be forewarned," Seamus instructed.

Abigail waved her hand over the dress and magically swapped the rags for the gown. Lily's face is filled with astonishment and gratitude. She looks to the sleevelet and the $\mathcal{L}$ is there. The gown is whole again.

Lily gasped with delight.

"I cannot believe my own eyes, if I did not just see it with them. What has just happened? I am wearing my dress now. You are like a fairy godmother. Thank you. One hundred times, thank you."

"Lily, we can be married now," Prince Ivan said with excitement, grabbing her by the waist and spinning her around, his metal suit clunking and groaning as he did so. Her wings grew brighter and light passed through them like prisms, sending sparks of colour dancing in the air.

"I shall send you back into your own time. As much as I would like to keep you close by, it is important you go back and exist at a time when you are most needed. We can't all stay clumped together in the present. Some of you," Abigail smiled wisely, "some of you are needed very much in the past, as your presence in the past affects not only your future, but all of us. And those of you from the present that might not know it, are actually from the future, here to educate your previous selves with the knowledge you will possess later on, so that you can teach it in the present time."

I gave Abigail a slightly confused look.

"As with our ancestors, they share their wisdom through the ages through voices they can speak through, books. It is up to you to decide to when you will best be able to share your own wisdom. Because sometimes the present is very stubborn to listen to the past, but also very hesitant to listen to the future. You could say humanity is afraid of its own destiny, because they fear it cannot be changed, when it can be." Abigail smirked. She spoke so much about the future, because that is where she existed.

"Alyson, you understand now, don't you?" Abigail took my hands into her own. I looked into her pale blue eyes and white hair. I nodded. She looked back into mine. I saw myself in them.

"Abigail?"

"I cannot tell you anymore, Alyson. Not yet. But I promise, you will understand. You are well on your way to discovering the true seeker, that which seeks the destiny of his or her own soul. But you must trust," she said with a smile. "Especially your Elders. They possess wisdom. And it is only through wisdom that you will survive what is coming. And because you choose to seek the truth, many will choose to fight you. But it will be a noble battle and one worth fighting for. The truth will bring peace, not just for yourself, but for all who walk beside you, and those who fly above you."

Abigail's words resonated deep within me. My heart felt like it gleamed from inside, and my forehead had light shining from it. I looked up. The eclipse had started and it made the fairegrounds very dark. The moon already had a ruddy glow. It gave it an eerie appearance. The moon looked like it was smeared in blood.

I looked to Abigail. She sensed it too. Something was amiss in the courtyard where we had portaled from.

"Lily, Ivan, my apologies for my haste, but I must go. Back to your own time. There's no time to waste. NOW!" she commanded and threw them into the chessboard. A portal sucked them in as though they'd fallen into a black hole. And then they were gone. No goodbyes or anything.

"Alyson. There is no time. He's back and he's at your school."

Abigail teleported us before I could even respond. We landed back in the courtyard. Only we weren't alone when we landed. I looked up through the open air of the courtyard and to the enclosed space. Hundreds of ravens stared down upon us, sitting perched on the walls. The sounds of them made my ears feel like bleeding. It was a horrible noise. Echoing inside the walls of sacred space, the noise sounded more like a vibration.

Sara still had a connection to Hremm Nevar, whether she knew it or not. Her time with him must've buried itself deep within her. I looked to where she sat on the ground and she looked completely frozen, and not just figuratively. She was!

"Sara?" I shook her trying to rouse her.

"Abigail. She's frozen!"

"Get her warm. Put your coat around her. He's drained her. Hremm Nevar is stealing Sara's life force to become whole again."

In that moment, Penelope the ghost dog came and sat next to Sara. I saw her glow. The dog gave every bit of its warmth into Sara. I realized that it was the dog who saved the gravedigger, at least for a little while. But the gravedigger would've probably have had to see him die first. How sad he would've been, knowing his pet died saving his life. I realized why the dog howled in the basement. Penelope wanted the gravedigger back. Penelope now was giving its life, again, to save Sara. Warmth entered Sara's body again and the ghost dog disappeared.

I realized it was Jeremy that had led Cameron to the ghost dog in the first place. Jeremy must've known. Could it be possible that somehow, Jeremy knew how to save Sara's life? Through a ghost dog? It was too tricky to ask questions that only the universe held answers to.

I wanted to thank the ghost dog somehow. I looked to the area of the missing headstones and had an idea.

The rest of the students stayed frozen in their time warp "hold" poses. Whatever position they paused in, was the position they stayed in. Jenny Fox's hand still looked like it hovered over a planchette that wasn't there.

"Alyson?" Sara spoke barely above a whisper. She had unfrozen. Sara looked around confused, but did not panic.

"How come she's not like the rest?" I whispered to Abigail.

"You will come to understand, and so shall she."

Sara stood up and dusted off her skirt. The ravens squawked louder. She looked up at them and then she started to panic. She fainted.

"Quick. Cover her or he'll be all over her!" Abigail shouted at me. I covered her with my coat.

The ravens simultaneously dove in and aimed themselves at Abigail. Abigail's eyes turned translucent silver. She held up her finger and from it sprayed a ray of white light all around us. The ravens bounced and ricocheted off her shield and went flying back into the atmosphere. Discouraged, the presence of Hremm Nevar left us. In his present scattered state, he was no match for us.

I had never seen Abigail's eyes like this. She glanced at me, but could not see me. She was blind. Her eyes went back to normal and she smiled.

"Do not be afraid. Yes, I am blind, but I can very much see."

"Undoubtedly. How did you know the eclipse had started if you can't see it?"

Abigail smiled. "The moon has an aura, just like you do. When it went from blue to red, I knew it was time. The right time for something magical to happen. The moon can give you several clues, Alyson. We are women. We change in cycles, just as the moon does. The moon affects our inner tides. We ebb and flow. You will understand much if you understand the moon."

I looked up to the night sky. The eclipse had passed over us and out of its final stages and the light of the silvery moon shined down once upon us again. It had happened. Abigail snapped her fingers.

Students chattered and laughed without concern or awareness that they'd missed a huge chunk of their evening. Jenny Fox looked at her hands and looked around at who stole her new toy. Too drunk to move, she leaned back and passed out, right next to her two dimwitted girlfriends.

Ethan and Cameron came back with some punch in little drink cups.

"Thanks," I said smiling and taking the cup.

"Are you lovely ladies going to stay out in the cold all night, or do you want to dance?"

"Oh you know I do!" I jumped and almost spilled the punch. "Let's go."

Inside the gym, the school's Halloween dance had taken the place of the chairs on the floor. Most of the parents had gone back home and a good majority of students remained.

Ethan and I danced, alongside Sara and a very reluctant Cameron, who barely swayed enough to call it dancing, but really, he just stood there and bobbed his head. Ethan took a break from dancing and pulled me aside.

"Want to go outside?" he whispered.

"Yeah," I said softly.

We went outside through the school's front door and sat on some nearby steps. The music from the gym was loud enough to migrate to the air outside. It was dark, crisp and cool in the air. Not a cloud in the sky. Just stars. Lots and lots of stars. I looked back down to Ethan and our eyes locked.

Ethan put his hand behind my neck and pulled me in quickly. "Let me finish that kiss we started." It made me giggle. This time, no one watched us, except for the moon, and she didn't mind one bit.

Chapter 20
ANCESTRAL VOICES

My affections for Ethan ran deep. After our kiss last night, I had to come home. Temptations overwhelmed me whenever I was with him. Still, I fell asleep hugging my pillow pressed near my face.

I could've kissed him all night long, stopping only to catch my breath. His cologne lingered in my hair. I wrapped it underneath my nose like a moustache and smelled it. Ethan. My beloved was with me. I fell asleep in lucid dreams, about nights under the stars, lost in a slow dance.

Morning light shined in through my bedroom window. Shadow lifted his head and then lowered it again, putting a paw over his nose to shield his eyes. Emily still lay curled in a tight ball. So much had happened the night before and the new day seemed to wash it away clean, like the tide cleansing the shore.

Stretching and greeting the morning sun, I pulled the covers back and got out of bed and ran downstairs, fuzzy slippers and all.

Mom had been painting, touching up her work. The painting in the living room once again had a white raven painted, perched with the girl with long flowing black hair. There was also a new addition to the painting.

"What's that? Is that?" I looked in closely.

"Yes. Isn't he cute? It just came to me and so I painted him in. He just makes me want to call him George or something cute like that. Isn't he adorable? I'd swear I saw his whiskers twitch at me – must be the paint fumes."

Whether she knew it or not, this painting had significance. My mother had a great and talented gift, both of being creative and with her magic. Sadie looked down to the tiny mouse in the painting. Her father's spirit was with her again. She smiled at me and resumed her pose on the canvas as my mother's gaze hit it.

"You know, I've wanted to paint something outdoors, but lately, there's been all these crows around and I didn't really want to paint those."

"No! No... you shouldn't paint those! They're ugly!" I yelled running at her with my arms up in air.

"Honey. Calm down. They're just birds."

Ha! Just birds. If only she knew.

"Oh, I know. But let's paint flowers or something else instead." *Unless it's a flower that shoots daggers out of its petals, I think we'll be safe.* Knowing my mother too had a gift, but she didn't know it yet, told me I had to keep an eye on her too.

"Okay. How's the homework coming along?"

Homework? You mean I have to rescue things in the magical world and still do homework? Life is so unfair!

"I'll get right on that."

I went upstairs, looked at the books and went back to bed. It wasn't restful sleep but rather lucid dreaming. Ethan and I were having our first fight, but then looking more closely, it wasn't Ethan… and it wasn't me.

We must've been in our late twenties, but it was very old surroundings, like in an old Western movie. We were in the back room of a noisy tavern. A brothel. Long brown hair cascaded down to my swollen belly. I was pregnant. The man was Seamus. His hair, gelled back, slick. He tucked at his suspenders and stuck up his chin at me. I yelled at him, rather, pleaded with him.

"Bella, I have to go away. You'll be fine without me. I promise. I'll always find you." He waved and pulled the door closed behind him. As it closed behind me, time sped up and I reopened the door to see two men standing in the rain before me. They presented me with a letter. I opened it and read it in slow motion. He had been killed. I dropped the letter and it fell to the ground.

"Are you alright Madame?" one of the men asked.

"Don't ever call me Madame again!" I shouted and pulled a tiny pistol out from my garter belt, shooting at both of them and missing on purpose. They ran off. I closed the door and opened my palm. There was the rune. The rune of Gebo, the gift X. Just like X means a kiss. His fate had been sealed, but his gift was given. I carried life within me. I passed the mirror and glanced at my own reflection. It was someone else. A past life. Of mine or Abigail's I did not know.

The image in the mirror spoke to me, although they were not my words. "Alyson, take note of this dream. Lily needs your help. You will know what to do next."

I sat up from my dream, sweating and jolted. "Bella?" I tried to remember it. It started to fade away. I quickly grabbed my dream journal and jotted down anything I could remember. I would have to ask Abigail about it later.

I closed the dream journal and looked at its simple cover. It read:

> *Always believe in the power of yourself, to live your dreams and achieve great wisdom, for anything is possible if you close your eyes and open your heart and remember the visions imparted upon you in your dreaming mind.*
>
> *A dream is a wish your heart makes.*

I had only recently begun to capture my dreams in a journal, but I found they spoke to me in ways I'd only begun to understand. I wrote them down daily, and with practice, I was able to remember them more easily.

I discovered it was also through my dreams that Emelia and Abigail would visit. Dream power – communicating via telepathy while asleep. It was something Emelia had done since I'd first met her. She told me it would take a lot of practice, but one day I might be able to do it also.

"If only you had your full powers," Abigail said to me, as she'd entered my room.

"Full powers?"

"I cannot go into it now, but you will be embarking on a great journey in the near future. The very near future. And it involves your past."

"My past?"

"It is almost time. You will know when," she added.

There was a long pause. I half expected her to go ahead and tell me, but she didn't. Instead, I decided to ask her about my dream.

"Abigail?"

"Yes, Alyson?"

"Did you ever have any other children? Is Lily, your daughter?"

She nodded.

"But from a long time ago. Another lifetime. I was called Doña Bella. I was an orphan, a brothel madame and gypsy, but not by choice.

It was a way of life I could afford. I had no skills other than those that came naturally to a woman. Women were not taught to read or write back then, although we had desire to. Seamus taught me. Once I learned to read and write, he taught me skills I never knew existed, magical skills and those skills we did write about – in special books, books of all kinds of magic. Those books were passed to a new generation of witches – good witches – wise women sent with intuitive and divine gifts, healing gifts, protection, guidance, wisdom, creation… the traits needed for any good mother to tend to her children. Ultimately we are guided by Elluna and the Great One, but it is Seamus who was brave enough to walk the Earth among humans and teach his knowledge. Seamus is responsible for my magic, and thereby yours as well."

"Your magic?"

"Yes. Seamus is probably the greatest Elder that ever lived and walked the Earth. As you may have concluded, Seamus is only half human. His other half is Divine. He is also my soul's true love. He captured my heart in ways I had never known. It went beyond the physical. I knew it the moment he'd said my name. Something within me stirred. My love for Seamus ran deep. This is why his death was so painful. His life was taken wrongfully for crimes he didn't commit. I was pregnant at the time with his daughters."

"Daughters?"

"Lily and Rowen were twins. Rowen died at birth. She is the portrait you will never see, but the voice you will always hear. They both are angels, separated at birth." Her voice shook.

"Rowen. Emelia told me about Rowen!"

"Yes, her story is filled with heartbreak. Lily was left behind. I could not bear to raise her alone. I could barely afford to feed her. But a rich woman came to my caravan one day and offered to help me raise the little girl. She offered me a solid gold piece. I told her there was no money that could possibly replace the loss I felt. So she cast me out into the desert. It is where I cried out for Hremm Nevar to take my life, so that Rowen could live. He agreed, for a price. He took my life and Rowen became alive again, but imprisoned inside of a tree for all eternity until someone finds her."

"That's horrible. I didn't know that. Where is she now? Have you found her?"

"Yes. She is not very far at all, but still untouchable to us. I am unsure how to release her from her imprisonment. In the interim, she speaks to us through books."

"Why did you seal Lily inside of a ring?"

"It is true, Lily lived a better life, being raised and trained as a princess, but she wasn't real royalty. At least not to anyone else's knowledge. Lily kept her secret hidden from everyone. The Queen snubbed her and told her to marry a Prince if she wanted to have the crown. So the Queen ordered every Prince from every nation to ask for her hand in marriage. She turned her head away at all of them and said her heart would only beat for true love. She said true love was something worth waiting for and no crown or gold could ever buy that. "I may not be a Princess, but I'm far more a Lady than you'll ever be," Lily told the Queen and revealed her angelic wings to her. The Queen, jealous of her and in anger, locked Lily away. As Lily wept, the Queen wept in separate chambers. Her loneliness made her even more bitter and spiteful. Her tears changed into something dark."

"In her loneliness, the Queen commanded one of the knight chess pieces to come alive on her chess board. It was Prince Ivan that arrived. The Queen tried and tried with loving advances towards him, but never could win his affections. Because the Queen cast a spell for true love, but she who is easily blinded by money and gold will miss it. It was Lily that caught the eye of Prince Ivan, as he saw her in a window. He couldn't see much of her, but he saw her eyes. It was in her eyes that he saw love. Their souls met and could not rest until they were married. The Queen, in her jealousy, sent Prince Ivan through time in an attempt to heal her own broken heart and distance any attempts for Lily to be seen with him. But Lily, being one of my daughters and thus possessing a natural gift of magic, found her way to the fairegrounds to Seamus in his current life. Seamus revealed to me his true nature. I made a promise not to tell anyone and to this day I have kept it. I also promised Seamus I would keep Lily hidden from the wrath of the Queen. So we agreed on a plan, to hide Lily in a ring. It was there that she remained protected, existing within a ring, and safe from the Queen as she waited for Prince Ivan. The Queen sent many minions in to find Lily. She even sent an imposter King. It was because you wore the ring and Lily's wedding dress, that he tried to go after you."

"I can't believe you trusted me enough to have me wear the ring. What if something happened to me?"

"I made sure you were prepared dear. Don't you remember the ghost in the house? The ghost with the glove? You're getting stronger. It's not just Hremm Nevar that lurks in the shadows."

"So the Queen must've been somehow working with Hremm Nevar."

"Hremm Nevar seeks those who are suffering from broken hearts or unrequited love. He seeks those who seek him. For when there is an absence of love, ... there is death, and pain, and suffering. Hremm Nevar gives false comfort to those who trust in him. Such as Sadie, who fell innocently into his hands after broken hearted with Harding. And your friend Sara, who wept for the loss of her friend

Jeremy. And how do I know this? Because he came to me too. I wept for the loss of Seamus. And he came to me. As Belladonna, he had power over me. But now, now I have seen and touched The Great One. I have powers Hremm Nevar will never possess and is powerless against. He knows he can never charm me. Because I am love. I use love to heal. Pure love. It can't be recreated with anything that isn't from the heart itself. As long as I surround myself with love, pure love, he cannot charm me. He cannot get through. This is why Hremm Nevar couldn't touch you, Alyson. Because you are in love and surrounded by love. But beware the times in your life that you suffer a broken heart or a crush, and keep mindful of how you learn from them. Or you may be at the hands of Hremm Nevar and this time, unprotected."

I continued to listen to Abigail and I agreed with her wisdom. "It's *love* that defeats Hremm Nevar? But Sadie loved him."

"Yes. She loved him, but did he love her? Hremm Nevar gives false love, but does he actually seek it? Can Hremm Nevar feel emotion? According to Sadie, his human side can."

"He has a human side?"

"Yes, there is a moment between when he transforms into his vampire self from his raven self. Like when the sun meets the horizon on the ocean, he becomes human. It is in that instant that he becomes vulnerable. He is like a dragon with a single scale missing. Hremm Nevar has a weak spot."

"But how do we kill him? How do we kill him when he is scattered into a million birds?"

"It is an unfortunate answer I must give you, but alas, his kind gives us no other choice. We must wait."

"Wait?"

"One day, Hremm Nevar will be whole again and we will be able to seek his vulnerable spot. For now, just avoiding look directly into his eyes – the eyes of his minions. If his ravens recognize your soul, they will pluck your very eyes out."

I winced in Abigail's description.

"Alyson, forgive me, I must return to the painting at once. Something is amiss." Abigail teleported just as she had arrived. I sensed something was wrong as well. I flung aside my covers and ran downstairs to the living room. Abigail flew around the painting frantically. Sadie was gone! Black raven feathers were left in her place.

I flung open the front door and a raven haired girl in a white dress ran through the snow. She looked back over her shoulder to see flocks of ravens chasing her. Though she did not scream. She turned around and faced them directly.

I held onto Emily as we watched Hremm Nevar swoop toward Sadie. Sadie did not waver her stance. She did not protect her face or shield herself. She did not prepare for the arrival of death. She was not afraid to face it.

Hremm Nevar's birds gathered together and hovered briefly above Sadie. He paused. There was a moment where I couldn't look. She would be attacked. But he didn't attack. He just hovered. He dropped a single black feather and flew off. Sadie reached down and picked it up.

"For protection," Abigail said with a smile. "He's called a truce. He gave her a feather, a part of himself, just as he took part of her. It's a peace offering."

"He didn't kill her?" I said to Abigail shocked.

"He couldn't. He loves her. Sadie has charmed death himself. She called to him when she was most defeated, when all seemed lost and heartbroken. She called for death. But when he came, she fell in love with him. I should know. I once called to him too. It is why she knows him."

Sadie walked back through the snow as she saw us standing in the doorway. It was a little more than unnerving. Bolts of lightning crashed to the ground behind her, even in the clear sky, and as she entered the house, she simply smiled and walked past us, the black feather clutched close to her heart.

Chapter 21

FROM INSIDE THE BLACK HOLLOW

"Where do you think he's hiding?"

"I see him not too far from water, but I cannot see where exactly," Abigail stared off into the space in front of her, her eyes going silver. "No. I am mistaken. It is not water I see. He is not on this plane. I see him amongst the stars. He is inside the Black Hollow."

"What is the Black Hollow?"

"The Black Hollow is a place that lurks in the depths of darkness, as light would be to a star, the Black Hollow is to a black hole. He has flown into the iris of the eye, where he waits. Hremm Nevar has disappeared from my sight." Her eyes went back to normal, although she was still blind. "He may be out of view for now, but he will return. There is always someone here on Earth that calls him back when the *black hollow* takes over their hearts – hearts filled with bleakness and despair, searching to fill their empty void with anything that would take their pain away. Hremm Nevar gives false comfort. No matter how difficult your life may seem, you must never call him to you. Be careful what you wish for as you might get it."

"I will – I mean, I won't. I won't call him."

I ran my fingers alongside the binder of the great book. Our book. The book of the seven sisters.

"Will he keep returning?" I asked.

Abigail let out a deep sigh. "I wish I could answer no. I wish we succeeded in capturing him, but it was only temporary. Hremm Nevar exists *because we let him*. He returns to help those poor heartbroken souls to feel comfort and love, albeit false love and comfort, but they are so desperate they do not know the difference. The question remains. Does Hremm Nevar have the capacity to love? Is all hope lost or can there ever exist a glimmer of hope within one so dark?"

"There is only one person I can think of that would know and be able to help us the most. Sadie."

Abigail nodded. "As demented as she may appear, in her madness, she has moments of wisdom. She may enlighten us as to a way we can perhaps not defeat Hremm Nevar, but put him ever to rest, and thus able to harm no more. We might have to go into the underworld ourselves first, in order to emerge forth with wisdom and insight, and light can be reborn."

"Go into the underworld? You mean, like Hades?"

Abigail nodded.

"The Black Hollow."

I took a deep sigh and opened the cover of the book. The seven ovals shimmered on the faded parchment page. At the heart of the page was a seven pointed star. Each oval radiated from a point. At the center of the star was a spiral. The floor shimmered and then quickly faded again. I thought it was just my imagination.

I looked at the oval that was my portrait. I now recognized her as the woman that was in my reflection that night I first spotted the black owl. She is me, but from a different time – a different life. Her portrait smiled at me and gave a wink, before resuming a completely still pose. Still, those eyes haunted me. My eyes. Who was she?

Once again, the blackness of the empty portrait frame intrigued me. Knowing there was a face within, only made me want to see it more. A face of purity. I knew it was a face I probably would never see, at least not with my own eyes. It would be like looking directly into the sun. I would be as blind as Abigail.

The sixth sister. She is the key.

She is the

Spinner of the Thread of Life,

Weaver of Fate

and Deliverer of Destiny.

A voice without a face that speaks the way angels do – with love and grace. A magical scribe of an instrument of music sung from the soul. Her song is much more than a doorway; it is a key that unlocks both the future and the past, linking them both to the present and providing a gateway – a stargate to hidden knowledge.

Her poetry is a dance, a prophecy of revelation.

Her words are wisdom.

Knowledge is power; wisdom is the key.

Also by Kristin Groulx:

The mis-adventures of Alyson Bell
Young Adult Paranormal Romance Series:

Book One: *The Ghost of Colby Drive*
(ISBN 978-0-9811315-0-4, July 2007)

Alyson Bell, new to the rural town of Hollow Creek: a town rumoured to be haunted by a ghostly spirit and a cat with more than the usual nine lives. Alyson unwillingly transitions into her new life, facing everyday teenage obstacles (bosoms and boyfriends), and hurdling over supernatural mysteries only *she* is predestined to encounter. Does one girl have what it takes to piece together the myriad of clues left behind in her century-old house to end a *cat*-astrophic curse, vanquish an evil soul-stealing vampire and still have time for a relationship with her new boyfriend, all before the next full moon?

Book Two: *The Curse of the Moonless Knight*
(ISBN 978-0-9811315-1-1, August 2008)

It is the season of Samhain, also celebrated as Hallowe'en. The crisp of Fall is in the air. Spirits are amiss in the town of Hollow Creek when a portal that should've stayed closed, is accidentally opened. A medieval knight, misplaced in time, links sixteen year-old Alyson to an extraordinary discovery about herself, and her family. Embarking on a quest for knowledge, Alyson learns that sometimes in this magical world, you have to close your eyes… *to see*. And in order to forgive, you must first open your heart.

Book Three: *The Oracle of the Missing Dryad*
(ISBN 978-0-9811315-2-8, September 2009)

Sometimes the pages just write themselves... as though, the spirit of the wood still lives between the text, dancing between pages and weaving magic. Alyson meets a tree dryad who helps Alyson on her latest adventure, that is, until the book the spirit is hiding inside of gets stolen and it's up to Alyson to travel through time to find her! For she holds the key that unlocks both the past and the future, and her prophecy is revealed.

Book Four: *The Crystal Goddess and the Wish Keeper*
(ISBN 978-0-9811315-3-5, October 2010)

Coming soon!

Available at
Amazon.com and Barnes & Noble

A tribute to my favourite RenFest...

The Kansas City Renaissance Festival offers a day like no other to eager visitors from across the Midwest. This year guests will also enjoy the antics of the all new Washer Well Wench show all seven weekends and bagpipe shows until the end of the Festival. The Gypsy Musical will perform on the Crown and Rose Stage 5 times daily, and the Barbarians have taken over the forest with fights scheduled several times each day and Barbarian Battles scheduled twice each day at the jousting arena. By far the rowdiest shows each day star the Knights of Noble Cause Productions, national joust troupe, with shows at the Renaissance Downs 4 times each day in all variances of battle and competition. And, guests can find cooling mists throughout the show this year to keep everyone comfortable!

The world famous turkey legs are of course on their way to Canterbury as well as a host of other treats found only at the Renaissance Festival. Shopkeepers bring out their very finest of wares, for the harvest always brings a multitude of visitors intent on great shopping.

The Kansas City Renaissance Festival is located in Bonner Springs, Kansas (just outside of KC, MO). Their website is www.kcrenfest.com.

(I am not affiliated with them... just a fan of their elaborate faire, and a suitable likeness was used as inspiration for the faire scenes in this book.)

A bit of lore from days ago

In this season of Samhain,

we are reminded of other wondrous worlds existing side by side with our own, and we are invited to play, laugh, don disguises, delight in small miracles of human friendship, use common sense, and free our hearts to explore who and what we truly are.

... At the heart of the Celtic Otherworld

grows an apple tree whose fruit has magical properties. Old sagas tell of heroes crossing the western sea to find this wondrous country, known in Ireland as

Emhain Abhlach, (Evan Avlach)

and in Britain, ... Avalon.

At Samhain, the apple harvest is in, and old hearthside games, such as apple-bobbing, called apple-dookin' in Scotland,

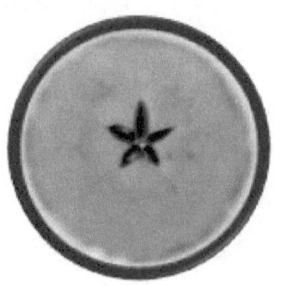

reflect the journey across water to obtain the magic apple....

with the **star** in the center

A little astronomy...

-→ With all eclipses, something ends and something else begins. During an eclipse period, you may feel like you are walking across a bridge to a brand new place, with no turning back from where you started. The door behind you latches, and locks. You can't go back because after the eclipse you will know more and understand things that were never clear to you before. In that sense, you really can't go home again.

... the Seven Sisters ...

The Pleiades' high visibility in the night sky has guaranteed it a special place in many cultures, both ancient and modern. In **Greek mythology**, they represented the **Seven Sisters**, while to the **Vikings**, they were **Freyja**'s hens, and their name in many old European languages compares them to a hen with chicks.

To the **Bronze Age** people of Europe, such as the **Celts** (and probably considerably earlier), the Pleiades were associated with mourning and with funerals, since at that time in history, on the **cross-quarter day** between the **autumn equinox** and the **winter solstice** (see **Samhain**, also **Halloween** or **All Souls Day**), which was a festival devoted to the remembrance of the dead, the cluster rose in the eastern sky as the sun's light faded in the evening. It was from this **acronychal rising** that the Pleiades became associated with tears and mourning. As a result of **precession** over the centuries, the Pleiades no longer marked the festival, but the association has nevertheless persisted, and accounts for the significance of the Pleiades astrologically.

The Pleiades is an open star cluster which is visible to the naked eye in the constellation Taurus. The Ancient Greeks saw seven stars in the cluster, and named them after the Pleiades, the seven daughters of Atlas and Pleione. According to myth, the hunter Orion was in love with them and pursued them until the gods took them to safety, transforming them first into doves, and then into stars. Telescopes have shown that there are up to 500 stars in the cluster.

Other literary sources...

Anonymous (English, 16th Century): *Greensleeves,*

from *Faire, Sweet & Cruell (*Bis CD 257): track 9

Of all English Renaissance tunes, this is the most familiar, partly because of its modern use for the Christmas carol "What Child Is This?" However, it was a wildly popular tune in its own day, and was arranged in endless different ways. Here we hear it sung much as it must have sounded in the 16th century. Although the text speaks in the voice of a man spurned by his lady love, it is here sung by a woman, which would not have bothered a Renaissance audience one bit. They had little concern for the gender of the singer of a song so long as the voice was a pleasant one. The message was conveyed by the words and melody, and not by the person of the singer.

Alas my love, ye do me wrong
to cast me off discurteously:
And I have loved you so long,
Delighting in your companie.

Greensleeves was all my joy
Greensleeves was my delight:
Greensleees was my heart of gold,
And who but my Ladie Greensleeves.

I have been readie at your hand,
to grant what ever you would crave
I have both waged life and land,
your love and good will for to have.

Refrain: Greensleeves was all my joy, etc.

Thou couldst desire no earthly thing,
But still thou hadst it readily,
Thy musicke still to play and sing,
And yet thou wuldst not love me.

Refrain: Greensleeves was all my joy, etc.

Greensleeves now farewel adieu
God I pray to prosper thee,
For I am still thy lover true
Come once again and love me.

~ * ~

Additional Sources:

Scene from Dracula: (school play script)

Abraham "Bram" Stoker (8 November 1847 – 20 April 1912) was an Irish writer of novels and short stories, who is best known today for his 1897 horror novel *Dracula*. During his lifetime, he was better known for being the personal assistant of the actor Sir Henry Irving and the business manager of the Lyceum Theatre in London, which Irving owned.

www.ingramcontent.com/pod-product-compliance
Lightning Source LLC
LaVergne TN
LVHW091529060526
838200LV00036B/540